FINAL EXPOSURE

OTHER BOOKS BY STEVE CARLSON

STEVE
CARLSON

FINAL EXPOSURE

Thomas Dunne Books
St. Martin's Minotaur ⚹ New York

This is a work of fiction. All of the characters, organizations, and events portrayed in this novel are either products of the author's imagination or are used fictitiously.

THOMAS DUNNE BOOKS.
An imprint of St. Martin's Press.

FINAL EXPOSURE. Copyright © 2008 by Steve Carlson. All rights reserved. Printed in the United States of America. For information, address St. Martin's Press, 175 Fifth Avenue, New York, N.Y. 10010.

www.thomasdunnebooks.com
www.minotaurbooks.com

Library of Congress Cataloging-in-Publication Data

Carlson, Steve, 1943-
    Final exposure / Steve Carlson. —1st St. Martin's Minotaur ed.
        p.   cm.
    ISBN-13: 978-0-312-38384-8
    ISBN-10: 0-312-38384-3
    1. Women photographers—Crimes against—Fiction.   2. Murder—Investigation—Fiction.   3. California, Northern—Fiction.   I. Title.
    PS3603.A7533F56   2008
    813'.6—dc22   2008023602

First Edition: October 2008

10 9 8 7 6 5 4 3 2 1

To Quinn and Rebecca
Long may they reign

ACKNOWLEDGMENTS

People *think of writing* as a lonely profession. That's not totally true. Granted, there are untold hours at the computer, but no book is written in a vacuum, least of all mine. I feel that diverse points of view and the knowledge of others help make a story rich, realistic, and in many cases, more factual.

My friend John Braislin not only supplied the title for this opus but helped me in understanding some of the problems associated with the hard of hearing.

My old pals Jim Tattersal (public and private law enforcement) and Jim McKenzie (FBI) helped keep me on track in dealing with the police, FBI, and all things legal.

My appreciation also goes out to the hearing-aid specialist David Reamer for his time, expertise, and for teaching me the facts and possibilities concerning the deaf and those, sometimes, temperamental devices.

Phil and Kelly Gahr were instrumental in helping set the locales for this story, for which I am grateful. Debby Trautman was generous in aiding me to "find the money trail."

Of course, none of this would matter a bit if it wasn't for my favorite publisher Ruth Cavin and her extraordinary good taste in loving this story. Thanks also to her assistant, Toni Plummer, for her quiet, efficient help with it all.

And nothing would quite be as good as it is without the labors of my wife/editor/critic and head cheerleader, Mary Ann.

Thank you all for a most enjoyable journey.

FINAL EXPOSURE

David Collier hadn't expected unemployment to feel this good. He had been officially out of work for about an hour now and already felt lighter than he had in months. Of course, his law firm insisted on calling it a "leave of absence" but that was all right. He knew he'd never go back.

David learned a long time ago that it wasn't necessary to like his clients, or even to believe in them, but lately it had gotten worse than that: David found himself actively disliking his clients. He saw few redeeming values in any of them and had come to resent any time spent in their presence or on their behalf. That, he realized, was not conducive to imparting the best legal advice or for his own personal happiness.

So, he quit. David was not the most popular man around his old firm at the moment but they would just have to deal with it. At thirty-eight, they considered him in his prime, certainly not at an age to start all over. The fact that he was unhappy did not seem all that relevant to them.

"A lot of people are unhappy. So what?" seemed to sum up their attitude. David thought those unhappy people should quit and start over also, but he let it go. It wasn't necessary for them to approve. The only approval he needed was from Rebecca, and thank God she did. Thank God.

He'd been a lawyer long enough to know that he was good at it but that he didn't want to do it anymore. He wanted to be a writer. He'd always wanted to be a writer and now he was finally going to have a chance to give it a shot. Pretty exciting stuff.

David had always thought it strange when he ran into people who were good at something they disliked. Life didn't seem like it should work that way but here he was, the personification of the concept. After a lot of commiseration, it had finally felt good to make a decision and act on it. Change at thirty-eight didn't feel too early (or too late, for that matter) to try for happiness. Actually, it felt just right.

He was looking forward to the future for the first time in way too long and was ready to get on with it. David was driving his 1970 Morgan (the last year they imported the "classic") up Highway 1 on a rare sunny San Francisco morning, approaching the 101 and the Golden Gate Bridge, heading out of town. The Bay shimmered brilliantly in the sun and the traffic was moving along at a good clip. Another rarity.

The Golden Gate Bridge. My God, how many times had David driven over it? Hundreds of times, at least. Now that he and Rebecca had moved north of the city, it had become a twice-a-day occurrence. He was looking forward to not having to do the daily commute to work but the trip itself never bothered him, especially driving the bridge.

The Golden Gate had a thousand different personalities and David loved them all. She shone in the sunshine, glistened in the rain, and seemed to play in the fog. Sometimes she'd show a spire here, then hide it only to reveal another one farther down.

Sometimes she'd hide totally, when visibility was about a foot in front of his face.

David's favorite view of it though, was probably when it was half and half: fog covering the bay and the bridge itself, but with the majestic towers rising through the clouds into blue sky above. Very dramatic.

Although, he had to admit, there was also not a whole lot wrong with the present day he was having. The sun shone brilliantly: blue of sky and blue of bay providing a crystal clear backdrop for the bridge's orange vermilion color.

It hadn't been nice enough to put the top down for weeks, but it was down today and the sun felt great. A box of personal files rested beside him.

Halfway across the bridge, his attention was drawn to a tan-colored truck with canvas sides barreling down the other side. In a glance he saw that it represented everything he disliked about city traffic: it was belching smoke; the driver was going too fast, weaving in and out of lanes as if being one car length closer to wherever actually made any difference; and he was on a cell phone.

Very few people sped or drove recklessly on the bridge. The obvious reason was that it was a long way down if they screwed up, but David thought it was actually more out of respect. No matter how many times people drove it, they were experiencing something special and they knew it. Well, most people knew it. Not that idiot. David just shook his head.

David noticed that he was shaking his head a lot lately. He just didn't get the world anymore. Sometimes he felt seriously out of touch. It even showed in his choice of cars. He loved his little full-fendered Morgan but even he knew it really didn't belong to today's world. Here he was, driving a car that hadn't n imported for over thirty years (something about too small a wheelbase), a car hardly anyone under forty had even heard of, and finding a mechanic and parts were getting progressively more difficult.

He had looked into a new version of the Morgan that was being made and imported to the U.S. but it looked like any other fancy, expensive car. Definitely not the classic. But he wasn't going to worry about that. There was no problem here. His little car was one aspect of David's life he had no intention of changing. He was going to hang in there as long as he could.

He wished he could feel so certain about the world. Sometimes he looked around and wondered, "What happened?" The hatred, the killing, the polarity, the fraud, even the way people dressed, the way they acted, the music they listened to, the TV shows they watched . . . Wasn't he way too young to feel like a dinosaur? Could he have outlived his time so soon?

These thoughts were just mental meanderings while he drove, definitely not depressing. Actually, David was looking forward and was excited about it. He was totally his own man and was free to do whatever he wanted.

David smiled. Every mile he put between himself and the city made the smile a little bigger. Yes, it was definitely time for a new start.

The fashionable, upscale, La Bonheur jewelry store was in the heart of the Financial District. It occupied the main floor of an impressive five-story building there. The floors above were rented to accountants, attorneys, or to other businesses that did not need foot traffic.

4

It was 10:00 A.M.; opening time. Two middle-aged female employees were talking by the front door, waiting for the manager to arrive with the keys. He soon appeared, exchanged perfunctory greetings with the ladies, and went to the door as a third employee, a young girl, ran to join them.

As soon as the door was opened, the manager went to a side wall and turned off the alarm before it had a chance to sound. He then reset the alarm to daytime/workday mode.

It was a morning seemingly like any other. Coffee was made, computers booted up, Venetian blinds opened and raised, displays assembled. No one noticed the four-inch hole that had been drilled through the ceiling back in a corner. They also didn't notice the small microphone that hung down through it a couple of inches.

The two floors above them had been leased a month earlier to an import/export company. Seeing those floors today, one would question the truth of that. They were empty, bare, totally devoid of furniture. The only activity was in the corner of one room in the office directly over the jewelry store. Four men of Middle-Eastern descent, wearing workout sweats, were huddled around the small hole in the floor.

The area around them was cluttered with equipment: ropes, bags, two chain saws, unmarked canisters, gas masks, and a tape recorder. Plugged into the recorder was the cord to the microphone that dangled through the small hole. The men were silent. One, appearing to be the leader, a man named Bashaar, was listening to the activity below with earphones.

The jewelry store was just about ready to open its doors to customers. Most of the morning chores had been completed when the manager crossed to the large A & E walk-in safe housed in a side room and dialed in the combination.

Upstairs, Bashaar held up his hand, both to ensure maximum

stillness from the group and to alert them to get ready to act very soon. Silently, they slipped on their gas masks. The two largest men readied themselves over the chain saws without touching them. A smaller, younger man, Ameen, cradled a three-inch-diameter tube in his fingers. They all froze and listened.

Dialing in the last of the numbers, the manager opened the large outer doors. With a key and a combination, he then opened the inner doors. When they were opened, they settled into their tracks with a distinctive, solid *clunk*.

That was the sound Bashaar had been waiting for. He took off his earphones, carefully pulled the microphone up by its cord, and nodded to Ameen. The smaller man poised himself over the hole and lined up the canister carefully. After checking to make sure everyone had their gas masks on securely, he pulled the pin, activating the device; gas started spewing from it as Ameen dropped it. At that moment, both large men fired up the chain saws and proceeded to work, cutting a large hole in the floor.

As the manager turned from the safe, everyone heard the sound of something rather heavy being dropped. As soon as the manager saw what was happening, he called to one of the women.

"The alarm. Quick!" He barely got the last word out before gagging and falling, unconscious.

The alarm was two strides away from the woman. She made one. The sudden inhale of a gasp was all it took. Very quickly the employees were all down and quiet. They didn't even hear the din of the chain saws cutting through their ceiling.

When the hole was large enough for a man to easily pass through, Bashaar nodded to one of the others. Ropes, that previously had had one end bolted to the floor, were tossed down through the hole. The men followed. Bashaar was the last to go, stowing away in a backpack everything left behind except the chain saws.

Ameen had been the first down the rope. He was pleased to see the four people unconscious on the floor behind the display cases. He went to the windows, lowered and closed the Venetian blinds, then turned on the lights. The two large men had already started scooping the contents of all the cases into the large bags they'd brought down from above.

When Bashaar came down, he unhurriedly opened the back door. There, backed up close to the building, was the tan-colored truck with the canvas sides. More canvas had been added to meet the building, forming a protected corridor from the store into the truck.

The occupants of the truck, also in gas masks, silently joined the original four in making trip after trip from the store to the truck, unseen by pedestrians, until nothing, not even the jewelry on the employees, was left.

The men closed the back door to the store, climbed into the truck, and closed its doors. The driver, after taking off his gas mask, took down the canvas tarps, threw them in the seat next to him, and casually drove off. Less than ten minutes had elapsed. No alarms were sounding.

2

David's father, Marv, had worked as a dye master at a paint company. It was good, creative work and he felt fortunate that it established his family firmly in the middle class. They took vacations to the Grand Canyon and Disneyland and all was well.

His mother, Trudy, kept the books for a TV repair company for a while but her steadily worsening arthritis finally forced her to quit. She'd been at home for most of the years David could remember.

Nevertheless, Marv felt good about the future he knew he had established for them. His company had a good retirement plan and had a matching funds setup where he could donate even more money to the retirement account and the company would match it. Every extra cent went into the fund. Marvelous.

Growing up was mostly fun for David. He would have rightly described himself as a "normal teenager." His family wasn't wealthy but they certainly weren't poor. He didn't get everything he wanted but, then again, he never went without anything important.

All that changed one day when David was a junior in high school. His dad came home looking like he was about to cry. Then he did cry. David had no idea what to do. His dad was a rock, *his* rock. He'd never seen him that way. Neither had Trudy.

Listening in on the ensuing conversations between his folks, David learned that the paint company had gone belly-up; worse than that, everyone had lost their retirement . . . all of it. Another company bought up the hardware and machinery and hired a few of the displaced workers of the former company, but since Marv was only one year away from retirement, he was too old.

At sixty-four years old, Marv Collier, after a lifetime of work and smart planning, found himself without a job, with no retirement, a sick wife, and a teenage son.

The little town of Medford, Oregon, which was having employment problems anyway, couldn't accommodate the influx of older workers cast upon them. No good jobs were available.

Since he also lost his medical insurance when the job stopped, Marv had to sell the house to keep paying for Trudy's medication. They moved into a trailer in the outskirts of town and both were real sorry about the money they'd promised David for his education.

Marv finally got a job working in a concession stand at the country club. It didn't pay much but it helped augment the $600 a month he was trying to live on from Social Security.

He spent his days making hamburgers for other men his age who were enjoying their retirement playing golf. He'd always wanted to play golf, but that was one of many things that were to be done "later."

After a couple of years of that, Marv died. There wasn't really a particular reason, his heart just stopped. David knew why. Because there was no reason to wake up in the morning, simple as that. He died from lack of interest. Trudy followed a month later.

David was a sophomore at Southern Oregon University in the neighboring town of Ashland. Suddenly, David felt very alone, like he'd been cut adrift. Even if his folks had been old, sick, and poor, they were still his folks. He never knew the simple comfort in that until they were gone.

David had always wanted to be a writer but, after what happened to his dad, the urge to be safe was overwhelming. Productive, yes. Even creative if he could manage it, but, *safe*. That was the main thing. Writing was definitely not safe. He'd find something else.

While in school, he lived in his parent's trailer, which was cheaper than an apartment, and whenever he wasn't in school, took over his dad's job at the concession stand.

One day David's life changed dramatically. It was "new members day" at the country club. About fifteen new members and their sponsors were having a shotgun golf tournament. Many happy faces. Two in particular got David's attention big time. One was Jim Keely, former president of the now-defunct paint company . . . and Judge Meriwether, the judge that had presided over the paint company's breakup. . . . The judge that had ruled there had been no intentional wrongdoing by the company . . . and the judge that had decided that there was nothing to do but pray for the poor folks who'd lost everything. Sometimes, life was tough.

"I told you you'd be a member one of these days," the judge told Keely, hand on his shoulder. "It took a little longer than I figured but it's good to have you here now."

"Thanks, Judge. I appreciate it. I really do."

He really did. David could see that. He was a very happy man, a very happy, *prosperous* man. David could also see that.

The image of those two men stayed with him. Was it really just coincidental that those two were old friends? Had they been friends before the company failed? How did Keely get his money? Was he one of the few who managed to get a good job afterward, or had he been able to keep his money? Maybe *all* the retirement funds didn't go under.

David shared his thoughts with his economics professor who thought it was an interesting problem and made a class project out of it. He steered them all, telling them what to look for, where to look and, later, how to decipher what they found.

What they discovered was that a large portion of the company's retirement fund had been invested in a franchise of Honey Baked Hams. David had always liked them and, so far, didn't see that as a problem, except that this was one of the very few Honey Baked Ham franchises that didn't make it . . . plus, even when it was apparent that this particular franchise was failing, the retirement fund continued to fund it ("giving it every chance to make it" were their words).

The frosting on this ugly cake came when two of David's classmates, who were helping on the project, discovered that two of the principal shareholders were the brothers of both Jim Keely and the honorable Judge Meriwether.

Granted, they were invested through company names, but if two undergraduate students could find who the parties really were, why couldn't the feds, or the police, or whoever-the-hell-it-was that was supposed to look into these things?

The professor thought "sunlight" would be the best way to deal with this particular situation. Get it out in the open. David started taking his camera to work with him. It took a couple of weeks but, one day, there they were again. He got a couple of good shots of Keely and the judge setting up the golf cart and, even later, having martinis after their game.

Another student/coconspirator found that the men had gone to separate colleges but shared the same fraternity. They'd known each other for a while. Yet another student in on it all worked for a local radio/TV station in Medford and, through them, had contact with the *Mail-Tribune* that covered all of southern Oregon.

Soon news stories and headlines followed: "Businessman and Judge—Old Friends." "Conflict of Interest!" "Retirement Plans Defunct for Employees but Not for Management." "Workers Lose Everything, Boss Retires in Luxury."

That started such an emotional groundswell of anger and lawsuits that it culminated with the judge being knocked off the bench and into his own retirement. Keely's assets were diminished severely when a good portion was divided among the nearly fifty former employees who'd gotten nothing.

David's share in this was about ten thousand dollars, enough to finish college (if he kept working—which he did). It also set a course for his life. He really liked the feeling of getting the bad guys. Justice felt good. It also felt good knowing his folks would have been proud of him.

He decided to go into law.

3

Water shadows flickered from the red bulb of the darkroom as Rebecca Collier lifted another photograph from the developing tray. This print joined the others that had been hung up to dry. The darkroom was small and cluttered with boxes that hadn't been unpacked yet.

Rebecca was in her element. She always felt more at peace in a darkroom than anywhere. She loved everything about it: the technical aspects of it, the creative freedom, the total privacy, even the smell of the chemicals. All of it.

She wore jeans and a plaid shirt tied up over her waist and was, as usual, barefoot. Her pixie face, short dark hair, and long, lean frame complemented each other beautifully. She was one of those women who looked terrific in whatever she wore. She didn't need makeup or accessories and hardly ever wore them. They just weren't necessary.

She stood back and surveyed her work so far. Surrounding her, in the muted red glow of the darkroom bulb, were drying photos of grand old mansions. There were shot after shot of these exquisite homes and attendant gardens and grounds, which were manicured to their finest. They were some of the loveliest homes in the country.

One shot seemed out of place. Most of the mansions were

photographed from three or four carefully chosen angles, some quite close. This particular shot seemed to have been taken from a distant hill.

The house was magnificent, its grand portico supported by rows of Doric columns. However, it was also apparent that it had slipped into disrepair. Its grounds were dried up, paint was peeling, and what shrubbery there was, was in much need of trimming.

Also setting this estate off from the others was a huge barn out back. Several men could be seen milling around the yard. There was only one shot of this mansion.

Feeling that she was on the right track, Rebecca settled back to her trays, ready with another batch.

The little town of Stinson Beach was really only a few blocks long. It was located in west Marin County on the other side of the peninsula from Sausalito, about a half hour north of San Francisco. Shoreline Drive, which leads from Highway 101 to Stinson Beach, has more switchbacks than Lombard Street, making it one of the most winding roads in California. The drive was generally considered worth it because of the charm of the little seaside community, the beach houses that flanked the village (some in the millions of dollars) and, of course, the beach itself.

David and Rebecca's beach house was a bit north of Stinson Beach. They were far enough away to feel remote and secluded but close enough that they could pop into town if they'd forgotten milk or wanted to go to one of the restaurants.

They had a vacant lot on one side and neighbors on the other that they never heard nor saw; the neighbors were either very quiet or else they were never there. Many of the houses in that area were second homes, frequented only in summer or on occasional weekends.

David and Rebecca had sold their San Francisco Victorian, made a good piece of change with it, and after a laborious look at every beach house in Northern California (seemingly) they found their little treasure.

It was fairly old, two stories, and they considered it quite funky. The outside was dark brown weathered shake that handled the extremes of weather there just fine. Their front yard was actually a walkway/arboretum that connected the beach house to Shoreline Drive, which connected them to the world. It was thick and lush, a bit overplanted, with a wide variety of plants that thrived in the foggy, damp weather of the area.

In back was a weathered redwood deck that ran the whole back of the house, with a table, chairs, lounges, and stairs that went down to the beach. The ocean took over from there and filled the senses as it did the landscape as it continued on forever.

The first and, so far, only major change they'd made to the place was to convert a small storage area into Rebecca's darkroom. Everything else was perfect.

David came in the back way, stomped the sand off his feet, opened the sliders, and stepped into his and Rebecca's future. The entire back of the house was glass, looking over the redwood deck to the ocean beyond. The house was totally empty at the moment except for a stereo and a bottle of champagne in an ice bucket, both setting on the floor by the fireplace.

David was carrying a handful of wildflowers he'd picked from the lot next door. He looked for something to put them in and was pleased to find an empty glass jar under the sink. That would have to do.

He set the flowers next to the champagne.

"Rebecca," he called out.

"Just a second, honey. I'm just about through," came the muffled answer from the darkroom on the other side of their little house. "Give me a couple of minutes."

"You got 'em," David said as he sat down on the floor, surveying their new world. Funny, he mused, how things turned out. Rebecca knew exactly what David was going through because she had just done the same thing.

She had been a young whiz-kid in the escrow business, having her own firm by age twenty-nine. David attributed that to the fact that Rebecca was probably the most organized person in the world. (Whenever David would mention anything about that, she would reply, "Of course! I'm a Virgo," as if that took care of any questions he might have had on that subject.)

She had had a very successful company but, like David, only a portion of her was satisfied by it. What was missing was the creative aspect, the artist in her. That found its release in her photography. David loved her work, as did the few others she'd shared it with. She had a sensitive eye and a sure hand . . . a natural.

Her anonymity was about to end, David felt certain. Rebecca sold her company to her best friend and had been devoting herself solely to photography for the last few months and loved it. Her first project was a collection called *California Mansions of the Thirties*.

She'd been shooting all over California and had quite an impressive collection. Equally impressive was the publisher that was already on board, waiting only for her to finish. Perfect.

It took David a little longer to wrap up his respective cases and clients but he finally had. Law had been good to him. After a brief stint as a prosecutor, he had switched to defense. His thoughts were to protect the little guy from getting beaten up by the system. It had definitely been safe, but the thrill of getting the bad guy was decidedly lacking. Actually, more and more he felt he had been hired to defend exactly those bad guys. He'd made a good chunk of money, and still was, but it was time to move on.

David was anxious and ready to proceed with his new occupation also. He wondered how long it would be before there would be a publisher waiting for him to finish a project.

"They're beautiful. Where'd you get them?" Rebecca's voice startled David out of his reverie. She knelt down and smelled the flowers he brought her.

"Next door. We have a whole lot full of them."

"Wonderful. Thank you," she said. "And I love your vase."

"In keeping with your decor, my dear," David said, looking around at the emptiness.

"I'm going after the 'uncluttered look.'"

"You succeeded. How's it going? Need any help?"

"No, thanks. I've got a couple of rolls left but I'm through for today."

"Good. How about a walk?"

"Perfect timing. I even cleaned out the trays." She reached down to help him up. "Let's get out of here."

They exited through the kitchen sliders and practically ran down the deck stairs to the beach. David quickly took off his shoes and left them on the stairs. They both agreed that nothing was better than bare toes on the beach.

Rebecca Ramos grew up in Carmel, California, daughter of Stephen Ramos, owner of the prestigious Ramos galleries. These were two of the more successful of the multitudinous art galleries in Carmel. As a smart, pretty girl with money, life was nearly idyllic for young Rebecca.

That all changed when a truck took a wide turn and slammed into the car driven by her mother, who was dropping off Rebecca's ten-year-old brother at school. Her mother suffered a few broken bones. Her brother was killed. Rebecca was fourteen.

Even though it was deemed that Rebecca's mother had done no wrong, things were never the same between her folks. The mother, of course, was devastated; the father always seemed to have an air of suspicion in the back of his mind that she could have done *something* to have gotten out of the way of that truck. They divorced three years later.

Rebecca bounced back and forth between the two until she went off to college. She was immensely thankful that she only had to put up with that for a year. It was bitter and sad and all-encompassing in its destruction of two good people.

Although it was certainly not pleasant, Rebecca did not include herself in the "destructed" column. She felt bad. She missed her silly little brother like crazy but she would make it. Still, her folks were so consumed by the dead son, sometimes Rebecca felt like raising her hand and saying, "I'm here," just to remind them that they still had one living child.

She went to Berkeley with a major in art and a minor in economics. Although she didn't need the money, she worked part-time at an escrow firm to make some money of her own. Daddy's pockets were deep but any money asked for or offered seemed more and more to have price tags on it.

Economics won out over art mainly because the break in economics came first. The break, in this case, was a simple awareness that she knew how to run an escrow. It made perfect sense to her and once she learned how to run the checks and inquiries, what forms were necessary, where to get them and how to fill them out . . . it was a matter of routine, a routine she could teach others.

Escrow houses all sold the same service. Very seldom was one actually "better" than another. They all had to do the same drill and comply with the same laws. Rebecca saw that what it came down to was marketing. She also saw that men comprised 90 percent of their clientele. (The wives would buy the house but the men got the paperwork.)

After graduation, she went to work for a large escrow firm and started her own two years later. She hired young, attractive, smart women, trained them well and paid them better. She didn't mind the so-called political incorrectness of it at all. The customers were happy, her employees were happy, they performed a necessary service, did it well, and she made a pot full of money. She was also bored to death after five years.

A new wrinkle came into her life, making things seem a little more worthwhile: the man in the elevator. The firm where this tall, dark, and handsome type worked occupied the top floor of the building where Rebecca housed her company.

They arrived at work about the same time and, sometimes, after working late, even left at seven or eight o'clock together. It started with cordial smiles and nods, but soon led to introductions. His name was David and he was a partner in the law firm upstairs. She soon noticed that arriving and leaving for work constituted the high points of her days.

It moved quickly onto the next level one day, when she was asking about him and found that he'd been asking the same people about her. They both laughed about it in the elevator and made a date to meet for drinks. They never looked back.

They married two years later. David was very good to Rebecca and her folks, who never did reconcile. The parents had both smoked, but it was the father who came down with lung cancer. After an excruciating year, in which he could hardly breathe, he mercifully died.

Her mother went on to live another five unhappy years and died from a heart attack . . . with a burning cigarette by her side.

Her folks hadn't spoken to each other for their last ten years.

Rebecca buried them on either side of her dead brother. She hoped she learned whatever lesson lurked in all that pain. Nothing sprung to mind but, she thought, something big enough to ruin three lives should have a lesson, a moral . . . something. Until an epiphany of some sort came along, she considered those plots the end of a tragic tale and proceeded to get on with living.

Over the years, experience and conversations with David led them both to feel that life did not have to be painful. Moments would happen, of course, but not everything . . . moments. That led to talks of what they both would really like, their dreams. That led to some big decisions that led, in turn, to their new lives at the beach house.

Life, for the moment, was exactly what both had dreamed. It was a fine time.

4

The beach was practically empty. Multiple sets of waves chased each other to the shore. Overcast skies blended with the ocean into one gray mass. David and Rebecca held each other easily as they walked along. Theirs was a close, comfortable love that couldn't help but show forth whenever they were together.

"We didn't get a chance to talk much about it last night," Rebecca was saying as they walked. "It was hard, wasn't it?"

"Yeah."

"How do you feel?"

"Nervous, happy, sad, elated, confused. You know . . . the usual," David replied after a moment. This wasn't the time to go into exactly how hard it had been to leave the firm he helped start, the tears in his secretary's eyes, leaving good friends. He got a lump in his throat just thinking about it. What would happen if he tried to talk? No. They'd go into all that later.

David chuckled to himself. Wouldn't the ladies around their law firm be amazed by his emotions at the time. His nickname around the office, supposedly behind his back, was "the volcano." David was quiet and mild-mannered . . . usually . . . but get on the wrong side of an argument, or a case he felt particularly strong about, and watch the eruption! He could be as strong, confrontational, vitriolic, acerbic, and just as downright mean as the next lawyer, if it was necessary. After the trial, he'd smile, shake everybody's hands, and leave like nothing had ever happened.

"Any second thoughts?" she wanted to know, bringing David back to reality.

"No. Not really."

They walked silently for a while, then Rebecca proclaimed, "I'm very proud of you."

"I haven't done anything yet."

"Excuse me," she corrected. "You've taken the first giant step. Do you realize how few people ever commit to anything?"

They walked farther. There was nothing to say to that. Maybe she was right. Well, he was certainly committed, he did know that.

"I think I'm going to like being married to a writer," Rebecca added.

"Writers are notoriously hungry."

"So, we'll live on love. No calories."

"Oh, right. We'd hate to get you all the way up to a hundred pounds, wouldn't we?"

They both laughed, held each other a little tighter. David then turned them around and looked back at their house.

"It isn't exactly *Tara*," David said.

"Tara didn't have an ocean."

"That's true."

"Oh, David, this is just too good," Rebecca said as they started walking slowly back toward the house. "A new house, new careers."

A dark man with a windbreaker was walking down the beach toward them.

"New neighbors to meet."

As they passed, David looked over to the man and smiled. "Hello."

Bashaar walked silently by, looking at them a bit too intently before he remembered to nod slightly as he continued walking.

". . . or not," Rebecca added with a smile.

"How's your shoot coming?" David asked, changing the mood.

"Great. I'm just about through. I'm really just one great old behemoth away. I've only got one shot of it on this roll, but I'm going to have to show you this one. It's sad."

"Sad?'

"It's outrageously gorgeous but no one has taken care of it in years."

"Is it empty?"

"No, I've seen people there. A few, actually. Could even be military."

"Really?" David said, surprised. "You don't usually hear mansions and military in the same sentence. Army?"

"Yeah, but I don't think *our* Army. What's Shelly?"

"Armenian."

"Maybe they were Armenian, something like that. They also didn't seem real accommodating. I don't know if I'll be able to fully shoot it or not. It would make a nice contrast to the other pieces."

"I hope you get it."

"Me, too."

They continued walking, enjoying the moment. The sun dropped below the cloud level, shooting rays of light over the water.

"Going to be a pretty one," David said, softly.

Rebecca followed his look, started to nod, then panicked.

"Oh, my God. C'mon, quick!" she said, grabbing David by the hand and running back toward the house.

"What is it?"

"Timing! Run!" is all Rebecca said as she continued on as fast as she could.

The previous conversation was left behind. David left his shoes where they were as they bounded two steps at a time up to the deck. Rebecca led him to the sliders opening into what would be his writing area.

They figured it was originally meant to be a dining room but the table they had in the kitchen would do just fine. They decided this would be the perfect writing area for David. From his desk he could see and talk to Rebecca when she was in the kitchen, could see into the living room and the fireplace on one side and, of course, the expanse of ocean through the floor-to-ceiling glass sliders on the other. Not bad.

Still breathing heavily from the run, Rebecca said, "Okay, now stand right there and close your eyes."

"Rebecca, what are you—?"

"Just close your eyes," she said, stopping him. "I have a little housewarming present."

He closed his eyes; she went to a nearby closet and struggled to bring out a large, heavy rolled-up rug.

"Actually, it's a very large housewarming present."

"Now, you shouldn't be—"

"Do you like sunsets, or not?" she said, cutting him off again.

"I love them."

"Then open your eyes."

David did, seeing her standing next to the large roll.

"What did you do?" he asked.

"Find out," she replied, motioning to the roll.

He took it from her. Laid it down and unrolled the most

beautiful Navajo rug he'd ever seen. The primary color was maroon offset by marvelous patterns in black, gray, and gold.

"To help you write," Rebecca said, pleased with the stunned look on his face. "You've always wanted one."

"Only my whole life. Oh, Becca, it's perfect. I can't believe it." He took her in his arms. "I sure do love you."

"I sure do love you right back."

They kissed, holding each other very tightly. Between kisses they sank to the floor and stretched out on the new rug, each wrapped around the other.

The sun sank even lower on the horizon, splitting clouds and sea, sending colors kaleidoscoping everywhere.

When the sun decided to fully set, it left the sea view from the house decidedly black. The two naked lovers were still on the rug, clothes in piles around them, lit softly from a light in the kitchen. Melodious strings from the stereo accompanied the scene as did the chilled champagne, which had been moved over to them and now appeared empty.

"The future is going to be so great," Rebecca said.

"I hadn't noticed a whole lot wrong with the present," David said, taking another sip of his champagne. Rebecca smiled.

"Want to have a baby?" she asked.

"What?"

"Sure. We're not too old, are we? This could be the perfect place for them. The little nippers could run around on the beach . . . not a bad way to grow up."

"Are you trying to tell me something?"

"Not yet," Rebecca replied seductively, as she set her champagne glass down and started after David with a mission. They melded into each other's arms, surrounded by the soft shadows of the night, feeling a contented happiness that both had craved for a long time.

t was a warm, sunny, clear day, perfect for moving. Rebecca and David had commandeered about ten of their friends to help and had made their first beach party out of it. Most of the hauling had been done. Furniture had been haphazardly set about and boxes were everywhere. Most of the crowd had already discovered the beer, the deck, and the beach. It was a relaxed group of old friends.

Chuck DiLucca and David were best friends. That's "were" as in past tense. When David first got out of law school, he worked as an Assistant California District Attorney, prosecuting the bad guys. Tall, dark, and macho, Chuck was a young officer on the San Francisco Police force and soon befriended his "cohort in crime," as he referred to David.

They were the "dynamic duo." Chuck would nab them, David would put them away. What a team! They, and their respective ladies of the moment, would take trips together: through the wine country, Vegas, Palm Springs, etc. They had a great time and thoroughly enjoyed each other.

That started to change when David went into private practice. Suddenly, he was no longer a prosecutor but a defender. His job now, as far as Chuck was concerned, was to get the scumbags off.

They found themselves hanging out less and less. The brakes were totally applied to their friendship when David was hired by a defendant that Chuck had personally arrested. David hadn't known that, only finding out when the trial began.

At first, David didn't know what he should do. He even considered removing himself as counsel, but the case he'd worked up was a sound one. Parts of his certainty were in the borderline ethics and strong-arm tactics of the arresting officer—even if it was Chuck.

David won the case handily and the defendant went free. Chuck was livid. The two men had a drink together later that night and became so vocal in their discussion that the bartender had to ask them to hold it down or take it outside.

They opted for outside, walking away in opposite directions.

The final nail in this particular coffin (as if it needed one) was when David successfully defended another of Chuck's collars. That did it. Chuck couldn't even be in the same room with David and wasn't for many years.

About two years ago, David and Rebecca had run into Chuck and his wife, Margie, at a fund-raiser. The men's estrangement had been so total, neither man had met either wife. There was a little discomfort between David and Chuck but not as much as they would have thought. The ladies, having no past history, immediately hit it off. David and Chuck found they could actually talk to each other and a fragile friendship started again.

For a time, everyone seemed to be getting along just fine . . . except Chuck and Margie. They'd been married seven years and had, evidently, spent the last four of them bickering. A suspected dalliance of Chuck's kicked it over the edge. Margie threw Chuck out and filed for divorce.

David and Rebecca got calls from each of them, telling the sad tale from their respective points of view and asking for the compassion and understanding of a friend. More than once, Chuck could have been found at David and Rebecca's house, watching football games, with Chuck preparing to spend the night in the guest room, while Rebecca was out consoling a distraught Margie who hadn't quite figured out how to get on with the rest of her life.

A messy divorce ensued, during which Chuck and David became much closer. A year later Margie was killed in a traffic accident. Chuck was so upset, one would never have known the terrible things they had said about each other a mere year earlier. Chuck, David, and Rebecca were now fast friends.

Almost. There was another side of Chuck that David wasn't quite sure about. The questionable practices David had defended against years ago were still part of the way Chuck did business. David knew that. He also knew that many of the ravings of the indignant Margie were true. David and Rebecca hadn't seen this side for years, nevertheless, David knew it was there.

It was never like before. Still, things seemed to ease up even more when David retired from the law. He and Chuck talked to each other on the phone every week or so and saw each other at least once a month. That seemed to work for everybody.

At the moment, Chuck was carrying half a couch through the front doorway, with David on the other end.

"Where do you want this, babe?" David called out to Rebecca, who was chatting with a small group on the deck.

"Oh, just anywhere," she said. "We'll scoot it all around tomorrow."

Both men gladly set it down right where they stood.

"This looks like 'anywhere' to me," David said, tired. "Thanks Chuck. That's it, isn't it?"

"Unless you want to bring in the trailer. It'd make a hell of a planter."

"C'mon. I'll buy you a beer."

As the men started for the deck, another man came in, Shelly. He was small, dark, late thirties, of Armenian descent.

"Am I late?" he asked.

"Oh, perfect timing, Shell," Chuck said. "We just brought in the last piece."

"Sorry about that, guys. I got stuck at a showing." Shelly came in, shook hands with David and Chuck.

"No worries," David said. "Finding this place for us forgives you a multitude of sins. C'mon."

The men walked out to the deck. David meant what he'd said to Shelly. He felt he owed him big time. He and Rebecca hadn't thought it would be that difficult finding just the right beach house until they started looking. Shelly was their real estate agent. David had known him cursorily for years but it wasn't until they spent most of the last year looking at places with him that they really got to know him.

He was the sturdy soul who led them to anything that remotely had "beach" in its description: by the beach, close to the beach, beach view, and, of course, their favorite . . . on the beach.

They figured Shelly must have shown them at least seventy houses before they finally found the one they were looking for and Shelly finally got his commission. It was a win-win, and Shelly was now considered a friend in the highest standing, even if he did show up late.

6

David, Chuck, and Shelly walked out on the deck, retrieved some beers from the large galvanized tub, and small-talked with the assembled group. The ladies from Rebecca's old company were there, as were casual friends and coworkers of David's. The biggest, tallest, and loudest of these was David's former law partner, Sol Freeburg, who was just replenishing his beer.

"This is going to be nice, Dave," Sol said, looking around approvingly. "There's a good feel here. You're still crazy, but at least you're going out in style."

"Why crazy?" Shelly wondered.

"Why crazy?" Sol repeated in his booming voice. "This is a very successful man you're looking at here. This genius is hanging up a practice most attorneys would kill for." Sol turned to David. "Tell me, does the world really need another novel?"

"I'll be writing other things, too, Sol."

"You bet you will, like letters to friends—please send money." Sol laughed at his own wit. "Seriously, we all wish you the best. God sometimes looks after the fools of this world; maybe you'll be one of them. You got any contacts?"

"We'll soon find out."

"There's always a desk for you, buddy. Know that."

At that moment, Rebecca's voice came up from below where a fire had been going. "Come and get it! Burgers are burnin'!"

Chuck was the first to move. "Excuse me. You really don't want to get between a cop and free food."

Shelly followed him, leaving David and Sol for a moment.

"Thanks for it all, Sol," David said warmly. "I mean it."

"I know you do."

The old friends shared a hug (the manly type, lots of patting) and started down the stairs and met Rebecca coming up.

"We're out of beer down there," she said.

"We have another case."

"And I'll bet you know just where to find it."

"Actually, I do." David turned to Sol. "Catch you later." Sol continued down to the beach as David and Rebecca went to another galvanized tub on the far side of the deck. David poured out the excess water and started to pick it up when he noticed Rebecca looking out over the scene. He joined her.

"Good friends," she said, huddling under his arm.

"Sure are," David agreed. They watched the people below for a while. Everyone seemed to be having a good time, the gathering centered around the fire on the beach. It was a comforting sight.

"Do you think we're doing the right thing?" Rebecca asked after a moment.

"I hope so. I do know I've never been happier."

"Sometimes I wonder if we're being realistic at all or just dreaming."

"Wait a minute," David said, turning to look at Rebecca straight on. "Are you talking to me about being realistic? I've only wanted to write since I was twelve; because of you, a twenty-six-year-old dream is coming true—and you're talking about being realistic?"

"Because of me?" she asked.

"Becca, you're the only person in my life that doesn't think I'm crazy to do this."

"With your talent I think you'd be crazy not to."

David threw his arms out wide. "I rest my case."

Rebecca smiled, then cuddled back under his arm again. "I guess the scary thing is, where do you go after perfect?"

"You don't go anywhere. That's where you hang out."

That sounded good. She liked that. "Sure do love you," she said softly.

David looked back at her and was about to speak when Chuck's voice boomed out, "Hey! About the beer?"

"Oh, sorry. Be right down." David turned to Rebecca, gave her a smile and a quick kiss, grabbed the tub of ice and beer bottles, and carried it down the stairs. Rebecca followed.

He set the tub down next to the empty one and looked back at his friends, dramatically accented by the fire.

"Uh, sorry about your marriage not working out, guys," Shelly said as everyone cracked up. Yes, it was a grand gathering of friends. Just the way it was supposed to be.

Two days after the beach party, the place looked considerably better, but the weather remained foggy and overcast. Boxes still dominated the scene but the furniture, at least, had been placed in some sort of order.

Most of David's activities had been centered around his work area, which now appeared ready: desk in place, computer hooked up, all set in full view of the ocean. The Navajo rug dominated the room and gave it a classy, warm look. David sat behind his desk looking out over it all. Pretty darn good, he was thinking.

"Shit!" Rebecca was obviously frustrated by something in her darkroom.

David couldn't help smiling. "Hark! Is that my delicate little flower?"

"Damn it! I lost a roll of film," Rebecca said as she came out of her darkroom. "It's probably behind those . . ." She suddenly became aware of what she was looking at. "Oh, David. I love it."

"So do I," David said, beaming.

"It's perfect," Rebecca said, walking barefoot over the Navajo rug. "You will be able to write wonderful, wonderful words here."

David swiveled his chair around. Rebecca knew that cue, came around the desk, and sat on his lap.

"Thank you, honey," David said, holding her.

"T'was my pleasure," she said before kissing him.

"Now, all I've got to do is think of something to write."

"I have faith," Rebecca said, relaxing into his arms.

"Well, that faith might get put to the test pretty quickly," David said, not letting her go. "You remember my story about the young man in his twenties who meets his father for the first time?"

"Uh-huh, I love it. It makes me cry."

"I sent it off this morning," David stated simply.

"Oh, I'm so glad," Rebecca said, straightening up. "There's so much hope in that one. Just promise me when you get rich and famous, you won't go getting all weird on me."

"Well, it'll be a chore, but I'll try." David squeezed her a little tighter. "Want to fool around?"

"Yes, as a matter of fact, but let me find that roll of film first. I've almost got this wrapped up," she said, reluctantly getting off his lap.

"Go get 'em!"

Rebecca gave him a not-so-ferocious growl as she headed back toward the darkroom. Suddenly, the doorbell rang. She changed direction, midstride. "I'll get it," she said and continued on into the living room and the front door.

When she opened it, Bashaar was standing there in a long coat.

"Mrs. Collier?" he asked.

"Yes."

Bashaar calmly brought a pistol with a silencer on it out of his pocket, raised it to eye level, and shot Rebecca in the head.

7

David *was still arranging* his desk when he heard a *thump* from the other room. He looked up.

"Who is it, hon?"

When he got no answer, he got up from his desk and went into the living room. "Becca?" As he rounded the stairs, David saw the grisly scene: Rebecca lying in a growing pond of blood with the killer standing over her.

When Bashaar saw David he quickly raised his gun and fired again, barely missing. David bolted for the back of the house, Bashaar right behind. David had reached his workroom slider when Bashaar turned the corner and fired again. This one hit David in the leg, the concussion throwing him through the partially opened door, onto the deck.

David half-climbed, half-fell off the deck onto the beach, surrounded by the early morning ocean fog. He limped next door as fast as his painful leg would allow.

"Help! Help! There's a man with a gun here! He's shot my wife! Call the police! Help!"

Most of the houses along this stretch of beach were raised above the sand and high tides by pylons. David just reached the bottom of his neighbor's house when a bullet dug into one of these, inches from David's head. Damn! Why couldn't these people ever be here? Realizing shouting gave away his position, David got very quiet. Painfully, he worked from pylon to pylon, hoping the ocean fog would help conceal him somewhat.

David was fully in shock, non-thinking except for being more frightened than he ever believed possible. When he reached the other side of the house, he forced himself up an incline that would bring him to the street.

He cautiously looked around the corner and saw Bashaar back by their beach house, looking the other way. David started hobbling in the other direction as fast as he could. Even through the fog, the visibility was good enough for Bashaar to notice David's movement.

Bashaar started unscrewing the silencer when a woman's voice was heard calling from the beach side. "Mandy! Where are you? You get back in the house this instant. I mean it!"

Not wanting to draw attention to himself, Bashaar screwed the silencer back on and stepped between two parked cars. He steadied himself on one and started taking careful, but still somewhat rushed, two-handed shots, thankful that there was no traffic on Shoreline Drive at this time. Bashaar cursed the silencer under his breath for disrupting his usual uncanny accuracy.

David, of course, knew nothing of this. He continued to run, erratically, hysterically, pain shooting up his leg, as Bashaar quietly fired off rounds. After the fifth shot, David's head seemed to explode. Suddenly, the world and everything in it turned black.

The typically bland armory sat baking in the midday sun. It was a large, unadorned metal building, with not a tree to be seen on the grounds. The perimeter was marked by a chain-link fence that encircled the building, a few trucks, and the handful of soldiers who were milling about.

A large garbage truck pulled up to the guard station out front. Identification and small talk were exchanged before the truck was waved in and proceeded directly to a large Dumpster at the back of the armory. No one paid it any mind.

Two men in City Maintenance uniforms climbed out of the truck and started hooking up the Dumpster for emptying. Two others, who had kept themselves out of sight, also climbed out of the cab and ran, unseen, to the back wall of the armory. Ameen was one of these men, carrying with him two canisters similar to the one dropped in the jewelry store.

The other man quickly and quietly drilled a four-inch hole through the corrugated tin exterior wall. Ameen set a small timer on each of the canisters and pushed them, one at a time, through the hole, hearing them land on the other side. Then they ran back to the truck and waited.

The two explosions from inside the armory caused the soldiers to instantly become alert. They shouldered their weapons and carefully entered the armory. Another man in maintenance uniform who was hiding behind a parked car out front knocked out the guard at the entrance, who had also turned at the sound of the explosions. The "maintenance man" then stuffed the guard down into his small booth, making sure that he couldn't be seen. He ran to join the others.

The initial two workers disconnected the Dumpster from the truck, put on gas masks, and opened the two large doors to the armory. They were pleased to see the ten or twelve soldiers lying on the ground, unconscious. They returned to the large garbage truck and drove it inside. The other men, also in gas masks, closed the doors behind it.

Surrounding the truck were, literally, hundreds of different types of rifles, pistols, ammunition, grenades, bazookas, and boxes of what appeared to be explosives.

The huge rear of the truck was opened and the men quickly and efficiently began loading the arsenal into the truck. They seemed to know exactly what they wanted and where they could find it.

Within a short period of time, the truck was full. The drivers climbed in, another opened the doors to the armory and closed them again when the truck was safely out. He then climbed in the truck with the others and drove away. The guard was still not moving. There was no sign that anything at all had happened.

David's eyelids blinked a couple of times as he tried to deal with the shards of light penetrating through and to bring the world into focus. He could barely make out that an attending nurse noticed his movement. She quickly ran off, returning with a doctor.

The doctor started talking to David, asking him questions, but David heard nothing. The doctor continued to try to make contact. David blinked a couple more times when things started to get fuzzier, but he couldn't make anything more clear. He still heard nothing as everything around him started to fade until it all again turned to black.

8

D avid tried again *to return to consciousness. As before, the bright light was difficult to face. He let a little seep by his eyelids, then a little more. Bit by bit, he got acclimated until he could open his eyes and see the nondescript hospital room he was in.*

There was no one around, but that was all right. He still felt pretty groggy and didn't really care to see anyone right then anyway. Except Rebecca. An empty feeling in the pit of his stomach hit him as he remembered the last time he saw her.

Could she have survived that? Please God, have her live. It looked horrible, gruesome, but sometimes people lived through things like that. Didn't they? Please let her be one of those cases.

As David slowly awoke, he became aware of the total silence around him. He knew hospitals were never noisy places, but this was different. As he was beginning to question it more, a nurse casually looked in and was surprised to see David's eyes open. She smiled, came over to the bed, and started talking to him.

Another hollow feeling went through David. He couldn't hear a thing. Nothing. He tried to talk to her, to tell her that he couldn't hear but when he moved his jaw the right side of his head seemed to erupt. He grimaced in pain and closed his mouth. That would have to wait.

The nurse, seeing him hurting, silently said something else to him and left. A few minutes later a doctor returned with the nurse and the same silent talking commenced. As disconcerting as it was, that would have to wait, too. More important than his hearing, more important than anything in the world: how was Rebecca?

He gritted through the pain of moving his jaw and managed to say, "Rebecca." His voice sounded strange to him, like he was talking into a metal rain barrel, but they heard him. They also didn't know what to do except exchange glances. Maybe they didn't know what they should say. Was he strong enough to hear the truth?

Unfortunately, their concerned vacillations told David everything he didn't want to know. The hollow feeling in his stomach gave way to a boulder in his throat that only got bigger. It couldn't be. Not his sweet Rebecca. The love of his life. His . . . his . . . He broke down in uncontrollable heart-wrenching sobs. No, not his Rebecca.

The doctor and nurse realized that this was not the time for them to talk to David. They left him alone, alone with his devastation. No, Not his Rebecca!

Over the next few days, David learned that he had been in a coma for nearly three weeks. A small amount of hearing returned to his left ear, rather like people whispering in another room. He became aware of sound but not enough to understand what the noise might be.

Rebecca was dead. David wanted to return to the blissful nothingness of the coma.

A bullet had struck the right side of David's head, above the ear. It entered and kept going, grazing his brain on the way. Exactly what the ramifications of that would be were unknown for the moment.

Dr. Mandell had been working with David on his hearing. Since David still had head wounds, for their session that morning the doctor was using a large soft headset that they'd used before. The doc-

*tor gingerly placed the earphones around the heavy bandages pro-
tecting David's head and over his ears.*

Sound crackled in the earphones as connections were made and
David reentered the realm of the hearing.

"Still okay?" Dr. Mandell asked when he got the earphones
in place.

David nodded.

"Good. The results of the first tests are in and I'm afraid it's
like I suspected. There will be no further hearing in your right
ear. The auditory nerve was damaged, but obviously, hearing
can be continued in your left ear with the aid of a hearing device,
so we have something to work with there.

"As for your leg injury," the doctor continued. "The muscles
were damaged quite severely but the bone was not broken and you
seem to be mending nicely. It may bother you some, but I imagine
you'll regain most, if not all, of your leg movement in time. Key
words being: in time. All right," the doctor said as he stood. "I'll
be back in a few minutes and we can run some more tests . . . see
what got chewed up in that brain of yours besides your hearing."

When Dr. Mandell left, Judy, an attractive nurse who had
been standing off to one side during this exchange, approached
David's bed.

"This may not seem like good news to you," she began, "but
given the severity of your injuries, I think you should be considered very lucky."

David didn't react to this. Nurse Judy also left the room,
passing Chuck in the doorway.

"I don't think you're lucky at all," Chuck said as he pulled a
chair up to David's bed. "In fact, I'd say you are about the un-
luckiest son of a bitch I know right now."

David strained to look over at him. "Rebecca?" he asked, hopefully.

Chuck was surprised at this. "Dave, they told you. They had to have . . . she's dead. You did know that, right?"

David sunk back into his bed, nodded his head. "Yeah, I was just hoping maybe . . ." How would he finish that? Hope it was all a dream, maybe? Sure, that would work. Anything but the reality.

"The funeral was a couple of weeks ago. You've been out of it for a while now, remember?"

"The funeral?" David's devastation over Rebecca's death had only gone as far as that. He could hardly get his mind around that, let alone thinking any further. "How? I mean . . . who? . . ."

"It was a joint effort, Dave. I kinda oversaw it but, Sol, Shelly, a bunch of folks chipped in. You two have a lot of friends, you know?"

David nodded slightly, noticing that Chuck had phrased that in the present tense, and was grateful. "Thank you."

"It was our privilege," Chuck said, gently.

Silence sat between them for a moment as David, again, tried to come to grips with everything that had happened.

"Listen, I don't have a lot of time here," Chuck said. "I've taken over this case personally. I hope that's all right with you."

David's look showed that he appreciated it very much.

"All right then, forgive me but I have to play Dick Tracy now," Chuck added, moving ahead. "First big question, did you see who did it?"

David nodded.

"Good. The doctor told me that it's tough for you to talk right now, but try your best. Describe him."

"Man . . . dark hair . . . dark complexion . . ." David began deliberately, his words sounding like he had a mouth full of mush. "About five-seven . . . slight build . . . early forties . . . raincoat."

"Dark complexion as in black? Latin? Foreign? . . ."

"Foreign."

"Arab?"

"Maybe."

"Oh, great. That's all we need. Had you seen him before?" Chuck asked, taking notes of David's answers.

"Maybe on the beach," David said after thinking a moment.

"Does he live around there?"

"I don't know."

"Anything else?" Chuck asked, coming closer, sitting on the side of David's bed. "C'mon, think like a lawyer again when you were beating my ass. You know what I need: scars, pockmarks, tattoos, an accent, a limp?"

David thought for another minute, then shook his head no.

"All right." Chuck hesitated. He knew these next ones would be tough. "Can you think of anyone who would want to kill Rebecca?"

David thought. Even the concept was difficult for him to consider. Kill Rebecca? God, no.

"Maybe something to do with her childhood?" Chuck persisted. "Jealous friends or relatives? Enemies?"

David shook his head. Rebecca had been the sweetest person on the planet. How could anyone want to kill her?

"She just started this photography thing, didn't she? What was she working on?"

"California mansions of the thirties."

"So she was shooting a bunch of old mansions? That's a real hot-button topic," Chuck added dryly.

"Pictures in the darkroom."

"No, they aren't."

"Yeah. They are."

"I looked."

"Chuck, Rebecca had been working all morning," David insisted. "They were hanging everywhere."

"We've searched the house, Dave. Believe me, there are no pictures hanging in the darkroom."

David sank back into his pillow, feeling even more defeated. Chuck went back to his notes.

"Maybe I'd better look into that after all. What could be such a big deal about a bunch of old mansions?" Chuck said, almost to himself. "It does look like we're dealing with a pro here, though . . . the execution-style murder of Rebecca, using a silencer. . . . By the way, that probably kept you alive. A silencer blows the hell out of accuracy past five or six feet. He had to be very good to get you at all. You were really too far to—"

"Chuck?" David interrupted.

"What."

David looked over to him earnestly. "I want to kill him."

"Hey, pal, get in line," Chuck said, trying to calm David down. "This guy is not going to walk, believe me." He stood. "You just take care of yourself. Let me get going on this. Mend! That's an order. I'll see you soon."

Chuck gave David a gentle pat on the shoulder and left. David stoically stared off into nothing, having no idea how to face this new, awful world he found himself in.

Three days later, David was propped up in bed, half-asleep. The fewer bandages on his head attested to his improvement. Judy entered with another nurse, Pam.

"Now, this is more like it," Pam said, looking at David.

"Here's my candidate for most likely to receive mouth-to-mouth resuscitation. A young, handsome, recently widowed writer cast adrift in the world . . . I could get into that."

Judy looked at her, amazed. "How can you talk like that right in front of him?"

"Oh, it's all right," Pam said. "He's deaf. He can't hear a thing without the machine."

"Uh, Pam . . . I think you'd better take another look."

Pam looked over to David, who held her gaze for a moment, then started to smile. He then held up the main unit of a smaller hearing aid he'd been fitted with. He'd heard it all.

"Oh, my God," Pam cried, totally mortified. She turned and ran from the room. David and Judy shared a chuckle.

"How are you doing?" she asked.

"All right, I guess. I'm ready to get out of here."

"Always a good sign," Judy said, as a bell in the hallway chimed. "Well, I'm being summoned. Try not to break any more hearts. I'll be back."

Judy left, leaving David alone with his thoughts . . . thoughts that no one should be left alone with.

9

A few days later, David was in a wheelchair, looking more like a person and less like a mummy. He talked with Chuck, who sat in one of the two chairs in the room. David still seemed quite weak.

"I wish I could say we were hot on his ass, but so far we've got bupkas. But don't worry about it, we're just getting started."

David nodded. "I know."

"So this hearing thing works pretty good, huh?"

"Yeah, it's doing all right as long as I point my good ear at you. I still miss a word now and then but . . . it's all right. It gets a little creative on me sometimes. I picked up a local jazz station yesterday." Chuck laughed. "You think I'm kidding. . . . I really did! It was weird." They both smiled a moment. "So what else is happening in the wacky world of law enforcement?"

"Oh, we're having a lot of fun. We've got a United Nations Middle-Eastern Peace Conference going on for a few weeks, with a couple of hundred Arab honchos over here, each one wanting to be taken care of like he and his group are the only ones here. These guys are maddening enough trying to deal with one on one. I can't imagine a whole room full of them.

"Plus," Chuck continued, "we've got terrorists or somebody

stealing jewels and guns and explosives. . . . Somehow these guys got hold of some of that Russian gas they used when all those kids got killed over there. It's an opiate called fentanyl, but they seem to have laced it with something else, too. It'll knock you out with one breath. It's supposed to be nonlethal but we've got at least three deaths so far anyway. People with weak hearts, respiratory problems . . . you know. The problem is trying to figure out what they plan to do with this stuff."

The door suddenly opened and Sol and his wife, Kay, came in. She crossed immediately to David.

"Oh, David, we heard that you were up and could hear again. We're so glad. Comas are so scary. We just wanted to say how absolutely terrible we feel and if there's anything we can do . . ."

"Thank you, Kay."

"We're so sorry you missed the funeral. It was so lovely . . . if there can be such a thing. Reverend Clark did a beautiful ceremony."

"He married us."

"I remember. He is so fond of you both. . . . Well . . . was . . . I mean . . ."

"Thanks so much for taking care of the arrangements everybody," David said. "I can't tell you how much that means to me."

"We were all glad to do what we could. You're not the only one who loved Rebecca, you know?" Kay said.

David smiled. Like Rebecca had said a lifetime ago, looking over this very bunch at the beach house, good friends.

"How much longer are you going to have to be here?" Sol asked.

"Probably a couple more weeks. You ought to see me in my walker. Pretty darn impressive." David knew they meant well, very well. He owed them, big time. Even though he was not in the mood for this at all, the least he could do was to act cheerful for their sakes. Their voices seemed to run together and he had to concentrate very hard to understand what people were saying to him.

The door opened again and Shelly came in.

"Good to see you up," he said as he came over to David.

"Hey, Shelly."

"How are you feeling?"

"Oh . . . fine. Now wait a minute," David said, looking at his room full of friends. "This can't be a coincidence. How'd you swing it? Isn't there supposed to be a limit?"

"We just got a little devious," Sol answered. "We noticed who your neighbors were and all asked for different room numbers."

"Are you going to let them get away with this, Officer?" David asked Chuck.

"Well, we have been known to turn our heads for a worthy cause," Chuck said with a smile.

"Will you be going back to the beach house?" Kay asked.

"Kay!" Sol was embarrassed by his wife's lack of tact.

"It's all right, Sol," David said easily. "I really don't know. But, whatever happens . . ."

The door opened again, this time admitting nurse Judy, who was first surprised, then appalled.

"What is going on in here?"

"Appears to be a gathering of friends," David said.

"Well, you can just 'gather' yourself out of here," Judy said strongly. "Visiting hours are over. Please leave . . . quickly and quietly!"

Judy left. The room was quiet for a moment as everyone looked sheepishly at each other.

"It was still a good idea," Shelly said.

Chuck was the first to rise. He came to David and shook his hand. "Hang in there. I'll let you know what's happening."

"Thanks Chuck."

The rest of the small group came by, wishing him well, offering best wishes and sympathy. When the last of them left, the toll showed on David. He was exhausted. He was just sitting, staring, recovering, when Judy came back in.

"I can't believe that," she said, still upset. "You're coming along nicely but you're not strong enough to—"

"Judy," David interrupted. "I don't want any more visitors."

"You can have *some*—but just one or two at a time."

"Listen to me, please," David said as emphatically as he could. "I don't want *any*! Not even during visiting hours. I'll tell you when I'm ready."

"Mr. Collier, a visitor now and then is good for you. You're just not ready for a party. People actually aid the . . ."

David got an idea midway through her speech. He took out the control for his hearing aid and, quite deliberately, so Judy could plainly see it, turned it off. *Judy's voice was instantly reduced to an unintelligible murmur. She continued to talk silently to him until she realized what he had done. She looked fed up with him and angrily stomped from the room. David stoically watched her go.*

Atop a building adjacent to the hospital, a dark figure moved to the edge of the roof and looked down. Through the hospital window, he could see David in his wheelchair. Bashaar was pleased that the city was still so noisy at this time of night. That would come in very handy, he thought, as he started assembling a sniper's rifle from its metal case.

49

David collected his thoughts for a moment and placed his hearing aid on the table next to the bed. *Without the aid, David's world was mostly silent. A gentle, underlying sound like wind blowing through trees provided a rather constant backdrop. As the doctor's experiments had shown, David could hear very loud sounds but might not be able to identify them. He would just be aware that something had happened.*

David noticed a TIME *magazine on a chest across the room and started to wheel over to it, then stopped. He decided to walk across.*

He laboriously got out of the wheelchair and attempted a few unsupported steps. Pain shot through his leg but he made it two steps, stopping to rest at the open window. He looked out at the active city below, wondering briefly if he would ever feel like rejoining that world.

Bashaar could hardly believe his good luck when he saw David present himself as a target standing in the window. Bashaar quickly assembled the last two pieces and got himself in position to fire.

Having caught his breath, David continued lurching over to the bureau and retrieved the magazine. He looked back to the wheelchair on the other side of the room, not remembering the room being so large.

Bashaar pulled back the rifle and waited patiently for David to light in one spot. His sniper position was well protected and he felt safe there. He could easily wait David out.

The return trip to the wheelchair was arduous but he did it. All right! One small step for man, and all that. He felt a sense of accomplishment as he collapsed back into his chair, took a few deep breaths, and proceeded to look through the magazine.

David was nicely centered in the window. This was what Bashaar had been waiting for. He slowly raised the rifle, steadied it on the small wall surrounding the rooftop, and took aim.

Damn! The light was all wrong for reading. David wheeled himself back, toward the wall where the light was brighter. Yes, that was better. He started to read again.

Bashaar was cursing David as he tried to readjust to the new angle David had just created. This one wasn't nearly as good. Bashaar climbed over heating ducts, around transoms, and still couldn't get a full shot. Ah well, at least David wasn't moving anymore. Bashaar knew he was an expert marksman. He could see enough of David to get the job done.

Once again, he took aim.

Silence enabled David to concentrate fully on whatever he was doing. He had quickly gotten engrossed in an article in the magazine and hadn't noticed anyone coming into the room. Suddenly a

*hand grabbed his shoulder and spun him around. There, talking to
him, her voice a hardly discernible hum, was nurse Judy.*

Bashaar patiently drew his rifle back. He watched and waited.

*As Judy continued talking silently to David, he turned, got his
hearing aid, and put it in.* The sounds of the city and Judy became clear.

". . . I've told you that before!" Judy said, angrily.

"What do you want?" David asked.

"I want you in bed. I thought you were going there when
your group left."

"I decided to read."

"It's almost eight-thirty. You can read in bed."

"I haven't gone to bed at eight-thirty since I was ten and being in bed is not going to help me a bit at this point."

"Why aren't you wearing your hearing aid?" Judy asked.

"Because there is a lot of *noise* in the world, Judy," David
said pointedly. "I now have the ability to tune it out."

Disgusted, Judy started for the door, turned. "Will you go to
bed soon, please?"

"Yes, I will go to bed soon," David answered, perhaps a bit
too loudly.

Nurse Judy left. David sat quietly, trying to calm down.
Then, again, *he took out his hearing aid and returned to his article.*

Seeing the nurse leave, Bashaar readied himself. It wasn't perfect but he thought he could make it. After carefully scoping
David in, he squeezed off a shot.

The window by David was open but had a screen. *Silently, the bullet tore through the screen and lodged in the wall behind David, who jumped. What was that? He had heard something but? . . . He looked around, saw nothing different. No one had come back in. Oh well, he knew there were going to be a lot of things he was going to have to get used to. Strange bumps and bangs were probably a part of it. He returned to his magazine.*

Bashaar was furious that he had missed the shot and started running back to where he'd left the rifle's case when he noticed David hadn't moved. He was still sitting there. How could that be?

Bashaar looked around. No one seemed to notice. What the hell, it looked like he was given a second chance. He again settled in, and took steady aim.

David was still reading when once again the screen silently tore open. *This time the bullet slammed into the wheelchair, spinning the chair and throwing David brutally to the floor. He cried out as the bullet ricocheted off into his bad leg.*

The sounds of the city covered the crack of the rifle but the sound the bullet made hitting the wheelchair, plus David's cry of pain, brought nurses and doctors running. David was on the floor, thoroughly scared and confused.

"What was that? Look, what the hell? What happened? My God, was he shot?" The medical staff was as frightened as David.

Eventually professionalism took over and David was returned to the bed, with attention given to his chewed-up leg.

Nurse Judy hated the look of painful bewilderment on David's face as he was given a sedative and wheeled down to the OR where they could assess and, hopefully, repair whatever damage had been done.

She took a cautious look outside the window after seeing the holes in the screen, but there were only dark, empty rooftops across the way and the noisy clatter of the city. Bashaar was gone.

10

A *bout fifteen minutes north* of the beach house was the little town of Bolinas. It wasn't much more than a wide spot in the road, but it sported a B&B, a couple of restaurants, a feed store, the Bolinas/Stinson elementary school, and a white slat Catholic church and cemetery. The cemetery was historical, very old, with headstones dating back to the 1800s. Eucalyptus groves intermingled with massive redwoods to give it a picturesque charm that would have done Norman Rockwell proud.

Chuck and his partner, Murray Townsend, a large black man in his mid-forties, stood by their unmarked police car, parked in the church's dirt parking lot, as David limped off into the cemetery. His hearing aid was in, head bandages now were minimal, and he walked with the aid of an ancient, beat-up cane that used to be his grandfather's.

He noticed that many of the old headstones had settled and fallen over and was surprised at the number of young children buried there. Many had their whole lives written out: lived 6 yrs. 3 mos. 14 days.

The site was gorgeous, as was the day. David noticed that he could see the water of the bay through the eucalyptus trees. Lovely.

Following Chuck's directions, he soon came to a red-hued stone with the simple markings,

REBECCA COLLIER
1974–2007

David just stood, staring, having no idea what to do or say. Realizing he had to do something, he choked back the lump in his throat and tried to speak.

"Uh . . . I'm sorry I missed the funeral. . . . I was still in a coma. . . . I heard it was beautiful. . . ." He stopped, feeling stupid talking to a piece of stone. He'd felt the same way talking to his parents. It just didn't work.

But, Rebecca! Was this all that was left of Rebecca? It couldn't be. Frustration added to his feeling of empty, overpowering sorrow.

"Goddamn it!" he said, but quickly retracted it. "No, no, I mean . . . well, I don't mean *that*." David wasn't sure about how he felt about God but if He was around somewhere David certainly didn't want Him damning anything . . . not with Rebecca . . . not anymore than He had already damned them.

"I mean . . . you're here and I love you and we have everything . . . and now you're not? How am I supposed to deal with that?" The futility of it all flooded over him. He almost walked away as his loss hit him even harder. He tried to fight back the frustration and pain but didn't quite succeed.

"What am I supposed to do now?" David waited. No answer. "I hope everything is good with you . . . wherever you are. I don't even know. I don't even have an idea."

He looked sadly around at the hundreds of other uncommunicative stone sentinels, mute representatives of entire lives lived, and read again his wife's sole testimony: Rebecca Collier,

1974–2007. A dash. A whole life summed up in the dash between the numbers. Not right.

"Damn it, Rebecca, we had it all! Everything we'd worked for was coming true. We just had so little time. We hardly got started." He looked again at the surrounding, silent stone forest, when it came to him. How he and Rebecca had both felt looking at their parents' headstones; how hopelessly inadequate they were to convey anything of the person lying there.

Suddenly, it became very clear. That could not be allowed to happen with Rebecca. "I know one thing I have to do. There has to be more than this. The world has to be a bit different because we came along. Something of us has to be left behind. Some tracks. Footprints. Something to show that we were here.

"If I don't, that means that it was all for nothing: our love, our lives, our hopes, dreams . . . all of it. And it was much too beautiful to be for nothing." David stared off into the distance with a new resolve. "I may not come back here anymore, Becca. I'm not real good at talking to a chunk of rock; besides, you're not here. I'll see and feel you at the beach, at our house . . . in your darkroom." He started to break down again but forced himself not to, just for another minute.

"I'm going to go now. If you can hear me, I guess you know how I feel and what I'm thinking. If you can't . . . if you can't . . ." The implications of that question hit him hard, much harder than he could handle right then. He started to leave again, but turned and looked back at her stone another moment.

"I sure do love you."

David turned and walked slowly back to the car.

As Chuck, Murray, and David pulled up in front of the beach house, David realized that he hadn't been the only dinosaur living there. Parked out front was Rebecca's 1962 Porsche Speedster. She loved that little car like he loved his Morgan. It was good they had found each other, they belonged together.

Those were David's thoughts as he silently got out of the police car and walked through their lush arboretum to the front door. He cautiously opened the door to the beach house, which looked like it had the last day he'd been there . . . except for a shiny spot on the floor just inside. The freshly cleaned, waxed area where Rebecca had lain . . . where Rebecca had died.

David hesitated a moment, then walked inside, carefully avoiding the waxed spot, followed by Chuck and Murray. Cursorily checking the place out as he walked, David went directly to the darkroom.

He opened it, stepped in, and was practically knocked down by the overwhelming feeling of Rebecca's presence in the darkroom. This had been her passion. Vestiges of that delight remained. David knew coming back to the beach would be rough but he hadn't anticipated this. Anger soon overtook his sorrow when he became aware that all the pictures that had been there were gone.

"No pictures," Chuck said when David stepped out of the darkroom.

"The killer must have taken them," David said tightly.

"Why would anyone kill for a bunch of pictures of old mansions?" Chuck wondered.

"Did you see any of them?" Murray asked David.

"Not that batch," David said as he crossed to a large box full of photos. "But she'd been working on this project for a while. I guess they weren't interested in these."

Chuck and Murray started looking through the pictures. Shot after shot of grand old mansions that looked to be straight out of *Architectural Digest*.

"Mind if I take them?" Chuck asked.

"I want them back," David said.

"You'll get them," Chuck said as he sat down, motioning for David to do the same. "We've got a problem here, Dave. Whoever is after you is still out there and I have no reason to believe that his reasons for killing you have changed any. Bottom line, I don't think you're real safe here. Why don't you get out of town for a few weeks? A getaway right now might do you some good."

"I've been away, Chuck. I want to be home."

"And I want to keep you alive. C'mon, just for a while. Give us a chance to get this guy."

"I really don't want to."

"I know you don't and I hate asking you, after all you've been through, but I think you'll also realize it's the smart thing to do. I can't keep an eye on you here, you're too vulnerable. Just disappear for a while. Don't even tell me where you're going. If I have any news, I'll get you on your cell."

"Let me think about it," David said after a moment.

"Fair enough, but don't think too long," Chuck replied as he stood and picked up the box of photos. He and Murray headed for the front door.

Before they quite got outside, Chuck had an afterthought. "Do you have a gun, Dave?"

"No."

"Want one?"

"No."

"You sure? It might not be a bad idea."

"Maybe later," David said, after hesitating.

"Listen, how'd you like to 'batch it' with me for a while?" Chuck asked, trying to make it sound like a spontaneous, fun idea. "You've sure helped me over a couple of rough spots when

I needed some help. Let me repay the favor. Besides, I could use the company."

"Thanks, Chuck," David said, "but I've got to do this sometime. It might as well be now."

"All right, then. Lock the doors after us, don't let anyone in, and get back to me, okay?"

"Yes, sir," David replied.

"You take care," Murray said on his way out.

"Thanks, Murray."

When Chuck and Murray left, David turned and surveyed what was left of his world, memories flooding over him. Something in one of the boxes caught his eye. He limped over to it and picked up a framed four-by-six-inch picture of Rebecca. He set it reverently on a small end table.

He looked around again. Everything looked so different. The house seemed devoid of life. His loss seemed unbearable. He looked over at the picture . . . then over at the shiny spot, then walked back to his writing area to get away from it. The first thing he saw there, dominating the room, was the Navajo rug.

It was just too much. Maybe Chuck was right. Maybe to get away from everything for a few weeks would be good. It might be a bit soon to come back. David slowly sat in the middle of the rug, reliving their last memories. Bit by bit, he gathered the rug around him and held it very, very tightly. Much of that evening was spent right there.

11

The next morning, David packed a small suitcase, put Rebecca's Porsche in the beach house's one-car garage, and left. He was headed south through the multitudinous switchbacks on Shoreline Drive, thankful again that he was driving his small sports car. His Morgan was made for those roads. He was on his way to one of his and Rebecca's favorite places in the world, Big Sur.

For Rebecca, growing up in Carmel, the Sur was only a half hour or so away but the feel was of a different world. Their first road trip together was to there, and David soon grew to love it as Rebecca had.

Since David was in no hurry, he opted to take Highway 1 the whole way down instead of the faster I-5. It would add a couple of hours to his trip but, so what? He'd canceled all his appointments, and besides, it was prettier. If he was going to have to do this he might as well give himself every chance to enjoy himself. A top-down ride along the coast might just be the ticket.

Well, almost. It was too cool and foggy for the top down for the first leg of the trip. It finally cleared and warmed up enough at Santa Cruz to pop the top. That was more like it. It turned out to be good timing because the coast started getting more beautiful each mile he got closer to Monterey.

As he knew it would be, this was also a tromp down memory lane. Nearly every place David looked, there was something he and Rebecca had seen or done. The Monterey Peninsula brought up memories of the famous jazz festival that they'd gone to twice. They loved Pebble Beach and had always wanted to eat at Roy's at Spanish Bay. They'd never quite gotten to that.

David had also always wanted a round at Pebble Beach to be in his memory banks but hadn't managed to get his game up to the point where it would be more than a humiliating experience. He might not make that one in this lifetime.

Memories hardened a bit when he got closer to Carmel. Rebecca's parents were both good people but it had been horrible to see what they did to each other out of a grief they didn't know how to handle. He didn't stop at the town on the way down. Perhaps he'd go back and explore a bit later. Or perhaps not.

Big Sur is one of the most dramatic spots on earth. Mountains and lush forest come down to the edges of sheer cliffs that fall straight down hundreds of feet to the ocean below. Sometimes there are beaches at the bottom, sometimes the cliffs end in jagged rocks severely buffeted by the relentless surf.

Scattered throughout the forest are inns and lodges of all varieties and all price tags. Their favorite had always been the funky little place called Deetjen's. Legend had it that Grandpa Deetjen built his initial cabin there, a bit after the turn of the century, before the highway was put in.

The fact that the road got built right outside his door turned out to be a mixed blessing. Gone was his peace and quiet, but it sure made it easy for folks to come visit him . . . and come they did. Very quickly Grandpa Deetjen ran out of room, so he started building more of them. That continued until he ended up with about twenty rooms of varying size.

It's questionable whether Grandpa had any skill, training, or even talent at building. His creation sprawled around an acre or so, stuck off into the trees alongside a stream that snaked its way across the property. There wasn't a plumb line in the place but it didn't matter. The place was so popular, he had to open it to the public.

Some walls have cracks between the boards where you can actually see through to the outside. One has ivy growing in from outside, through these cracks and throughout the room. The ivy is trained and guided around the room as if they meant for it to be there. By now, they do; it's called "the Ivy Room."

The feeling is rustic, funky, charming. The dining room has a brick floor, barn wood walls, is heated by a Franklin stove, and dinner comes with classical music and the best food in the world. David and Rebecca liked it a lot.

David thought it was amazing that an old guy with a hammer could throw up these boards as haphazardly as he did and have the effect come out as appealing as it had. David knew if he tried something like that, it would come out looking like a slum.

David checked into a room called "Faraway." As its name implied, it was the farthest room away from the office. If he was going to get away from it all, he might as well go all the way. Besides, this was the room he and Rebecca had stayed in on their last trip there.

It was also heated by a stove, and had a small patio that looked out over the brook. Huge Douglas firs, ponderosas, and redwoods towered over everything, permeating the air with the smell of pine.

He took a nap that afternoon, started one of the three books he'd brought, ate in the rustic dining room and wondered if he would ever get used to dining alone. Alone. That was perhaps the dominant word right now. At home, at least he had his friends; here, there was nobody. Of course, at home, someone was trying to kill him. He should probably remember that.

One night he read on a flyer that a movie was being shown at the local Grange. *Start the Revolution Without Me* was always one of David's favorites, even if they never had figured out how to end it. It just quit. Very strange.

He showed up at the appointed time at the country meeting hall. It was nearly full. A couple of young girls were playing their recital pieces on the piano that was up front by the flags. Folding chairs had been placed in neat rows.

The movie started about on time and had run for ten or fifteen minutes when it stopped and the lights came on. David wondered what was wrong. It turned out that the coffee was now ready, so it was time for refreshments. Everyone got up, got some popcorn and a Coke or coffee, sat back down, and they started the movie again. Ah, small-town Americana. Rebecca would have loved it.

Down the road a bit from Deetjen's, on top of a jut of land overlooking the sea and cliffs, is Nepenthe. It is one of the more spectacular views on the planet. David and Rebecca had spent many an hour with a cup of coffee or a glass of wine gazing out over it all. This trip was no exception, except that it wasn't quite the same alone. Nothing was quite the same alone.

12

A *few days later,* still at Big Sur, David had finished his books and was getting a little antsy. He decided to go to Carmel after all, and found that . . . not that much had changed. Some galleries and restaurants had different names now but, basically, David couldn't remember downtown Carmel changing much since he first was there years ago. It was in its own little time warp.

Driving past the lovely home where Rebecca had been raised was sad. As was seeing her father's galleries, now sold and renamed. Lunch at Clint Eastwood's Hog's Breath Inn had always cheered them up. It was still there, but again . . . not the same. He didn't know exactly what he had been looking for, he just knew that he hadn't found it.

Still searching, since he was so close, David decided to eat at Roy's at Spanish Bay, see if he could enjoy it for the both of them. Roy's, the restaurant, wasn't that much different than any other nice restaurant. What made it exceptional was its location.

It was perfectly placed on a promontory of land jutting out into the ocean. With a picturesque beach and the blue, blue water of the Pacific on two sides and the magnificent Spanish Bay golf course on the others, beauty was everywhere.

People were starting to congregate on the outside patio. Of

course, the sun was riding low. David imagined the sunsets here would be outstanding. He took his wine and joined the small throng outside.

The second thing David noticed, after admiring again the superb setting, was that he was the only person there alone. He was surrounded by couples, families, and small groups of friends. He wondered if he would ever get used to that.

He'd just sat on the side of a brick planter, leaving the chairs for the groups, when he thought he heard, very faintly, a bagpipe. David checked his hearing aid, even turned it up a notch. Yes, that's exactly what it was. From the expressions of those around him, they'd heard it, too. Some actually seemed to have been waiting for it.

With gathering expectations, everyone continued to listen as the pipes drew ever closer. After a few minutes, a marvelous sight came into view. Around the bend of the promontory, down by the water's edge, walked a solitary piper in full regalia.

He slowly walked and played until he reached the beach in front of his rapt audience. Then, perfectly timed with the sunset behind him, the piper turned and headed up to the group. He stopped only yards from Roy's patio on what David was to learn was Spanish Bay's eighteenth hole. He was also to learn that this happened nightly.

It was said that, in Scotland, a piper was dispatched every afternoon at this time to summon the golfers back in. Day's end.

David and the rest of the patio contingency were transfixed as the kilted piper continued to perform for another fifteen minutes or so before walking, still playing, back into the ocean fog that was accompanying that evening's nightfall.

Everyone was moved. None more than David who so wished that Rebecca could have experienced that. It was everything she had loved.

Dinner was fine, but after that extraordinary experience, David's solitude seemed even more severe. He wasn't getting used to it. He seemed to be missing her more.

In this melancholy, he realized one of the reasons why traveling alone was no good for him: he needed someone to say "Look at that!" to. He wasn't good at just soaking it up for himself. Especially not something as poignant as what he'd just seen. Intellectually, he knew he should be able to do that, but . . . it didn't seem to work that way.

It was perhaps a little too brisk to have the top down as he drove back from Spanish Bay that night, but he always kept an extra jacket in the trunk for just such an occasion. It was a shame to put up the top and cut off the evening view of the surrounding mountains and forests. He put on the jacket and toughed it out.

He had just reentered the Sur and was surrounded by its mammoth trees when he noticed his left hand was shaking. It started small, like a vibration, but quickly got so big he had to take the hand off the wheel for safety.

Just as he got concerned about the hand, he started feeling dizzy. He'd had moments like that in the hospital, but not for a while now. That, too, quickly got worse. The road seemed to curve off to the right in front of him, then to the left. He knew he'd better pull over and stop now!

As he started to slow down and pull over, the road moved again and threatened to slam him into a low white guardrail. In David's diminished mental capacity, his first thought was for his car. He could just imagine the damage it would do if he hit it, so he swerved to the right and missed it.

Unfortunately, what that did was put him between the

guardrail and what it was protecting cars from: in this case, a sheer drop-off of over three hundred feet. David had continued to stand on the brakes and was relieved when he finally stopped without hitting anything. He sat still for a few moments until his head started to clear.

When it did, David was afraid to move. There was just enough light for him to see that his car rested inches from the cliff, inches from the guardrail, on a small sliver of land hardly more than four feet wide. (Remember about the Morgan having such a small wheelbase? If he'd been driving a Hummer, he would have been toast.)

As blurry as everything had been for him, David was amazed at what he had done there. He didn't think he could thread that particular needle at his most alert. Of course, if he had been alert he never would have tried it.

His hand was still shaking. Other body parts were starting to shake also but that was out of fear, much more understandable. Looking at the land around him, David was relieved that it hadn't rained recently. If that area had been wet at all, he and his little car would have slid off. Jagged rocks and pounding surf awaited below.

As gently as he could, David put the car in reverse and, as smoothly as possible, let the clutch out and slowly started to creep backward. He had stopped practically ten feet past the beginning of the guardrail. David kept his left hand, which was still shaking, on his lap. He knew he really didn't have control over it at the moment and didn't want it anywhere near the steering wheel. Better to do it with one hand.

Taking it a few inches at a time, David finally got the car back on the road. He just sat there breathing for a few moments, trying to get used to the idea that he was not going to be plummeting to his death. Then he realized that he'd better get moving before someone came along the road and slammed into him. That probably wasn't the best place to stop and reconnoiter.

David quickly, but deliberately, drove the rest of the way back to Deetjen's, where a hot bath and a scotch made him feel better.

The next day, David sat atop Nepenthe, with a great cup of coffee, watching the fog ebb and flow, as it did there sometimes. Quite a spectacle. His mind, however, was far away.

His exile wasn't working, for a number of reasons. This was supposed to be cathartic, helpful; instead, he was totally depressed. Even though Big Sur was one of his favorite places, there wasn't much to do there. How long could he just look out over the scenery, no matter how beautiful it was? With Rebecca, he could have sat there happily for days. Alone, he had to *do* something.

And now this new wrinkle with the dizziness and his hand! That bullet to the head may have caused more damage than he thought. He might not have that long to live even if nobody killed him, which also meant that he might not have that much time to leave the tracks he'd promised Rebecca.

The more he thought about it, the more committed he became to that promise. Something had to be left of their lives besides a few law cases and escrows. Something of their loves, their passions should be left. Those were the tracks that were necessary.

He also made another promise, this one to himself but with all the depth and intensity he could muster. The killer of Rebecca would be caught. He would not get away with it. To have Rebecca dead and her killer walking around was unacceptable. That would not happen.

Sitting there, soaking up the sun, David decided he'd have to get to work again. It was the only thing that made sense. Being "safe" was one thing, but dedicating your life to it, having that be the primary focus of living, didn't seem right. At least, not for him. No, now he had goals, big ones.

The anger inside him was burning. He wanted to strike, hard . . . but where? Who? He was going to have to keep a lid on himself and think. This was too important.

After a moment, he decided to pursue this problem like he had his parents' situation, like he had done for so many years when he actually had a client that he knew (really *knew*) to be innocent. He'd found that he could be pretty good at uncovering the truth of a situation. Actually, he'd learned that when he put his mind to something, there wasn't a lot he couldn't do.

He decided to start right then. Chuck was good at what he did and was probably three steps ahead of him, but that didn't matter. David needed to do this for David. He borrowed a pencil from the waitress, grabbed a couple of napkins, and started making notes.

> *Who would benefit from Rebecca's death? The photos*
> *had to constitute a threat of some sort. What kind?*
> *And to whom?*

But the ones he'd seen were all so idyllic. The only questionable one seemed to be the solitary picture of that neglected mansion that Rebecca was disturbed about. She said she only had one shot of it on that roll. That implied another roll, perhaps the one she couldn't find. The one she never found because . . .

No. Stop it! He wasn't going there. Misting up won't help; finding the son of a bitch that did it, will. Focus!

Back to remembering. She'd mentioned something about the military . . . that military types might have been hanging around that house. Damn, he wished he had that picture. He hadn't even seen it. But Rebecca had evidently been watching the place for a while. If she got a military feel out of it, there was good reason. Her judgment was sound. He could trust her.

Military. David couldn't think of a plausible reason why our military would be on the grounds of an old mansion. . . . And what was it Chuck had said about someone robbing an armory? Our military wouldn't be stealing its own weapons, but a private militia in need of arming might.

David realized that he was making some pretty big judgment jumps here but she had also mentioned that they looked Armenian, like Shelly. Actually, that took in practically all of the Middle East. David knew that racial profiling was unfair to a lot of people, but he couldn't really help making that particular jump. If most of the terrorist acts are being committed by young Middle-Eastern men, when one hears of young Middle-Eastern men in a strange military situation, it would be foolish to not pay attention.

More notes:

> *Try to find Rebecca's lost roll of film. Might have pictures of old mansion. Could men be military? Could they have anything to do with the robbing of the armory? Was that what they were here for? Were there more?*

David started thinking . . . with that many weapons, there'd have to be a number of shoulders to hoist them. Even though he didn't know if he could identify the killer precisely, he did know that he was of Middle-Eastern descent. Another coincidence?

Okay, continuing this train of thought, say that there were a group of Arab-type militiamen in or around San Francisco. They would not want to draw attention to themselves.

Where could a group of Middle-Eastern men go where they would blend in? Where would they live? Eat? Together? Were they a unit? How many would there have to be for whatever they were trying to do? Would ten be enough? Twenty?

Well, it was a start, David thought, putting the folded napkin in his pocket. That was it. He was heading back. He wasn't going to let the fear of death stop him from living. Besides, he had promises to keep.

13

I t was midafternoon when David pulled up in front of the beach house. He realized he was taking a risk by coming back, but everything was just too important not to be involved. Knowing his little Morgan was quite identifiable, he pulled Rebecca's Porsche out of the garage, covered it with its tarp, and put his car in the garage. He didn't think that would necessarily fool anyone, but it seemed a little smarter than leaving his out front.

The house was as before: the boxes, the shiny spot. It didn't seem as though anyone had been there since he left. That was a good thing. David knew Chuck would not be pleased that he was back so, for the moment, he decided not to tell him. Instead he called Shelly.

"I'd like to take advantage of your ethnicity for a moment, if I could," David asked on the phone.

"What do you need?" Shelly asked.

"Where in San Francisco could a group of young Arab-type guys live without drawing attention to themselves? I was wondering about the Mission District?"

"Yeah, that's pretty international. It's gotten more Hispanic lately but it still might work. Noe Valley used to be a good bet before the yuppies discovered that it's the main place here that actually gets sun. It's become pretty trendy lately but that could also be a possibility. Probably the main place that I'd go to, though, would be the Tenderloin District. There are quite a few Middle-Eastern businesses down there, hotels and the like. Listen, I'm going to be down around there later. Want me to look into anything for you?"

"Actually, I'd love to meet you there. Would you have an hour or so?"

"Sure. I'll be free after five. Let's get together then."

That was perfect for David. They made plans to meet at five-thirty. Wondering if tiredness had anything to do with his hand and the dizziness, he lay down to take a quick nap so he could be sharp that afternoon.

Downtown San Francisco was trying hard to revitalize itself, with some areas having more success than others. The warehouse districts were becoming expensive lofts and the old Victorians, that a few years ago were just old, were now charming and were going for big bucks.

The Tenderloin area, try as it might, still looked pretty sad. Soon, David got an idea. Scattered around the neighborhoods were small, rather sleazy hotels, wall to wall to wall. Many, according to Shelly, were owned by Mid-East concerns. David thought that if he was putting together a small army, those would be the perfect places to keep them.

David had narrowed it down to three that seemed perfect. They were all appropriately shabby and no one was going to be asking a lot of embarrassing questions. Two were upstairs over businesses and all seemed like places where someone could hide and never be found.

He asked Shelly to try to get a look at the hotel registers to see who was living there, but they wouldn't go for it. It seemed that privacy went with the price of the room.

What might be helpful, Shelly suggested, was a fellow Armenian friend of his who was a cop in this district. Maybe he could find out who was staying there. Besides, he owed Shelly a favor.

David thought that was a fine idea. Shelly said he'd get in touch with him and see what he could do. Of course, he might be a little busy right then with that Middle-Eastern peace conference going on. With all the Mid-East dignitaries and their retinues to look after, Arab-speaking police officers were at a premium. Shelly said it had been days since the guy had a full night's sleep, but he would see what he could do.

Both men returned to their respective lives, vowing to contact the other as soon as they learned anything.

When he got back to the beach house, David figured he'd been bad long enough and called Chuck, who was not thrilled to hear from him. In fact he was irate and was on his way over.

David poured himself a glass of wine and waited.

"This is the stupidest damn thing you have ever done, David," Chuck bellowed. "What the hell were you thinking?"

"I got too stir-crazy too quick, Chuck. I can't just hang around. I have to be involved in it somehow."

"Bullshit! You're not going anywhere near this investigation. If you're not going to leave and be safe, stay put. Work just as hard as you want from the comfort of your own home. I mean it."

"I know you do."

"Where'd you go, anyway?"

David told him about Big Sur. Yeah, Chuck nodded his

75

head. He'd thought that's probably where David went. "Good place," he continued. "You should have stayed there."

David chose not to tell him about his physical bouts or his nearly fatal road incident. While he was at it, he also decided not to tell him about his exploits with Shelly. He did wonder if Chuck had made similar assumptions, but decided to wait to see what happened.

The men talked a while longer, with David assuring Chuck that he had no plans to go anywhere and that he'd let him know if something came up. Chuck reiterated all his warnings: keep all doors and windows locked, don't let anyone in, don't go anywhere, and call if there is anything out of the ordinary. "Anything!"

"Yes, master."

David was surprised how quickly the house became lonely when Chuck left. David had never been one to shun being alone, but having no choice in the matter, especially under these circumstances, made it quite different.

He nursed another glass of wine, sat on the living room sofa, and stared into the fire for a long time . . . trying hard not to look at the shiny spot.

The next day, as the sun was starting to burn off the morning fog, making everything seem much too cheerful, and David was halfheartedly trying to put things away in the kitchen, there was a knock on the glass slider from the beach side. The curtains were still drawn across them.

A flash of fear and anger went through him as he froze. He quickly grabbed a large carving knife and hugged the wall as he inched his way toward the curtains and the glass doors. Ever so carefully, he peeked around the curtain.

He was rather surprised to see a lovely, curvaceous lady in a white bikini standing there. She was holding a fairly large box.

Beside her was a seven-year-old girl holding a covered tray. Feeling silly about taking all these precautions, David quickly put down the knife, drew back the curtains, and opened the sliders.

"Hi. Are you David Collier?" she asked.

"Yes."

"Well, hi again. My name is Daley and this is my daughter Amanda."

"Hi," Amanda said, happily.

"Hello."

"We live a couple of houses down the beach," Daley explained, "and we heard about . . . well, everything and . . . I didn't even know if you'd be up yet."

"I didn't sleep real well."

"We have your mail and some food," Amanda cheerfully announced, holding out her tray as evidence.

"Yes, I collected it for you," Daley said. "I also thought you might not feel like cooking this morning, so I made you some breakfast."

"Well, thank you. . . . Uh, come in." They did. David took the tray from Amanda and set it on the counter. He then took the box from Daley. "Wow, this is heavy. Thank you. I never even considered how much it would stack up. This was very nice of you."

"No problem. And the tray is just French toast. If you're not hungry now, it's great cold."

That startled David a bit but he tried not to let it show. He was spared having to say anything by young Amanda.

"I have to go to the bathroom."

"Oh, honey."

"Well, I do," she persisted.

David smiled. "Just turn right past the stairs."

"I'm sorry," she said to David, embarrassed. "Amanda, you're supposed to go at home. You're old enough to know that."

"But, Mom . . ."

Daley took her through the living room and off toward the stairs. David looked distrustfully at the French toast, then scanned the papers. The Middle-Eastern Peace Conference seemed to dominate the front pages with evidently no breakthroughs in sight. Looking through the mail, he found two letters that interested him. By the time the ladies returned, David's mood was decidedly darker.

Daley noticed the mail but not the mood. "Good news?" she asked perkily.

"Not particularly," David said through clenched teeth. "This is a famous rejection slip for me. This other one is from my wife's editor, telling me that they are no longer interested in the mansion project because of the danger that somehow seems to be mixed up with it."

Daley was suddenly uncomfortable being there.

"I'm very sorry, Mr. Collier," she said, drifting toward the door. "We'd better be going now."

"Thank you," David said, so mad he could hardly speak.

"Well, it was nice meeting you. We'll see you around the beach," Daley said, trying to keep everything upbeat.

David just nodded as he opened the door for them and they left. He walked back to the stack of mail, glowered at it a moment, then swiped them all off the counter onto the floor. Letters flew everywhere. "Goddamn it!"

David's swipe nearly knocked him to the floor. He had to grab the counter to stop from falling. After a moment of feeling rather foolish he laboriously started picking up the scattered mail.

Later that day, David was on the cordless phone talking to his accountant while looking through some of the boxes still stacked in the living room.

"Do we really have to do this now? I have no idea where half that stuff is. . . . All right. . . . Wait a minute. I think I remember," he said as he walked back toward Rebecca's darkroom. "We put some stuff in here just to get it out of the way . . . give me a second."

Entering into the darkroom surrounded him with the same essence of Rebecca that overwhelmed him the first time. He took a couple of deep breaths, tucked the phone under his chin, and started going through some of the boxes there. He moved one aside and froze.

There on the floor between two boxes was a small roll of film. That could be the one Rebecca had been looking for . . . the one she may have been killed for. David picked it up. "Listen, Bob, I really am going to need more time to go through these boxes. Let me get back to you in the next couple of days. . . . Yes, I promise. . . . Okay, bye."

David clicked off the phone, looked again at the roll of film, and decided. Thankful that Rebecca had taught him how to use the darkroom, he started pouring solution into the trays, turned on the red light, and set the room up for developing.

A couple hours later, David knew he had something Chuck should definitely see.

Everything was perfect. The floor to ceiling bookcases, the rich wood, and the fine carved desk made this the perfect den for writing. The colors in the Navajo rug were further accentuated by the surrounding wood tones.

David was writing at the desk dressed in a white silk shirt, open at the collar, and a dark brown velvet sport coat, tailored to him perfectly. A marble fireplace and large bay window rounded out the room. It was truly . . . perfect.

"David."

He looked up to see Rebecca entering the room in a floor-length white dress with high lace collar, looking radiant. "You're working too hard. Come take a walk with me."

"I'm afraid you're right," David said, rising to meet her. "I'd love to."

They walked, arm in arm, out to the column-supported portico and continued on to the perfectly manicured grounds. They strolled past a picturesque koi pond and stopped by a rose-covered gazebo where they kissed.

Their kiss was interrupted by a doorbell. Rebecca smiled, gave David another quick kiss, and started for the house. "I'll get it."

David smiled at how lovely she was, running gaily for the house when something hit him. "Rebecca, no!" he called. "Don't! Rebecca!"

He started running after her. She laughed, thinking he was playing, and darted into the house.

The sound of her closing the door was like a loud gunshot as the door to the darkroom was also opened. David lunged out of the darkroom just as Chuck opened the door, scaring the hell out of both of them.

"What the? . . . David, you all right?" Chuck asked, quickly recovering.

David, who had just been jolted awake, leaned against the wall, holding his head in his hands, trying to get his breath.

"Didn't you hear the bell?"

"Damn it, Chuck."

"A nightmare?"

"Yeah."

"I didn't ruin any pictures or anything, opening the door, did I?" Chuck asked.

"No, it's fine. They're dry."

"What'd you do, sleep in there?" Chuck asked, looking hesitantly into the darkroom.

"I guess so. Must have dozed off in the chair. Didn't get much sleep last night."

Chuck stepped into the darkroom. Pictures were hanging everywhere. "These what you wanted to show me?"

"Yeah."

David also stepped into the darkroom, took down some of the pictures that were drying and laid them out on the kitchen table. They were all of the run-down mansion (which bore a striking resemblance to the mansion in David's dream). All were still taken from a distance and looked like companion shots to the one Rebecca had developed earlier.

"Looks like a great old place," Chuck said, looking them over. "Kinda gone to hell, hasn't it?"

David got a magnifying glass from the darkroom, handed it to Chuck, and indicated a couple of shots. "Check them out."

Chuck looked closer through the lens. The shots David specified were primarily of the mansion's backyard and huge barn. Rebecca had been right, the feel was definitely military. A group of men, in fatigues, with weapons, were milling around. Looking closer, it appeared the barn, although made to look old, wasn't nearly as old as the house.

David wondered how recently it had been added. And why? The house had been let go for years. If there wasn't enough interest to keep the house up, why build a big barn to go with it?

"Yeah. They didn't do that good a job on that, did they?" Chuck said.

"Do you think these men could be housed there?" David asked. "It'd probably be big enough."

"I doubt it," Chuck said still studying with the magnifying glass. "We don't know how many rooms inside would be bedrooms, but notice that there is just one car and the transport truck. I think they were brought here." He looked a while longer. "What the hell are they up to?" Chuck said, mostly to himself.

The large barn doors were partially open where a glint of something unidentifiable inside could be seen.

"Can you make that out?" Chuck asked, pointing to the glint.

"No."

Chuck went from picture to picture. Many were close enough to tell that the men were of Middle-Eastern origin. Some of the men's features could even be made out, but meant nothing to David.

"Anybody look familiar to you?" Chuck asked.

"Honestly, I don't know if I'd recognize him if I saw him. I just got a glimpse. It could be any of these guys."

"Or none of them?"

"Or none of them."

"It's too bad we couldn't let the killer know that you can't identify him," Chuck said. "He might not be trying so hard to kill you."

"Maybe I should take out an ad."

Chuck moved on to some shots where it was obvious that the men saw Rebecca taking the pictures and didn't like it. In the one that seemed to be the last shot of the sequence, they were shaking their fists at her, visibly upset. Some had started running toward her. The pictures stopped there.

"And Rebecca didn't mention anything about this?"

"No."

"Where is it?"

"I have no idea."

"If she was killed because of these," Chuck said, looking closer, "I'd sure like to know who they are and what they're training for."

"You going to look into it?"

"Damn straight. Having the right to bear arms is one thing, having your own armed militia is another. I'll find out a bit more about them first, though. Got to do it right," Chuck said, collecting the pictures. "Are these all of them?"

"Yeah."

"Let me see what I can come up with downtown. You're sticking around here, right?"

"I'm afraid so."

"All right. Hang in there. I'll be in touch."

"Thanks Chuck."

Chuck left, David closed the door and went back into the darkroom. When he went to empty the trays, he noticed that there was still one picture of the old mansion soaking. He got it, started to run to tell Chuck there was one more, just as he heard Chuck drive away. Too late. He returned to the darkroom, hung it up to dry, and went back to cleaning everything up.

ater that night, David was at his desk paying the bills that had accumulated during his Big Sur trip. He hadn't even thought about them. It was a good thing he came back early, he was already behind. On top of everything else, all he'd need was to be carted off to debtors' prison.

A "bong" and an icon told David that an e-mail message had just come in. He popped it up and saw that it was from Shelly. The message read:

> David,
> Here are the registers you wanted. All three of them!
> Hope you find what you're after.
> Shelly

David was impressed. He hadn't expected the whole registers, just a number of people or . . . He didn't know, but this was great. He wrote back:

> Shelly,
> This is terrific. Your friend must owe you one hell of a favor, that's all I can say. Thank him for me.
> Dave

David just started studying the registers when Shelly wrote back:

> *Dave,*
> *First of all, I introduced him to his wife.*
> *Second, I was best man at his wedding.*
> *Plus, they eloped and I kept the secret, against all*
> *odds, for over a month. They've been happily married*
> *now for 8 years, 2 kids, my God-children. So even*
> *with him working this silly conference, yeah, he owes*
> *me. Go get 'em.*
> *Shelly*

David smiled as he printed out the registers and started perusing them. The first was from one of the few stand-alone hotels on Hyde Street. It seemed to David that it would be a good place to have people coming and going with no one taking particular notice. It had the rather optimistic name of . . .

THE PARAMOUNT

1-A Bashaar	2-A Talha	3-A Mamnoon
1-B Makeen	Ubaidah	3-B OPEN
Abdul-Haseeb	2-B Ameen	3-C Jamaal
1-C Fuad	Fadi	Zaafir
Misbaan	2-C OPEN	3-D Abdul-Bilal
1-D Sameer	2-D Siraj	Fateen
Asif	Wajeeh	3-E OPEN
	2-E Abdul-Raafi	3-F Abdule-Bari
	Lu'ay	Thaqib
	2-F Tariq	
	Rabee'	

A pretty full hotel. David thought that definitely had possibilities. He went on to the next. That was the Newberry Hotel, which was upstairs, over a deli. The stairs were around back and it also was in an industrial area. Easy to hide.

NEWBERRY HOTEL

201—Mr. S. Lizarraga	301—Mr. & Mrs. Moughal
202—Mr. B. Chaudhury	302—OPEN
203—OPEN	303—Mr. C. H. Charles
204—Miss P. Gonzales	304—Mrs. A. Khan

That wasn't quite as interesting. Too few people to do the damage these folks had already done. It also looked like families and women in there, too. He doubted if that would be the case in a paramilitary situation like this one.

The next hotel was located over a bar. Again, stairs were in the back, lots of seedy noise out front, international crowd. A group could very easily not be noticed there.

THE STRAND

1. M. Littrell	7. T. Lee
2. K. Chopdat	8. A. Badar
3. OPEN	9. S. Rzeszutek
4. P. Oaxaca	10. OPEN
5. K. Rupel	11. G. Novara
6. M. H. Bhatti	12. M. Rahman

That one also looked interesting. It wasn't marked whether the boarders were men or women, but if only one registered and there were two or more to a room, that could be the right amount of bodies.

He called Shelly back and asked his opinion about The Paramount and The Strand. Did anything jump out at him? Shelly looked them over and laughed. He hadn't noticed it at first but, yes, something did jump out. All the names at The Paramount were first names. That seemed a little strange, didn't it?

David agreed, but it made perfect sense if maybe these people weren't supposed to be there in the first place or if someone *really* didn't want anybody to know who these people were, ever.

He thanked Shelly again, hung up, and went back to the register. Mostly two to a room, even though there were some empty rooms. Only two rooms had singles in them, one on each floor. They could be the honchos, David surmised. This very well could be a barracks-type of situation. Now, what to do next?

He decided, for the moment, that to sleep on it would probably be the best thing. He turned off the lights, checked the doors, and went upstairs, hoping he'd have better luck sleeping than he'd had the night before.

The next morning didn't bring clarity but it brought resolve. He knew he should call Chuck but also knew that if he did, Chuck would take the registers and tell him not to get ahead of himself. ("It could be a soccer team or something," David could hear him saying.) Then he'd tell him to stay in the house and Chuck would go off and try to solve the case.

Nope. David just couldn't do it. He was through sitting around. He had a quick breakfast, got dressed, and fired up Rebecca's little Porsche (his *stealth* car) and headed downtown. He wanted to take another look at The Paramount.

David felt like a cop, sitting there in the car with coffee and a doughnut, staking out the place. He'd love to see one or two men come or go, see for certain if they would fit the profile he was imagining.

Hyde Street was so busy he had to park at a side street nearly a block away, but he still got a pretty good look at the place. (He wondered if any of them had noticed the irony of hiding out on Hyde Street?)

David realized that if he was going to keep up this clandestine behavior he was going to have to rent or borrow a car from somewhere. The Porsche didn't quite stand out as much as his Morgan but he also wasn't seeing a lot of other Porsches around that neighborhood, even old ones. Maybe he should hunt up an old brown Ford somewhere.

Although he had been watching the front of the building, after a couple of hours, movement in back caught his eye. A truck pulled up in back of the hotel, a tan truck with canvas sides. David jockeyed the car around a bit to get a better view. Young men in civies were climbing in the back of the truck. The sides were then tied down and the truck drove away.

David gave it at least a block head start. He didn't want to be seen in his much-too-noticeable little car but it was also easy to follow them. The truck was higher than most cars so David could keep an eye on it from quite a ways back. The truck was heading for the Golden Gate.

Traffic was moderately heavy as he followed them over the bridge and up through Sausalito. David felt a small relief when the truck continued on past the Shoreline Drive exit, then wondered why he would feel relieved. Did he think the whole group of them was going to attack the beach house? Take him out for good? Well, even so, he was glad they were continuing north.

Traffic thinned out for a while so David dropped back. He moved closer when traffic picked up again as they approached San Rafael. He almost lost them a couple of times in the city, trying very hard to keep the little Porsche from being seen too often or too clearly by the truck.

They turned off onto Center Avenue and after a mile and a half or so, turned left onto Sir Francis Drake Boulevard. That led back to Olema and Bolinas and David's side of Marin. Where the hell were they going?

The area now was gently rolling hills, open farmland. Occasional clumps of trees were scattered around but it was mostly just yellow bald hills for miles. There was practically no traffic on these roads so David had to stay very far back. He lost them many times on these hills, only to find them again when they both happened to be on top of their particular rise.

About fifteen minutes later David topped one of these hills and found himself practically on top of the truck, which had slowed to turn off on a dirt road. David made a point of not looking over at them as he drove straight on until he was sure they couldn't see him. He then turned around and drove back slowly, carefully, trying to figure out where they'd gone.

He didn't want to get on the same road they had taken in case the driver came back, but found a parallel road about a half mile down. He took that. This road was also hilly. He drove back about half a mile and pulled over by one of the knolls.

He got out, took his cane, and proceeded to, rather laboriously, climb the nearby hill. It was worth it. He could see that the truck had pulled up to a large tent a quarter mile or so up the road.

David got back to the car and drove a quarter mile up his parallel road to another little rise. He climbed up this one and lay on the top, covered by a healthy grove of weeds as he watched below. He wished he'd had the foresight to bring his binoculars along but who knew he'd be ending up out here?

It was a large flat valley surrounded by low hills. Not a stick grew in that area. The tent was probably fifty feet long by twelve feet wide. Two Porta-Potties and a Winnebago were close by.

What happened next had been carefully orchestrated and it was obvious that the men had done all this before, many times.

They headed, single file, into the tent in their civies. (The register for The Paramount had listed twenty-four men staying in the hotel. David felt that seemed about the right number of men below him.) In less than fifteen minutes, they started filing out, armed with rifles, in fatigues, complete with packs and gas masks. They filed into formation until they were all present. Then, at the order of one who was obviously in charge, they put on the gas masks and started doing wind sprints, running as fast as they could to a marker about a hundred yards away. They'd regroup and do it again, four or five times. The one in charge timed each run.

Didn't Chuck say that the people who were robbing places, including the armory, did so with some of that Russian gas? The kind that knocks you out as soon as you breathe it? This was getting more interesting all the time.

Sixteen of the men then marched out to the center of this valley four or five hundred yards away and got into a tight group. At a signal from the main guy, they suddenly ran from the center, angled out rather like a pie slice, four to a group.

They ran about a hundred yards, with gas masks on, did five minutes worth of calisthenics, then ran back to the center and re-formed the small group.

They were given ten minutes to rest, then the whole exercise was done again. That happened four times, followed by a series of strenuous exercises. These guys were in great shape.

David figured he'd seen enough when they started back into the tent. The driver seeing the Porsche on the road again might be too much.

My God! Suddenly, something else hit him. . . . How had they known where Rebecca lived? The only way was if they had followed her . . . and she was driving her Porsche . . . this one that he was supposedly hiding out in. Yes, tomorrow would definitely bring a change of cars . . . if he could live through today. He couldn't believe that hadn't occurred to him sooner.

He limped back to the car as quickly as he could manage and headed home, careful not to kick up too much dust behind him on the dirt road. When he regained the highway, he stomped on the gas.

he next morning, David was having coffee on his fog-shrouded deck, feeling very alone. He and Rebecca didn't mind the fog at all; in fact, at times they openly enjoyed it. Now would have been one of those times. There was an otherworldly feel about being surrounded by fog, hearing nothing but the surf and beach sounds. But having Rebecca gone took all the allure out of it. He was back to simply having coffee in the fog. By himself.

He looked back over the list of questions he'd made at Big Sur. One that he hadn't gone after yet was eating. Where would these guys eat? Perhaps that would give him the chance to see some of them close enough to get a handle on where they were from anyway.

David left again on the all-too-familiar switchback leading away from his little beach paradise into the megacity bustle of San Francisco. The fog abated the farther south he got and by the time he reached the bridge, she was in her sunbathed glory. David drove alongside a runner on the bridge for the longest time. If you were going to take a run for a mile or so (actually 1.7 miles), could you find a better place than running the Golden Gate Bridge? David thought not. Interesting how some people want to kill people and others want to get out into the sun and run. What a strange species we are.

Once in the city David drove directly to the Dollar Rent A Car lot. They were a little surprised when he asked for the oldest, ugliest, dirtiest car they had. They took great pride in letting him know that they had nothing in that category.

David settled for second best and got a gray Dodge. That would have to do. Feeling a little more secure now, he returned to the Tenderloin district and slowly trolled the streets looking for places to eat within walking distance of the lovely Paramount Hotel.

He found four that could be good candidates but two were within three blocks. They were little greasy spoon–type diners that probably did a good (and cheap) lunch business. David was definitely the minority down there and felt a little exposed going into one of those places alone.

Again, it was Shelly to the rescue. No, he didn't have any plans for lunch and, sure, he could meet him outside this questionable dining facility.

It was called "Pedro's" but offered food from all over; tacos, sure, but also hamburgers, stews (good luck with that one), soups, and even a falafel. The place was set up like a dining car, booths along both sides. David and Shelly got there before twelve and got a booth in the back. David faced the wall with Shelly looking at the people who came in.

They had guessed well. It was a popular place. A number of Arab-looking types came in. A variety of languages could be heard around them, none English.

Knowing that the man who killed Rebecca, who almost killed him, could be in that restaurant right then, made David antsy. He wanted to turn around and look each one of them in the eye. He might be able to recognize the killer that way . . . of course, the killer might also recognize David and he didn't even have a gun. But then, he'd seen these guys work out. Even with a gun he'd be no match for them.

He forced himself to calm down. They were on a fact-finding mission, that's all. Hopefully, Shelly could pick up some words, some dialects that could tell something of the makeup of this group.

Not wanting to be seen there, David kept his back to the group the whole time. They had a marginal hamburger and a (quite good, actually) falafel and a few cups of coffee that you could have cut with a knife. They waited until nearly everyone had gone before they left.

They also waited until they got outside before they had any substantial conversation.

"From what little I could see," David said, "they could sure be our guys. The right ages, ethnicity, strong. What about the languages?"

"They were all over the place," Shelly said. "Mostly Arabic and Farsi but I think I even picked up some Turkish. A pretty international group."

"Rebecca's killer might have been in there. We might have been sitting right next to him."

"They were a pretty rough bunch. Any of them looked capable of most anything."

Shelly had more appointments that afternoon so he thanked David for the lunch (it had been David's treat) and left him. David was halfway back to the rent-a-car place when he figured he might as well use this nondescript car while he had it. He didn't quite know for what yet, but he'd think of something. Besides the Porsche probably wasn't that great an idea just yet. When he got home (the Dodge didn't handle the switchbacks nearly as well as the Porsche or his Morgan), he called up and booked the car for another day.

The excitement of it all had left him beat. He lay down and was asleep in about four seconds. He awoke as it was getting dark, made himself a drink and a fire, put a TV dinner in the microwave, and sat on the sofa, contemplating his next move.

Then he got an idea. His adrenaline might still have been charged from his exploits earlier in the day. He knew that if he went to Chuck with the information he now had, Chuck would make sure he never had the opportunity to get anywhere near this case again. He wasn't ready for that. Besides, he hadn't heard anything from Chuck about what *he* was doing. Did David have to solve this thing himself?

Well, if that's what it took, he would do it. His promises, his mission, were never far from the surface and it felt good to be actively involved, to be *doing* something. He was getting excitedly nervous just thinking about it.

David wanted to take another look at that field, maybe peek in that big tent if no one was around. Maybe try to figure out what they were doing, what they were practicing for. He was sure this militia, or whatever it was, was somehow tied to the big old house and that was directly tied to Rebecca's death. They were not going to get away with it and he was not going to sit idly by and watch Chuck and his cronies laboriously try to figure out what was going on.

He caught himself, as he often did, staring at Rebecca's picture. She was so lovely. She could have been a model. (Actually, David remembered, she had done some modeling in college.) The camera loved her. You couldn't take a bad picture of her if you tried, but this was one of the best. It even caught that subtle twinkle that lay behind nearly everything she did.

David forgot about the TV dinner. He spent the evening sitting alone on the couch, in front of the fire, with Rebecca's picture.

16

David was up before dawn. The other day, when he first saw them, the truck had picked up the men around 10:00 A.M. Knowing that most militaries like to do things in a uniform, consistent manner, especially training, he figured they'd probably be doing the same thing today. If he got there about 6:00 A.M., that should give him enough time to take a quick look around, perhaps learn something, and get out of there.

He was a little concerned about the Winnebago. That was probably for guards. No one would leave a tent full of weapons unguarded. He figured he'd go to the same place he'd been before. That protected him, and the car as well, while still allowing him a good view over it all. This time he would be aided by his binoculars, grateful that when he bought them, he'd gotten a good pair. These were terrific. He'd be able to look these guys in the face after all.

It was still dark when he left most of the city lights behind. A disturbing thought came to him; what if the tent wasn't there anymore? Everything there could have been packed up and gone in less than half an hour.

He decided to take a quick look first, before driving on to the farther road he had been on the other day. It was hilly surrounding the flat field, he could just inch over one of those hills and find out if there was still anything to see without making his presence known.

The sun was just beginning to come up when he turned on the dirt road leading to the valley. Suddenly, a cold chill went down his back as he saw two headlights turn onto the road right behind him. His eyes shot to the rearview mirror. It was the tan truck! No!

Damn it! Damn it! Damn it! What a stupid move. He berated himself repeatedly as he tried to get his panicked mind to work. He couldn't believe this was happening. Maybe Chuck was right, maybe he couldn't be trusted to act in an intelligent manner. He sure did a bonehead move this time. Damn it!

His first thought was to see how fast that Dodge would go. He could certainly outrun the truck but that would call even more attention to himself and he didn't know how far back this road went. They could also radio ahead . . . no, running for it wasn't going to work.

He just had to hope the road went back a few miles, maybe to some farms. If asked, that was where he was going. The truck was five or six car lengths behind him, going the same speed David was. At least they weren't trying to catch him or get him to pull over. Yet.

He didn't know what to hope for regarding the tent and what waited ahead. He supposed he could hope that he wouldn't come over a rise and find five guys with machine guns blocking the road. He could definitely hope for that.

He felt a little better when he topped the rise that led to the flat valley. The tent, Porta-Potties, and Winnebago were still there, but no men were blocking the road. There were only two men with cups of coffee standing outside the tent. They looked suspiciously at David until they saw the truck coming down the road behind him. They then started looking very official, getting the tent opened and ready for their troops, but they still kept a wary eye on David as he drove by.

David just kept on driving. He didn't even look over when he drove past. Nothing suspicious out there. Nope. He was going to keep on until he was totally out of sight. Then he'd decide what to do next. The first thing, though, was to get some miles between them, go visit a farm somewhere.

David soon realized how deceptively huge this valley was. He kept driving and driving but knew they could still see him, or at least, see the dust plume kicked up behind him. He was going to have to go to the back of a couple of small mountains that were ahead of him before he could be safely out of sight.

He was probably about two miles past the tent with another two to go when he rounded a blind turn and found that a good portion of the road had been washed away. A three-foot-wide gully cut through it, right in front of him. It was also about two feet deep. He quickly stood on the brakes, trying to keep the Dodge out of the gully.

It didn't work. He had been going too fast and, because of the blind curve, saw it too late to slow down. The car slammed into the far end of the gully, lurched to a stop amid a cloud of dust, with the front end of the car suspended in air, high-centered and thoroughly stuck. Damn it! So much for visiting the farms.

David's first concern was how this would look to the soldiers if they were watching. He got out of the car and looked off toward them, pleased that he couldn't even make them out. If they had been watching his dust they may have noticed that it stopped but, even so, he was pretty far away. He had to hope they didn't know the road was blocked and weren't that concerned about him.

He got out the cell phone that he had, fortunately, thrown in the car before he left home. Half the time he forgot it, but he was glad he had it then.

He couldn't get a signal. The hills around the valley were either too high or else the lack of population out there made it unnecessary to have any signal towers. Or both. David wished he'd spent the extra bucks to get one of those satellite phones. He was sure that would have worked.

He was also dismayed when he saw that his power was down. He couldn't remember the last time he'd charged it. Since Rebecca's death, there were a lot of little things like that that were going undone. He was going to have to wake up. Actually, it was a wonder his phone had any power at all. He quickly turned it off to conserve what little he had.

Now what? He was going to have to get to some higher ground to get a signal, but he was roughly in the middle of the valley so he could go either way. Heading back toward the main road would take him closer to the military guys, but he could go miles in the other direction and maybe find nothing there. He looked again at the huge gully. No car had passed that way in a very long time.

Still chastising himself for getting into this predicament in the first place, David pocketed the cell phone, slung the binoculars around his neck, and started limping back toward the tent, the truck, and the army, planning to circumvent it widely as he got closer.

It was crucially important that he stay alive. Tracks had not been left; Rebecca's killer was probably in the tan truck. It was not enough for him to try not to be captured, he *must* not! Period. Too much was at stake. Alert. He had to stay alert.

It wasn't long before his leg started hurting. Not planning to do any walking, he hadn't brought his cane. Another brilliant move.

He topped one of the hilly rises and quickly dropped to the ground. He scurried down to the low point of the rise and started running as fast as he could out into the valley away from the road.

What he saw was that the men had changed into their uniforms again and were marching en masse and armed down the road toward him. David had to get as far away from them as he could before they found the car. They would know he'd be around there somewhere and would blanket the area until they found him.

As he painfully ran, trying to keep to the larger bunches of chaparral sprinkled around, he realized he made another slight miscalculation. If Rebecca had been killed for what she saw while taking those pictures (basically shots of an old house), how did he think they wouldn't be interested in him driving casually by where they were doing their militia training—*illegal* militia training?

David had to rest a moment. He found an area pretty well covered with two-foot grasses, enough for him to lie down and not be seen . . . from a distance, anyway. He trained his binoculars on the group. The good news was that it seemed they hadn't seen him yet. The bad news was that they had already found the car and had dispersed, checking in all directions.

Wait. They weren't going in all directions anymore, they were only going in one. His direction. They must have picked up his footprints. If a car hadn't been there for a year or so, imagine how long since anyone walked there. Following his footprints shouldn't be all that hard.

David took a big breath and started running again, his leg really hurting now. He tried to jump from patch to patch of weeds and chaparral, hoping to cut down on the trail he was leaving.

He could see that he wasn't going to be able to outrun these guys. He wasn't really running to anything anyway, he was just running from them and had a large valley in front of him. With the pain he was feeling already, he knew this was not going to work. He needed a place to hide. And quickly.

When David stopped again, to catch his breath, he noticed his hand was shaking more than he'd ever seen it. He hadn't even noticed it while running but it was all over the place now. Terrific.

Soon, his leg really started bothering him and even gave out on him a few times, causing him to do a couple of face-plants on the desert. Now, instead of simply being scared half to death, he was also mad.

He had been heading toward a strip of tall green grasses and weeds, thinking that offered the best chance of finding a hiding place. When he reached the area, what he found was an old culvert that had been laid across the valley many years ago. The leaking water from it had created the strip, a little greenbelt. Many of the pipes were still around, some broken, some not. They were about two feet in diameter, made of corrugated tin, and had just about enough room for him to fit inside, David thought . . . and hoped.

He was quickly reminded of the old adage, *"Be careful what you wish for . . . you just may get it."* He was able to get in, barely, fighting past ancient spiderwebs. He only hoped the spiders had long since gone on. He was halfway in when he realized it was so tight that he was unable to get the binoculars in with him. He tucked them under the pipe as far as he could and covered them with dirt and grass and went back to trying to stuff himself in the pipe. He made it but there was no room left to move, hardly enough to breathe, and he only hoped that if he was not discovered there he would be able to get out again.

He had tried to erase any footprints or signs that he had been around there before getting in. Now, he waited. It wasn't long before he could hear voices. They were getting closer.

All of a sudden, he started hearing pinging. It sounded like Morse code, pounding on his pipe. He realized that his hand was shaking again and his wedding band was tapping against the metal pipe. He quickly rolled an inch or two, about all he could move, but it was enough. The hand quietly shook against his leg now. Hopefully, they hadn't heard it.

From the sound of it, two or three of the men wandered over by the pipes. They randomly kicked a few, speaking in one of the languages he and Shelly had heard at the diner. David was glad they hadn't chosen his to kick. It certainly wouldn't have had the ring the others did. More like a "thump." It would have been all over.

The military guys soon seemed to tire of the pipes and moved on. It seemed like David could still hear their voices for hours. He didn't move. He had to go to the bathroom, a spiderweb was tickling his nose, and he was extremely uncomfortable.

The pipe got hot around noon but, as the day progressed, it started getting chilly. David wore only a shirt. Again, he hadn't planned on hiking around much.

Later in the day, after an hour or two of silence, he started the arduous job of undulating himself, quietly, out of the pipe. It seemed a little more difficult getting out than it had getting in but that could also have been the fact that he hadn't moved for a few hours. It took a while. He'd scoot, wait, listen, then scoot a little farther.

Getting his arms clear felt wonderful as did finally getting a chance to relieve himself. Aah, the simple pleasures. He didn't dare stand or make any large movements. His plan was to wait until dark before he moved anywhere. So he sat, cold, hungry, angry, and depressed.

When it got dark enough for him to safely move, he did. Laying in the pipe and later, on the ground, didn't do his leg any good; in fact it hurt like hell. He managed to find a large stick that he could use as a cane. That helped a bit, but he was still making very slow progress. He belatedly remembered his binoculars and had to go back to get them.

It seemed to take him a couple of hours to reach the area where the tent had been. Everything was gone, even the Porta-Potties. Tire tracks were the only signs that anyone had ever been there. Knowing David was on the loose around there somewhere must have spooked them. They weren't taking any chances.

That was probably prudent on their part, David thought. After all, a large military tent full of uniforms and weapons could be fairly incriminating. He continued walking, first back to the dirt road leading into the valley, then back a mile or so to Sir Francis Drake Boulevard, a road seldom traveled at night.

It was dark. Not a moon in sight, or a car either, for that matter. David limped along for seemingly hours before the first car came along. David tried to flag it down, but they kept driving. He couldn't really blame them, it was a pretty questionable place to pick up a stranger.

Finally an old pickup came along, going slow enough that the driver could easily see David limping along; his headlights followed him like a spotlight. The driver decided to stop.

"You all right there, young fella?" said the grizzled gentleman driving.

"My car quit on a side road a few miles back," David said, coming up to the old man's window. "I could sure use a lift."

"I'm off to Olema. That do you?"

"Sure does," David said and started to walk around the truck to the passenger door. The old man stopped him.

"Can't do it that way. I work outta this truck. No room, I'm afraid."

David looked at the passenger seat and, even with little light, had to agree with the man. It seemed to be loaded with the tools of his trade: gloves, a construction belt, hand-belt sander, power drill, even what was left of yesterday's pizza.

"Just hop up in the back and make yourself comfortable. It won't be all that long."

David struggled his way into the pickup bed and looked around. Compared to the bed, the front seat looked relatively neat. Tool boxes, nails, ratchet sets, handsaws, power nail motors, and various other things were in the shadows everywhere. David had no idea what half of them were. One dark spot turned out to be a stack of lumber. That seemed good enough. David sat. The old man took off as soon as he saw David was set.

Fortunately, the old man had been right. David had walked farther than he thought and it wasn't that long a drive into Olema. It was a good thing because David was freezing. He tried to scrunch down behind the cab to avoid the wind but couldn't do it fully. It did give his leg a rest, though, so he supposed it was better than walking.

Once in Olema, the old man stopped at a restaurant/bar. David half fell out of the bed, thanked the gentleman profusely, and even offered to give him a few bucks for his trouble.

The old guy said it was no trouble worth paying for, wished David luck, and drove off.

It must have worked. David's luck started turning around that very moment. The first person he saw as he walked inside was a sheriff's deputy on a stool at the counter finishing up his dinner.

David sat down beside him, ordered a cup of coffee to warm up, and introduced himself to the officer. He asked if the deputy's rounds might take him south, like maybe around Stinson Beach? He quickly tried to explain the situation, about how the car ended up in the gully, and made some lame excuse about possibly buying a few acres out there and how he had just wanted to take a look. He chose to avoid any mention of the armed militia.

David realized that he didn't have a lot of other choices. It would probably take forever to get a cab out there, if it was even possible; he didn't want to explain anything to Chuck at three in the morning, and the rental car place wouldn't be open for hours.

As it turned out, the deputy was heading that way and, sure, he could give him a lift, and did. David was, once again, aware of the blessings of rural, small-town America. That never would have happened in the city.

A half an hour later, the deputy dropped him at his door. David thanked him profusely, waved as he drove off, and went inside, exhausted.

As tired as he was, he was also famished. The TV dinner of the other night was still in the microwave so he nuked it again and drew a quick bath. The coffee had helped, but not that much. He still felt chilled to the bone, and he'd always found that a hot bath was the most effective way to heat himself up.

He soaked in the bath, with a glass of wine balanced on the rim of the tub, eating his reheated TV dinner, which tasted horrible. He hoped he wasn't poisoning himself. Still, it was the high point of the day. Blissful sleep soon followed.

17

Dollar Rent A Car was not pleased when David talked to them the next morning. But, yes, they would appreciate directions for their tow truck driver as to where the car was disabled, and they tightly thanked him for that. Not knowing what he was going to be getting into when he and Shelly went for their clandestine lunch, David had taken out the extra insurance on the car that they offered, so, even in spite of everything, he owed them nothing.

Feeling rather fortunate, David prepared to fully face the music. It was time to call Chuck.

"Was that just me or didn't we have a talk about all this?" Once again, Chuck was fuming.

"Relax a minute. Sit down," David said to Chuck and Murray, who had both made the windy trek out to the beach house. "I've got a bit of a saga here but also some interesting news." They all sat down in the living room as David brought them up to date.

"Let me start at the beginning. When I was in Big Sur, I realized that I couldn't just sit this one out, that I had to be involved somehow. I started wondering about things, like this Arab military presence that Rebecca was concerned about, which we later saw in the pictures. Where could a group like that stay without attracting attention? My Armenian friend, Shelly, suggested the Tenderloin District. So, a couple of days ago, we went down there and checked it out, see if anything jumped out at us."

"I'm amazed something didn't jump out at you," Chuck said sarcastically. "And take your fool heads off in the process."

"Now, now. We got some good stuff. Take a look at these." David passed over the hotel registers. Chuck and Murray intently checked them over.

"I think you can see why we were interested in The Paramount; plus, the only names recorded were first names. There is still no official record of these guys. Later, trying to get a glimpse of some of these men in person, I staked the place out for a while."

"You realize this is getting worse all the time," Chuck said.

"Hey, I'm coming to the good part. I saw a truck pull up behind the place and take the men out of town, north of Mill Valley."

"How do you know that?" Murray asked.

"I followed them." Chuck was about off the sofa but David motioned for him to take it easy and continued. He told the whole story: about the guys working out, the running, the weapons, the gas masks, his lunch at the Arab greasy spoon with Shelly, his going back the next day, wrecking the rent-a-car, his close call in the pipe, all the way down to the sheriff's deputy who picked him up and brought him home.

Chuck and Murray just stared when David finished. They were having a hard time believing all this but sensed somehow, unfortunately, that it was probably true.

"Sounds like a typical day."

"They're not there anymore. Packed up and left," David added.

"How do you know?" Chuck asked.

"When I walked back to where they had been, everything was gone: the tent, Porta-Potties, Winnebago . . . everything."

"You really did all that stuff?" Murray asked, still amazed.

"Not my finest hours, I know," David admitted. "If I hadn't gotten caught, they'd still be there. I guess they figured they couldn't risk it with me still walking around knowing where they were."

"Shit."

"Remember The Paramount. They're all there."

"And haven't done anything illegal that we can prove," Chuck pointed out. "There's no crime in being listed by your first name. We will check out their legal status, though, as best we can." He glowered at David for a moment. "Please tell me I can assume you are through playing James Bond."

"I am."

"Good. This would have been great stuff if you hadn't scared them off, but maybe we can still get them." Chuck stood. "Listen, in your exploits, did you happen to learn anything more about that old house?"

"Not yet."

"Not ever! You're through, remember? I know you feel invincible but you're not. I'd kinda like you to hang around for a while, you know? You don't seem to get it that—"

Suddenly, the phone rang, causing all three men to jump. They laughed at each other as David answered.

"Hello. . . . Oh, hi Sol. . . . Just talking with Chuck and his partner. . . . No, that's all right. . . . Really? . . . Tomorrow? That's great. I'd love to. . . . One o'clock. You got it. . . . Hey, is my old parking spot still open? . . . Excellent. . . . All right, then. Thanks for calling. I'll see you at one. . . . You bet. Bye."

David hung up and jotted down the information on a pad.

"That's nice. One of my ex-partners' birthday is tomorrow. Having a little 'do.'"

"And you want to go. What were we just talking about?"

"Oh, come on, Chuck. I didn't want to hide out at Big Sur, I don't want to hide out here. Look, I promise I'll be careful. I'll go and come back. No big deal."

Chuck still didn't like it but knew he wasn't going to be making any more headway with David on that one. He pocketed his notes as he and Murray headed for the front door.

"Well, you did good and bad work," Chuck said. "Please let us take it from here. Keep yourself safe, alright?"

David said nothing. Chuck and Murray started to leave.

"By the way"—David stopped them on the sidewalk; they turned—"Arabic, Farsi, and even some Turkish."

"What is that?"

"The languages spoken by these guys in the diner. Thanks for coming out." David closed the door and smiled, seeing both men pull their pads back out and make notes of the new information. He walked back into the living room and saw Rebecca's picture . . . and hoped in his heart that he hadn't blown it too badly.

18

That night David lit a fire in the fireplace and proceeded to try once again to find the papers his accountant was after. He had made himself a scotch, had just retrieved a folder from one of the multitudinous boxes still stacked around, and paced casually around the house, sipping and reading.

David had done some more developing while he was cleaning up earlier. The four-by-six-inch picture of Rebecca had become an eight-by-ten-inch in a larger frame, and now sat on the mantel. It was a lovely picture and it was impossible to walk into the room without your eyes going to it. It made David so peaceful, seeing it there, but broke his heart at the same time.

Suddenly, David heard loud mariachi music blaring in his hearing aid! He dropped the folder—causing papers to scatter, quickly put down his drink—spilling half of it—and pulled the hearing aid out of his ear as fast as he could. *Casting him into his near silence.*

He shook his head to try to clear it. Damn, that was loud. Looking at the mess he'd made, he bent over to pick up the papers but got dizzy. He slowly stood, steadying himself on the end table. After a moment, his head seem to clear, and he tried again for the papers. As he reached out, his hand was shaking so badly he could hardly hang on to a piece of paper.

He silently sat there on the floor, defeated, his hand visibly shaking in his lap. He looked up to Rebecca's picture as if for strength. Despite what Chuck had said, David was feeling very mortal.

The next morning was a typical Northern California coast day. David walked alone along the chilly, misty, foggy beach. His hearing aid was back in and seemed to be behaving itself for the moment. The ocean sounds were loud, even threatening. Large pieces of driftwood lurked like misshapen nature lying in wait. Waves crashed and pounded, seagulls cut through the gray backdrop looking angry as they flew screaming by.

He limped back to his house, got a cup of coffee and, since he was still dressed for it, sat at the table outside on his deck, looking closer at the mansion picture that he still had.

Daley and Amanda were also taking a beach walk, saw him, and came over to the deck.

"Brisk this morning, isn't it?" Daley asked.

"Oh, good morning." David hadn't seen them come up. "Yes, it is."

"Would you like to take a walk?"

"Thanks, but I just got back from one. I don't think the leg is quite ready for another so soon."

Daley had come halfway up the stairs to better talk to David, knowing he didn't hear real well. She noticed the picture he was looking at. "What have you got there? Looks pretty."

David held the picture out to her. Daley and Amanda both came the rest of the way up the stairs to David.

"Have you ever seen this place?" he asked.

"Yeah, sure," Daley said, looking at the picture. "I don't know exactly where but I have seen it before."

"Great. If you do remember, could you let me know?"

"Do you want to buy it?"

"No, it's . . . personal reasons, but important. Here, keep this. I'll make some others."

"Okay, sure. I'll see what I can come up with." Daley took it, then started to head back to the stairs when she stopped. "Hey, how about coming over for dinner tonight? Mandy and I haven't had company for much too long."

"Yeah, can you?" Amanda excitedly echoed.

"Well, sure," David said, feeling cornered. How could he ask someone to do him a favor, then turn them down for dinner, even if he wanted to? "That would be nice. Thank you."

"Good," Daley said, going down the stairs. "And I'll think about that house. I know I've seen it. See you about seven." She and Amanda started back out to the beach, then threw back as an afterthought, "Come earlier if you want. We could catch the sunset."

They continued walking. David just watched for a moment, unsure of what he should be doing now.

A couple hours later, David was dressed and ready to go to his friend's surprise birthday party. Since the bad guys may be able to recognize Rebecca's Porsche, he put it back in the garage and, since the fog had already started to burn off, popped the top on his Morgan. He knew it was more memorable but he'd try to keep as low a profile as he could.

He knew he was going to have to do something with her Porsche: store it, sell it, keep it. Nothing seemed right at the moment, so he decided to pull a Scarlett and think about it tomorrow.

He climbed in and had just started backing out of the drive

when Daley and Amanda came running toward him, yelling, arms waving.

"Wait, David! Stop!"

"What is it?" David asked as he stopped, both running up to him. Amanda was holding a large glass globe.

"Thank goodness we got you," Daley said, trying to catch her breath. "I just went to start my car and—nothing, so I called the auto club but, you know, living out here, they won't be here for at least an hour and Mandy goes to the elementary school in Bolinas in the afternoons. Could you take her?"

"Oh, Daley, I'm sorry. I'm going into town, that's twenty minutes in the opposite direction and I have to be there at—"

"But this is a very special day for her," Daley interrupted. "It's show-and-tell, see? She found a Japanese net float on the beach the other day"—Amanda proudly held up her glass sphere—"and she's been so anxious to—"

"Daley, I really can't. It's important that I . . ."

David didn't get any further before Amanda started to cry. She looked a pitiful sight all dressed up, hugging her float, sobbing. David could argue with Daley all day but he couldn't fight that.

"All right, get in," David said, resigned. "At least I'll be so late I won't have to worry about spoiling the surprise."

"Thank you, David," Daley said, opening the Morgan's door for Amanda to get in. "Just for this, I'll make an extra special dinner tonight."

David forced a smile, nodded, and drove off.

David and Amanda drove in silence for a while before Amanda said, "I know you didn't want to take me."

"Oh, Amanda, it's not that," David said. "It's just that everyone was supposed to be there at a certain time to surprise my friend."

Suddenly, a large car, belching smoke, roared past them, honking. The driver seemed upset, yelling obscenities and giving them the finger out the window.

Amanda was concerned. "What was that man mad about?" she wanted to know.

"I don't know, honey. But I'm sure it doesn't have anything to do with us."

"Then why did he act mad at us?"

"Some people are just unhappy . . . and they seem to want to take it out on everyone else."

Amanda thought a moment. "I think I have a teacher like that."

David smiled. "Yeah, I had a couple like that, too."

They arrived at the school in plenty of time. Children of all ages were everywhere, playing, yelling, running. David was able to park close to the front of the school.

"Why can't people just be happy?" Amanda wondered aloud. She'd been thinking about this. "I'm happy. Mom's happy. You're happy, aren't you Mr. Collier?"

David hesitated a moment. Even if she was a child, she didn't deserve a lie that big. "I'm working on it, Amanda. But it does make me happy being able to help out a sweet little girl like you. You go have fun, okay? Be careful with your float."

"I will. Thank you," Amanda said as she got out of the car, gently cradling her globe. She quickly ran off toward a group of her girlfriends who were also holding various prized possessions, all jumping around, talking at the same time. David smiled and watched for a few moments before starting to drive off.

As his attention moved away from the girls, another sight made him stop cold. In front of him, also dropping off a child, was a pregnant woman who looked just like Rebecca. Well, maybe not exactly but definitely the same type. Enough to get his attention. Enough for him to be flooded by memories of unfulfilled plans.

He watched her send her little boy off, dreaming of what could have been. She then climbed laboriously into her SUV and drove off. David's own reality sadly came back to him as he also drove slowly away, melancholy and revenge vying for the dominant feeling.

19

David had arrived in town and was driving through the Castro District, heading for his old office near Mission Dolores Park. He found himself even more thankful that he didn't have to make that drive daily anymore. Besides the switchbacks out at Marin, there were no direct routes once he got in town. It was mostly surface streets and half the time they were crawling.

As he was musing about all this, he became faintly aware of sirens in the distance. As he got closer, they got louder. As he made the turn onto Church Street, he ran into a total traffic jam. Cars everywhere. No one was moving. In fact, most people had left their cars. David could see people crowding around police and fire trucks ahead.

An uncomfortable feeling came over him as he also left his Morgan and wove his way between the other abandoned cars, working his way toward his old office building. As he got closer he saw that the activity was actually centered around the parking structure next door. He arrived there in time to see ambulance attendants and firemen carrying a sheet-covered body from the structure and placing it in an ambulance.

David leaned on a nearby car for support, having left his cane in the car. He suddenly felt weak and dizzy. A man who had gone farther up came back to a woman near David. He over-heard their exchange.

"What was it?" the woman asked.

"A car exploded down there," the man said. "Killed a lady. Someone mentioned a bomb but I don't know. It's a mess."

The couple walked on. David sunk to the ground, leaning against the car, in shock, the pandemonium of disaster all around him.

"There's no doubt about it," Chuck said, later that day. "If you would have parked there first, you'd be dead now. She must have known you weren't there anymore."

Chuck and Murray were with David at the beach house again. David was still numb.

"Her husband is with the firm next door," he replied.

"Yeah, we talked to him," Murray said. "He'd told her she could use the parking space until it was reassigned. He feels pretty bad."

"I'm sorry about that, Dave," Chuck said. "I didn't want you to be around any of this but we have to deal with the reality of the situation now. So don't go crazy on me, all right? Murray's been guarding the Saudi contingency to this peace conference. He could use a little break. He's going to be your houseguest for a while. Hopefully, it won't be long."

"Do you have anything?" David asked hopefully, reading something in Chuck's last comment.

"Maybe. The bomb was in an attaché case and activated by the car driving over the detonator. Any car parking there would have done it. But the grip, the handle, was blown clear. If we can lift some prints from it . . . who knows?"

"And your phone is probably tapped," Murray added. "Remember, the killer knew exactly when and where you were going to be."

"We'll take care of that," Chuck said. "Don't worry about it. Well, let me get to work and try to find some answers. You going to be okay?"

"Hell, I don't know, Chuck," David replied after a moment. "I guess so."

"You hang in there. Murray, I'll be checking with you."

"Right," Murray said as Chuck gave David a friendly pat on the shoulder and left.

Everything very quickly got quiet. David and Murray had known each other from a distance for some time, which meant they were really just acquaintances that were now sharing the same house. Neither quite knew what to say to the other.

"Uh, look. I know this could be uncomfortable," Murray started out. "But try not to pay any attention to me, okay? I mean, I'll be wandering in and out but just ignore me."

"Sure." David sat, passively looking at the cold fireplace. Murray roamed around the house, familiarizing himself with the rooms, checking doors, windows.

"Did you know the lady?" he asked, coming back into the living room.

"No, just the husband. Three kids."

"Boy, that's tough."

Murray continued around the house. Given the enormity of his loss and all the pain and anguish around him, it was easy for David to ignore Murray.

The terrible reality of it all swept over him. His attention was drawn again and again to the picture of Rebecca on the mantel. Tears started to form but before they could fall, his sorrow turned to anger. The volcano was ready to blow. How *dare* this happen? How *dare* these good people be taken?

The more he thought about what was happening, the madder he got. Two wonderful women were dead and the son of a bitch who did it was still walking around . . . and trying to kill *him*! Why? What did he think David knew? How *dare* he, the bastard!

He couldn't take it anymore. In his fury, David got up, grabbed his cane, and walked determinedly out of the house to the deck. He attacked the stairs as best he could and stomped out onto the beach. Murray followed, wondering what was going on here.

David walked stormily along the beach, his anguish and temper rising rapidly. Murray followed attentively behind. How *dare* someone kill Rebecca? The sweetest . . . kindest . . . David walked as fast as his bum leg and cane would take him, then faster. His anger becoming fury.

He threw down his cane and tried to run. He and Rebecca had been perfect for each other. Perfect! Every muscle was pulling, stretching, but his leg couldn't keep pace with his desires. David fell, making him even madder. He tried to get up and run again but couldn't. He fell again, furious. He pounded the sand with all his strength, arms flailing, legs kicking, getting out his frustration and hurt until he was exhausted. He finally stopped and just lay there, panting.

After a long couple of minutes, David climbed to his feet, hands and arms sore, retrieved his cane, and slowly limped back to the house. Murray stood silently by the beach house stairs as David returned.

"Want a beer, Murray?" David asked casually as he walked by.

"No, thank you," Murray replied simply and followed.

Later that afternoon, David sat at the table on the deck trying to write. "Trying" was definitely the word. He was having a hard time sorting out his thoughts. Murray sat on the other end of the deck, keeping a watchful eye on David, but also seemed to be enjoying the ocean.

After a while, Murray asked, "So you quit being a lawyer to be a writer, huh?"

"Yeah."

"What kind of writer?"

David was not thrilled about having his thoughts interrupted, such as they were, and was definitely not in the mood for small talk, but what was he going to do? "I was going to start with short stories, then, hopefully, move into novels."

"Was?"

"Things have changed," David said after a moment. "Spending my time making up stories now seems kind of . . . inadequate . . . for now anyway," he added. "Later . . . who knows?"

David tried to go back to writing. After a moment . . .

"Is that a story you're working on now?"

"Not really. Just thoughts."

Murray didn't seem to have a follow-up comment so David was able to get back to it. His "just thoughts" were taking an interesting turn. He'd never thought much of life, death, and the meaning of it all but suddenly, what happened to a person after death became one of the most important things in the world to know about.

The waves seemed somehow beneficial to the thought process and soon David was making notes about the possible nature of God and the place of the soul in eternity, when . . .

"Uh, excuse me?"

David continued to stare at his paper a few seconds before looking up to Murray, who had come over by him.

"Just wondering if you'd mind if I made another pot of coffee?"

"Murray, don't ever ask permission to do anything again. As long as you're staying here, this is your place, too. *Mi casa es su casa* . . . all that. Okay?"

"Sure, okay. Sorry," Murray said, picking up the hardness in David's response. "I'll be right back."

Murray took a quick look around to make sure everything was still secure. "If you see any movement at all, step inside, all right?"

"Yeah."

Murray went inside.

Having his train of thought broken, David pushed his writing materials out of the way and leaned back, looking out to sea.

"Oh, Rebecca, why couldn't it have been me? You would have handled all this so much better . . . so much better. . . ."

His words became thoughts as ". . . so much better" became a mantra that coincided with the tide. The words then became "Becca . . . Becca . . ." then "Rebecca," forming a chant. Her name, the rhythm of the waves, all blended into one. David closed his eyes and turned his hearing aid up a notch.

The waves were crashing now with the sound of "Rebecca," gulls were screeching. He turned the sound up as loud as it would go. The waves were now thunderous, the birds, cacophonous! He was surrounded by sound, engulfed in it. Suddenly . . .

"SIR!"

David bolted upright, turning his hearing aid down as quickly as he could. Murray was standing in the doorway behind him.

"Jesus, Murray. What is it?"

"A lady called about dinner tonight. Guess you had some plans. Anyway, I told her you weren't going anywhere . . . so she's bringing it over here."

David had forgotten all about that. Damn.

"Who is she?" Murray asked.

"A neighbor . . . trying to be way too helpful."

"Is she the one with the kid? She knew where you were going today, didn't she?" Murray asked, wondering if he might be onto something here.

"Murray, it's because of her and her daughter that I'm alive."

"Oh, yeah. I guess you're right." Murray was still thinking about it when he went back to finish the coffee.

David sat a moment longer before reluctantly gathering his materials and taking them inside. The moment was lost.

20

Bashaar and Ameen were in a richly wooded office or den. It was nicely furnished with a desk, computer, filing cabinets, and a polished wooden table.

Bashaar was fitting a type of gas mask to Ameen. It fit over his entire head, with a clear faceplate from his forehead to his chin. A canister/filter rested in the nape of his neck.

"Start wearing it tomorrow," Bashaar said. "Let everybody get used to it. Tell them you have a sinus infection. A bad one. Contagious."

"They'll laugh at me," Ameen said.

"Good. They will remember then. We want them to be suspicious of nothing. Besides, you will have the last laugh, my friend."

Ameen smiled to himself as he looked in a mirror, modeling his new mask.

Daley set up a card table in the living room so they could have a nice dinner by the fireplace. David had put away a few more boxes to make the place a bit more presentable but couldn't get motivated to do much. Actually, he wished there had been a polite way to get out of it.

He begrudgingly had to admit that the dinner Daley brought

(Cajun catfish) was delicious and it was also nice that she brought enough for Murray, who insisted on not joining them. He sat on the sofa with a TV tray while watching a basketball game with the sound turned off. The sound came from Daley's favorite hard rock-and-roll radio station on the stereo, which was playing much too loud.

She must have gotten a babysitter for the evening because young Amanda had been left home. It was just David and Daley at the card table. She even brought a candle that burned between them.

Daley, once again, looked terrific, with a white halter top and skirt split all the way up to Nevada. Her white outfit and her light hair looked great with her nicely tanned skin and she knew it. Murray noticed it, too. She was also talking a mile a minute. David was having a terrible time.

"I still think it's just so amazing the way things worked out," Daley was saying. "I mean, I felt so bad imposing on you but I had to, you know? . . . And then it ends up saving your life? Incredible . . . And Mandy was so happy, well, she was happy anyway. I guess her net float was the hit of the day."

"Does the stereo have to be on that loud?" David asked.

"Oh, I'll bet it bothers your hearing aid, doesn't it?" Daley said, getting ready to change it.

"No. It's just awfully loud."

"Don't you like music?"

"I love music, Daley. But I'm not particularly crazy about *that* music and I especially don't like having to yell over it."

"Oh, sure. I'm sorry," Daley went over to the stereo, turned it down a very small bit, and returned to the table, Murray's eyes on her all the while. She started talking again before she sat down.

"Yes, that's better. I really think all this has to be karma, don't you? I mean, all this death and everything?"

Suddenly Murray's cell phone rang, mercifully shutting her up. Murray answered.

"Murray . . . Oh, hi babe . . . right in the middle of dinner . . . Yeah, that would be good. Catch you in an hour or so . . . Bye."

He pocketed the phone. "Sorry about that."

"Sure, no problem," Daley said, then took up where she left off. "Well, anyway, about karma. It was just their time, you know? I mean, that's why you were saved. You can't really believe it's just luck when you're talking about your life and everything."

Suddenly, the doorbell rang. David and Murray quickly exchanged a look. Daley jumped to her feet. "I'll get it."

"Sit down!" Murray said hard. She did.

Murray drew his pistol and held it to his side as he carefully opened the door. A small woman stood there.

"Hello. Is David Collier here?" she asked Murray.

"Who are you?" Murray asked.

"Judy West; I was his nurse."

When David heard this he got up and went to the front door. "Judy, hi. Come in, please."

Murray discreetly put his gun away as Judy came in. She was carrying a highly polished cane with a bow around it.

"Hi. I just thought I'd drop . . ." Judy noticed the lovely, sexy Daley and the candlelit dinner.

"Oh, this is Daley, a neighbor, and this is my 'bodyguard' Murray. This is Judy West."

They said hi's all around. Murray sat back down. Judy suddenly looked like she wished she was anyplace else. Embarrassed, she still forged ahead. "I just wanted to see how you were doing and . . . bring you a little present."

She handed him the cane. David was aware of her discomfort and wished he could do something about it. "It's great, Judy, thank you. You should see the old thing I've been using. Would you come in and join us?"

"No, please." She looked over again at the romantic sight. "I just wanted to say 'hi' and . . . I know I can get pretty crusty around the hospital sometimes, but . . . well, I just thought you might like some company."

"It was a good thought. Another time, maybe?"

"Sure," Judy said, getting ready to leave. She looked again over to Daley. "She's very pretty."

Judy stepped out the door and was gone before David could say anything . . . whatever that might have been. Murray came over, checked out the cane, and handed it back. "Clean."

David felt terrible as he walked back to the card table with the cane.

"Attractive lady," Daley said. "Did she say she was your nurse?"

"Yes."

"What a neat cane. Did you read the card?"

"Oh, no. I didn't." He hadn't noticed that there was a card.

"Well, read it. Really, you men. No sentimentality."

David found it, took it off the cane, and read it.

David,
I've had a bad month myself. I hope I didn't take it out
on you too much. Heal well.
Judy

He put the card on the table. Daley immediately picked it up. "Was she pretty bad?" she asked after reading it.

"No, she was fine. I think she's tougher on herself than anyone else."

"That's a shame."

"Yeah."

"You know, karma really does make you feel better when you realize that there's a balance. I mean, the bad guys may not have to pay much in this life, but, boy, will they get it in the next."

David's gaze drifted over to Murray, who was working hard to keep his face as stoic as possible . . . and the evening went on.

21

David, Daley, and Murray were out on the deck. Her dishes were on the nearby table ready for her short beach walk home.

"I have a lot to thank you for today," David said. "Directly, the lovely dinner and evening. Indirectly, my life."

"I'm very glad," Daley said softly as she stepped closer and gave David much more of a kiss than he was prepared for. She finally stopped, looking at David meaningfully for a moment before going to Murray and shaking his hand.

"Good night, Murray. You guard his body good now, you hear?"

"Yes, ma'am," Murray said as he handed her one of his cards. "If you ever see anything suspicious or have any problems, you just let me know, okay?"

"I will do it, Officer," Daley said with a smile as she tucked the card in her halter top.

"And thanks for bringing some for me, too," Murray added.

"My pleasure," Daley said as she picked up her dishes and started for the stairs. "G'night guys."

She left. They both watched her walk down to her beach house.

"That girl will never drown," Murray said, not taking his eyes off her.

"Yeah."

"Looks like she's after you."

"That's all I need right now."

"You know what your problem is?" Murray asked, philosophically. "You're a gentleman. Ladies love that stuff. You keep being nice, they're going to keep hanging around. I know what I'm talking about. There aren't many of us genteel types left, but the ladies love us."

David waited another moment by the railing, trying to assimilate the many changes around him. No, too big a task for one emotion-filled evening. He went inside, Murray right behind.

"I think I'll turn in, Murray."

"Yeah, I've had all the fun I can stand, too. I've been meaning to ask you . . . could I call you 'David'? Otherwise, I'm living here with a guy named 'Mr. Collier' . . . what is that?"

David smiled as he said, " 'Dave' will be just fine."

"Thank you. Appreciate it."

"You know, we've got a guest room upstairs," David said, starting to go up. "It never quite got put together, but—"

"That's all right," Murray assured him. "I'm a couch kinda guy. I'll talk to my wife for a while and hit it right here. Sleep good, Dave."

David nodded and headed up the stairs to his bedroom. About halfway up, he had a dizzy spell. He steadied himself on the banister, took a few deep breaths, and continued slowly climbing. Murray was already calling his wife on his cell and didn't notice this.

David and Rebecca lay nude après love on the Navajo rug. The scene was lit by sunset colors and shadows. Somehow the sky seemed more brilliant, the colors more vibrant, the sound of the sea even more melodic. Everything was soft.

This perfect reverie was disturbed by the doorbell. Even it sounded lovely. Rebecca kissed David, then got up to answer it.

David loved the moment. Seeing her, looking around at the lovely day, their charming house, then he looked back in the direction Rebecca had gone and screamed, "NO!"

He walked quickly around the corner and saw Rebecca naked by the front door, dead, with most of her face blown off.

David jolted upright in bed still yelling, "No! No, Rebecca!" He was sweating and still panting when he noticed the moon and streetlamps through the window. He noticeably relaxed. Thank God it was only a dream.

He then looked over to the empty side of the bed and just as quickly remembered the awful truth. He slowly lay back down staring at the ceiling in remembrance and pain. Awake for the night.

Ameen, wearing his helmeted faceplate, walked up to the guard booth stationed by the entrance to a large government facility. He showed his ID to the guard, who looked at him and laughed.

"What's with the new look, Ameen? Doing a little swimming?"

"Sinus infection," Ameen said. "Guess I'm contagious. Got to keep it covered for a while."

"Quite a fashion statement," the guard said as he buzzed open the door. Ameen passed through.

"Like a fighter pilot," Ameen said.

"Right. A five-five, rag-head, fighter pilot," the guard said, still chuckling.

Ameen casually gave the guard the finger as he walked on into the building. This caused the guard to laugh even harder.

That same morning, Dr. Mandell was at the beach house going over David's hearing aid. David sat in his silence until the doctor put it back in. Sounds of living crackled, then cleared as it settled in.

"High-intensity devices like these are so sensitive," the doctor said. 'Sometimes it takes a few adjustments to get them just right. How's this?"

"Seems fine."

"Good. Well, hopefully, this will do it, but any more problems, just let me know and I'll send a technician out."

"Will do. Thanks."

"How's your brain adjusting to this thing?" the doctor asked. "Are you having trouble following conversations or anything like that?"

"I miss some words every once in a while but I can generally follow. I'm not real good in crowds."

"No, and you never will be. Too much sound just overwhelms these little guys. If you watch people's mouths as they speak," the doctor continued, "I think you'll find that it's easier to understand them."

"It is." David said. "I've already been doing that."

"Good. How's everything else? Notice anything out of the ordinary?"

"My hands shake sometimes."

"So you mentioned," the doctor said, making a note in his book. "Have you ever felt dizzy?"

"Yeah. A couple of times."

"Really?" the doctor's interest was perked. "Have you fallen down?"

"Came close."

The doctor frowned as he made more notes. "How severe is the shaking?"

David tried to show the doctor how much it shook. "About like this."

"If you were holding a cup of coffee, would it spill?"

"Oh, yeah. It'd be a mess."

The doctor thought for a moment, then pulled out his pad. "I don't like prescribing anything until I know for sure what we're dealing with, but we've got to make sure we're going in the right direction. Take one of these every morning for the next week or so. They should help," the doctor said, writing out a prescription. "You could also have my nurse call this in if you'd like," he said, handing David the prescription. "When all this police business ends, give me a call. The bullet nicked the right side of your brain. I'll take another look at that MRI, make sure there isn't something we've overlooked. Anything else?"

"I think that's it." David decided not to tell him that he'd practically driven his car off a cliff. The next step after that would be the doctor telling him not to drive anymore. That wasn't going to happen. He'd just be careful.

Doctor Mandell stood. "All right. That adjustment should help with the hearing. Get that prescription filled soon. Give me a call as soon as you can. We should check you out again."

David said that he would and, with Murray, walked the doctor to the door. "Thanks for coming by," David said, shaking his hand.

"You bet," Doctor Mandell said as he looked around appreciatively. "Funny. I live in a town by the ocean and I can't remember the last time I was at the beach. It's nice here." He then turned back to David. "Take care now. Call me."

The doctor left. They closed the door and returned to the living room.

"I'll bet that's the first house call he's made in his whole career," Murray said.

"Thanks, Murray. I appreciate it."

"Hey, the power of the badge."

"I'm going to be doing some work in the darkroom, all right?"

Murray picked up the *TV Guide*. "Sure. I think there's a game on."

David first went to his desk and, while he was thinking about it, had the doctor's nurse call in the prescription to his closest pharmacy, a few miles up the road in Point Reyes Station. He set it to be picked up the next day, then went into the darkroom and closed the door behind him.

22

The red light lit the darkroom. David soaked up the feeling of Rebecca as he poured solution into the trays and looked for the negatives he wanted to develop. Murray had evidently found a basketball game on TV and had it turned a bit louder than David would have liked, especially there. David faced the darkroom with the reverence of a shrine. A basketball game didn't fit.

He took his hearing aid out, set it off to the side, and returned to the negatives, accompanied only by his thoughts.

An hour or so later, the fruits of David's labors were evident. Since he had given his copy of the one remaining shot of the old mansion in question to Daley, he made a few more. While they dried, a larger, sixteen-and-a-half- by twenty-inch picture of Rebecca soaked in the tray.

David could still feel Rebecca around him as he looked at her picture through the water. She seemed to move, animated in the gently moving water.

As he watched her gently sway, memories vied for attention, crowding in and over him.

"Do you like sunsets or not?" "I love them." "Then open your eyes." "Do you think we're doing the right thing?" "The future's going to be so great." "I sure do love you." "Sure do love you right back."

Suddenly, light poured into the room and Murray's hand reached in and grabbed David's shoulder and turned him around. Murray had his gun in the other hand, talking to him in a barely audible whisper, motioning him out of the room. David quickly scrambled to put his hearing aid back in.

Sound returned to him as David burst out of the darkroom, shocked to see Murray holding a gun on Shelly.

"My God, Murray. What is it?" David asked.

"I've been pounding on the door. Didn't you hear me?"

"No, I didn't. Shelly, what's going on?"

"You know this guy?" Murray asked.

"Of course, I know him," David said. "He's the guy who got the hotel registers for us. He also shared my celebrated lunch in the diner that you and Chuck loved so much."

"I remember that," Murray mumbled.

"The gun's not necessary, Murray. I also asked him to come over."

"As I mentioned to you," Shelly said to Murray.

"Well, from now on, if you're having friends over, let me know," Murray said as he put his gun away and returned to his basketball game.

Shelly stepped into the darkroom with David, leaving the door open.

"Sorry about that," David said.

"It happens," Shelly said. "A little more recently, what with one thing or another. Oh, before you give me your news, I just found out that our good ol' Paramount got sold about six months ago."

"Really. Who would want to buy that dump?"

"In this case, an overseas consortium, primarily involved in shipping."

"Can you find out who's behind it? An individual maybe?"

"I doubt it. It seems pretty well covered. Kingsnorth Bros., LTD, registered in England. Their main offices are in Pakistan, but they have a presence all over the Middle East."

"Kingsnorth Brothers. Doesn't sound Pakistani."

"I imagine it was designed specifically to not sound Pakistani," Shelly said.

"So, they bought the whole place," David said, mostly to himself. "My God, they must be planning something massive."

"Is this the one you were talking about?" Shelly asked, looking over a blowup of the old mansion.

"Yeah. I've got to find it. Does it look familiar to you?"

"No," Shelly said after studying it a moment. "Do you know where it is?"

"Shelly, if I knew where it was, I wouldn't need you to help me find it."

"I mean, what town? Is it around here someplace?"

"I think so. Rebecca never did drive all that far lately. No idea at all?"

"Not really, but I'm in a large office. Somebody should know something."

David gave Shelly a picture. "Good. Hang on to this. The police will probably want it for evidence."

Murray stepped into the darkroom doorway, took the picture from Shelly. "The police will definitely want it as evidence. This is from that missing roll, right?"

"Yeah. I found one more."

"It doesn't go anywhere." Murray walked out into the living room with the picture.

"Murray, we've got to find that house," David pleaded. "Shelly's in real estate. He can do it."

"If Chuck wants to release one, that's up to him," Murray said. "I can't clear it."

David saw the mail truck pull up out front and got an idea. He quickly headed for the front door.

"All right, I'll talk to Chuck later," David said on his way. "Oh good, the mail's here. Mind if I get it, Murray?"

"Yes, I mind. You know better than that," Murray said, as he went outside to collect the mail from the box by the curb.

As soon as he had gone a few steps, David limped quickly back to the darkroom and grabbed another picture of the mansion, and stuffed it inside Shelly's coat. "I made some copies. Get back to me."

"Will do," Shelly said, securing the hidden picture as Murray returned with a stack of mail.

"Most of it's junk," Murray said, handing it to David.

"Always. . . . Hey, thanks for coming over anyway, Shelly. I'll talk to Chuck about trying to get a picture for you."

"Sure, Dave. See you." Shelly started to leave, turned to Murray. "Next time I'll call ahead."

"Good idea," Murray said. After Shelly left, he followed David into the living room. "What's this 'mail' business? You know you can't do that."

"I just need to get out some, that's all. Get some air."

"Well, it shouldn't be too long now."

That perked David's interest. "Why?"

"Huh?"

"Do you know something?"

"Oh, no . . . not really," Murray waffled.

"Murray!"

"Hey, we can't go blabbing around about everything we're doing, you know."

"This kind of involves me, in case you hadn't noticed. Besides . . ." David said, indicating the empty room. "Who am I going to tell?"

"It's just that they got some good prints off the handle of that attaché case. They've got a suspect."

"Great. Who is it?"

"I have no idea." Murray said. "I'm not involved in that end of it . . . obviously, because I'm here . . . but they're looking for him. Chuck will keep you posted."

Murray's cell phone rang; he answered. "Murray . . . oh, hi, babe . . . I don't know. You'll know when I do . . . Uh-huh . . ."

As Murray continued on the phone, he made a motion to David that he may be on the phone a while. David nodded and went back to the darkroom. Rebecca's picture had soaked long enough. He hung it gently, looked at it a moment longer, then went back to the living room.

David mimed to Murray if it was alright for him to go out on the deck. Murray took the phone with him, checked outside to make sure it was clear, while keeping up his end of the conversation with his wife. He nodded to David that it was "all clear" and went to the far side of the deck where he could keep an eye out for David and talk quietly enough to not disturb him.

David took the mail and sat at the outside deck table. He took a moment to look over the ocean and digest the information he just got from Murray. The possibility of getting the man that killed Rebecca . . . well, it was huge. David thought about what he'd do if and when they eventually catch that guy. He'd like to have some time alone in a room with him, he knew that, but as for himself . . . he had no idea. He couldn't even imagine. Any thoughts of his future went as far as killing or capturing the killer and putting him away. Period. There was a big wall right there where everything stopped. There was nothing else.

He watched with melancholy envy as Murray talked freely and lovingly with his wife at the other end of the deck. A surge of emptiness made its way though him. It was the "what if" thoughts that were the worst.

After a while, he started going through the mail. After a few, he came across an envelope that got his attention. Trying not to get his hopes up, he opened it and read the letter.

It must have been good news because his face lit up immediately. He was sitting there, grinning broadly, as Daley walked up.

"Hi. How are you doing?" she asked.

"Actually, I'm pretty darn great. *Atlantic Monthly* is interested in publishing one of my stories."

"Great. How much are they paying you?"

"I don't know," David said. "Maybe nothing. It doesn't matter."

"The hell it doesn't," she replied strongly. "Don't let those turkeys take advantage of you. Start out on the right foot; let them know from the beginning that you're a pro. If they want you, they're going to have to pay for it. No money—no stories—period."

David just looked at her . . . then, "I knew you'd be happy for me, Daley. Enjoy your day," David said as he got up and went into the house.

Daley wondered if it was something she said.

Later that afternoon, Murray was watching a football game in the living room. David was on the phone in his writing room, not pleased.

". . . so what does that mean?" David asked the person on the other end of the line. "You will never handle a controversial subject because someone may not like it? That's a hell of a way to run a magazine."

David hung up, sat there fuming a minute, then called out to Murray.

"That's one of the great things about a telephone. If you don't like what you're hearing, you just hang up."

"Is that what you're doing?" Murray called back.

"No, That's what they're doing to me."

Murray chuckled and went back to his game. David just sat there, livid, wondering what to try next. A knock on the glass slider next to him made him jump. He looked up and saw Daley at the door.

Murray had also heard the knock and was immediately running into David's room, gun half drawn. He returned it to his holster when he saw that it was Daley. He half waved and went back to the TV. David got up and opened the doors.

"I'm really sorry if I said something wrong," Daley said from the doorway, not coming in. "I really am happy for you. I really am. I mean, sometimes I get nervous and excited and make a coo-coo out of myself."

"A cuckoo?" David asked.

"It's a technical term. I am sorry."

"That's all right, but thanks."

"I think you're going to like this better," she said, brightening. "I remembered where I saw that house. It's actually not that far away. Do you know that turnoff to Taylor Park by Olema?"

"Yeah. The one that goes to San Raphael?"

"That's the one," Daley said. "Sir Francis Drake Boulevard, I think it's called. Anyway, you take that east for a few miles until you see a sign to Camp Charlotte. Amanda used to be a Brownie. That's their camp out there. It's been a couple of years but we used to go there quite a lot. This road won't take you right by the old house but you'll be able to see it off to your left.

I'm sure it's the same one. I'll bet you could figure out how to get there. It's secluded down in one of those valleys, you know?"

David knew very well. No wonder the militants picked up their tent and left when they couldn't find him, they were just a valley or two away from this house, possibly their headquarters.

David stepped out on the deck, gave Daley a hug and a kiss on the cheek. "Daley, you're a dream. Thank you. You may have done more than you know."

"Good, I'm glad. Maybe one of these days you could tell me what this is all about?"

"I absolutely will," David said, starting to go back inside. "That's a promise. I'll see you later. Thanks again."

23

David went directly to the living room where Murray was still on the phone, watching a football game with the sound turned very low. An occasional grunt seemed all that was necessary for him to keep up his end of the phone conversation. Murray saw David enter and looked up at him questioningly.

"Daley remembers where she saw the house," David said, trying to contain his excitement.

Murray quickly straightened up. "Something's come up, babe. Gotta go. I'll call back later." He hung up. "Where is it?"

"Not that far; less than an hour. I can find it. Let's call Chuck."

"Won't do any good," Murray said, putting away his cell phone. "He's gone till tomorrow. Some Chamber of Commerce thing. He wouldn't be able to get a search warrant until then anyway."

"That shouldn't be a problem, should it?"

"You can never tell. Judges can be weird, you know that."

"But, Murray! What about the troops and the guns . . . gas masks! And the pictures were stolen. The killer didn't want us to have pictures of that house!"

"Now, don't get your knickers in a twist," Murray said, trying to calm David down. "Hopefully, it will be enough. We'll find that out tomorrow . . . then we'll *tell* you about it. You're not going anywhere close to that place."

"I have to, Murray," David said quietly but firmly.

"Get a grip, son. That's the last place Chuck will want you to be. You know that."

"Yeah, I do know that. I also know that I'm tired of getting *this* close to things and not have anything happen."

David crossed to the mantel and the picture of Rebecca, resolving even deeper that whoever it was that took her away from him will pay dearly. He then noticed that his hand was shaking again. This seemed to take him down a notch or two. Was he even going to live long enough to make it happen? He had no idea how much more time he had but he wasn't making any long-term bets. If he was going to make good on his promises, he'd better get on with it.

David went to his writing area and looked out over the sea, deep in thought. After a few minutes, a quiet determination came over him. He thought a few minutes more, then returned to the living room and sat down on the sofa with Murray, who had gotten back into his football game.

"Could I talk to you a minute, Murray?" David asked.

"Sure," Murray said, putting the TV on mute. "What's up?"

"You love your wife, right?"

"Hey, she's the best."

"What would you do if someone killed her?"

That got Murray's attention. He wished they could have had this talk a little later when the game was over, but he tried to force himself to answer David's question truthfully.

"I have thought about that," Murray said. "Unfortunately, knowing me, I'd probably go crazy. That would be first. Then I'd find the guy who did it and somebody, hopefully, would stop me from killing him. If not . . . all bets are off." Murray then went back to his football game.

"Then what?"

"What do you mean?"

"After your revenge," David asked after thinking a moment. "Where do you go then?"

"Try to start over, I guess," Murray mumbled, eyes back on the game. He hadn't thought about it that far.

"And how do you do that?" David said quietly, mostly to himself.

Murray's team just suffered a turnover and the game got outrageously exciting. Murray realized the importance of David trying to make some sense of it all and knew that he should try to help all he could, but another turnover! Now?

David didn't even notice that Murray wasn't really with him. That was all right, actually, another body was all he needed. David was as much in his own world, at this time, as Murray was.

"What's made it so tough for me is that I've just felt numb," David continued. "I didn't know what I wanted to do . . . didn't know what I *could* do . . . so I didn't do anything except look around a little." David thought for another minute. This wasn't accomplishing anything. It was time for him to get resourceful again. Determined. Think. What did finding the location of the house change? Anything? Maybe it was time to make something happen.

"You know, Murray," David said after a moment, "maybe there is something I can do."

"Good. Good," Murray said, nodding. It looked like his team might be getting the ball back.

"It all can't have been for nothing . . . it can't. I won't allow it. Just some tracks, that's all. Some footprints," David said, still deep in thought. "I've got some work to do, Murray, and I think I'm finally able to start doing it."

"Sounds good," Murray said. Yes! His team got the ball and with time on the clock.

"Well, thanks for talking with me," David said sincerely. "It helped a lot."

"Sure. You bet. Anytime." A touchdown was imminent.

David went back to his writing room. When David left the room, Murray turned the TV sound back on.

David sat again at his desk gazing out over the beach. Quickly, he decided and reached for the phone.

"Murray," David called out from his room. "Could you do me a favor and forget about what you might hear?"

"What?" Murray yelled back over the game noise.

"Never mind." David looked up a number from his address book and dialed.

"Mr. Moeller, please," David said to the secretary on the phone. ". . . David Collier . . ." After a moment, "Gordon, how are you? . . . Yeah, I know, it has. I want to thank you for the card, too. I appreciate it. . . . Good, glad to hear it. Listen, Gordon, the reason I'm calling, I'm finishing the project Rebecca was working on when she got killed. It's really quite charming and I thought it might be just right for you. . . .

"Well, in twenty-five words or less, it's a photo retrospective of some of the grand mansions built in California in the 1930s. A coffee-table book, really lovely. Architecturally, that was a pretty amazing time in our history and . . . No, there's nothing controversial about it at all. . . ."

From the look on David's face, Gordon's response to this was not what David wanted to hear.

". . . Gordon, forgive me for this, but Rebecca died working on this project." David said, firmly. "You said once to let you know if there was ever anything you could do for me. I'm letting you know. . . ." David took a deep breath and continued. "All right, let's try another tack. I'll make you a deal: you publish this book and I'll have a bonfire with my records of the Canadian stuff. . . . No, they're in my personal records. . . . All right, I'll send them to you and you can have the bonfire. . . . Fine, I'll get them to you as soon as it's finished. . . . Right."

David hung up. Well, he wished he hadn't had to do it like that but, at least, it was done.

Murray called out from the other room, "There wasn't a little friendly extortion going on in there, was there?"

"Why, whatever do you mean?" David replied innocently.

Murray grunted and went back to the game. David's look again took him back to the sea, his hand shaking steadily in his lap.

Later that evening, David was in the darkroom finishing framing Rebecca's large picture. He then took down the one he'd put on the mantel and, instead, hung the new one over the fireplace, above the mantel.

He stepped back and thought it looked great. It dominated the room . . . just as it should, he thought.

Still later, the fire had burned farther down and Murray's game was long over (he was watching the fights now) when David walked in from his writing area.

"Let me make sure I understand the situation, Murray," David said, standing by the couch. "I can't go anywhere; I can't know the name of the man suspected of killing my wife; I can't go near that house, in fact, no one can without a search warrant and there's no guarantee that we can even get one?"

"That's about it, Dave," Murray said. "A lot of it pisses me off, too, but those are the rules, and enforcing those rules is my job."

"Those rules used to be my job, too," David said, quietly, as he looked appreciatively at Rebecca's new photo, then smiled slightly as he thought, *But they're not anymore.*

"Well, I'm turning in," David said with an exaggerated yawn. "Good night, Murray."

" 'Night, Dave," Murray said, watching David go upstairs. He also yawned and went back to the fights.

T*he next morning,* Murray was asleep on the couch when David, still in his bathrobe, came quietly down the stairs, across the living room, and into the kitchen. Noiselessly, he took down two cups, then reached into his robe pocket and pulled out a box labeled "Sleepy-Time Capsules." He opened four of them, pouring the powder inside into one of the cups.

Having returned the box and empty capsules to his robe pocket, David then, quite noisily, opened the refrigerator and got some orange juice. The noise quickly woke Murray.

"Jesus! I didn't even hear you," he said, half awake.

"Sorry, I couldn't sleep anymore. Want some coffee?" David asked, already pouring them.

"Sure, thanks," Murray said, stretching.

"Cream and sugar, right?" David asked.

"Yeah."

David added the condiments to the special coffee and brought the cups over to the sofa. Since David took his coffee black, it was easy to tell which one went to Murray, who took it and thanked him. David sat down next to him, turned the TV on to the *Stock Market Review* and settled in to watch it.

"Sorry," David said to Murray. "But I never miss this. Investments, you know."

"Sure," Murray said, still stretched out over most of the couch. He sipped his coffee a few minutes, watching some of the program. Soon another news preview came on touting the last day of the UN Middle-Eastern Peace Conference being held at San Francisco's United Nations Plaza.

"Boy, they've sure made a big deal about that," Murray said.

"Wouldn't it be something if they could actually do something?"

"They probably could if all sides really wanted to. Everybody wants their particular version of peace and that's it. Nobody wants to compromise or work together. Pretty tough under those circumstances."

"I'll say. Chuck said you were looking after some of them. What was that like?"

"Oh, like being someone's servant that they think smells bad."

"That sounds like fun."

"Yeah, great fun." Murray grunted, rolling his eyes.

The program started with the announcer droning on about the future of pork bellies. "Oh, good. Here we are," David said as he made himself comfortable.

"Boy, that'll put you to sleep," Murray said after a few minutes.

"Sure will."

David and Murray sat quietly drinking their coffee, watching the boring program.

Less than an hour later, Murray was sound asleep and David was finishing making a hushed phone call at his desk. He came into the living room, already dressed and carrying a manila folder. He checked to make sure Murray was still comfortably comatose and let himself quietly out the front door.

It was another misty, gloomy day at the beach. As much as David loved having the top down on his little Morgan, the weather just wasn't cooperating. Up it stayed.

He threw the manila folder on the passenger seat, popped it out of gear, and slowly rolled the car back out onto the street, steering it through the open driver door. Once on the street, he continued to push it another hundred feet or so before getting in and starting the car.

Just one of the many pleasures in owning a small sports car, David thought, smiling, as he drove off down the street.

Bashaar and Ameen were in the same richly paneled office where Bashaar had introduced the strange diving mask Ameen had been wearing. On this day Bashaar was giving him more instruction. Ameen was still wearing the mask. The only difference was a small gas canister that was worn around his waist, and a rubber tube that led from the canister to a nozzle that he held in his hand.

Ameen was pushing a button on the hose as he waved it back and forth. The fine spray went wherever he pointed.

"Excellent," Bashaar said. "All you have to do is walk past them and wave." Bashaar stepped back, assessing his silly looking friend again. "Did everyone see you?"

"I even wandered the halls," Ameen said, his voice sounding rather hollow. "Oh yeah. They saw me."

"Did they make fun of you?"

"Big time."

"Good. Then they will think nothing strange as you walk by later today."

"And then, they will think nothing," Ameen said. Both men laughed.

Daley's instructions took him up north, around the tiny berg of Olema. This worked out fine for David, since it was close to

Point Reyes Station and the pharmacy where David's prescription awaited. He drove the few miles up there, picked up the prescription for his shaky hand, and took a pill as soon as he got outside. Wouldn't it be nice if that was one less thing he had to worry about?

He then crossed the street to take care of his other business. He knew that a branch of the real estate company Shelly worked for was located there. He dropped off the folder with a note and backtracked down the road a bit to the turnoff and headed for the mansion. It was eerie for him to be going down this road again since it was the same road that led to the field where the militants were playing. These were the same miles he had walked before the old carpenter picked him up. Not exactly his fondest memories.

Well, finding the mansion was David's main intent. After practically an hour of following Daley's directions to the letter, however, he still seemed to be missing the turnoff. He couldn't find the Camp Charlotte sign to save his life.

He finally flagged over a small local farmer driving a tractor that seemed way too big for him. He was going about three miles an hour on the highway, much to the joy of anyone coming up behind him. Fortunately, there wasn't much traffic on this road. He got passed a lot.

David asked him about the sign.

"Oh, yeah. Somebody stole it about a year ago," the little farmer said. He smiled, showing both of his teeth. "Probably someone with a sweetheart named Charlotte, I'd guess." He seemed to ponder that a moment. "Do people still name people Charlotte?"

David was sure that there was a constituency of Charlottes out there, probably less than there were fifty years ago but he was sure there were still some about. The old farmer seemed to feel better about that and proceeded to point out to David where the sign used to be. David had just driven by there about four times.

David also took a chance and asked about the mansion.

"Oh sure, the old Crawford place," the old man said, seemingly pleased by the memory. "Boy, that was a beauty. A real shame."

"What was a shame?" David asked.

"Oh, they had a lovely spread but none of their kids wanted to go into farming or even to try to keep the place up after the folks died. The kids fought about the place so much, they couldn't even come to an agreement about selling it. I think even they are dead now. It's just been sitting there empty for about the last thirty years or so. Some groups seemed to use it every now and then but not so much lately. It's pretty well gone.

"I could tell you some tales about Lydia and Grant Crawford, though, that you wouldn't believe. . . ." the little farmer started off, laughing to himself, settling himself on his tractor seat as if he wasn't going to be moving for a long time. "Those two used to get in the worst rows. I remember one . . ."

David realized it was then or never. He quickly jumped in, said he was sure the stories were terrific but that he was running late already, since he got so lost, and really had to run. He thanked the old farmer again, hopped in the car and took off before the old gent could get rolling again.

With the old farmer's directions, David took the road to the Brownie camp rather than the one leading directly to the house. He didn't really want to run into any of those militant types out there.

He drove back a mile or so, rounded a bend and there it was, off to his left, just like Daley said it would be. Immediately, he

153

could see the nearby hill from where Rebecca had taken the pictures, and drove to it.

The weather was still murky as David crouched down behind some foliage, scanning the house below through his binoculars and taking some pictures of his own with his cell phone. Although it was a lovely old place, badly in need of repair, David felt a foreboding just looking at it. Perhaps it was the knowledge that Rebecca had probably been killed for doing exactly what David was doing now.

A group of about seven men in civies were hanging around, as if waiting for something. Three cars were in evidence. While David was watching, two men, one carrying what looked to be a diving mask, came out of the house and headed for the cars. Everyone got in and started to leave.

As the car got to the gates, the driver got out and released two ferocious-looking Rottweillers from a chain-link cage nearby. He then locked the metal gates, returned to the car, and they all left.

As much as David would have loved to have followed them, the little, recognizable Morgan was probably not the best for that; besides, this might be a good time to get a closer look at the house. They wouldn't have let the dogs out if they weren't planning on being gone for quite a while. This might be perfect.

David sat there a while longer, trying to formulate a plan of action. When he finally came on one, he, too, drove away.

David was standing at a pay phone on the side of a mom-and pop–type market, a few miles away from anything, talking to a rather amazed Chuck.

". . . That's right. I'm there now. . . . No, don't be mad at him. I slipped him a mickey. There wasn't anything he could do. I'm even calling from a pay phone to your cell, so we know it's not tapped. See? I'm getting all this cop stuff down. . . . Because I knew if I was here, you'd have to come out and get me to make sure I don't get in any trouble, right?"

David held the phone away from his ear at Chuck's response.

"That's what I thought," David said back into the phone. He gave Chuck directions to the market and hung up. He had a few things to do before Chuck arrived. In spite of everything, he couldn't help smiling a little to himself as he went inside.

It was practically an hour later when Chuck arrived, furious but resigned. They left the Morgan and took the unmarked patrol car to the hill where David had been watching the house. Chuck looked through the binoculars.

"When I got here," David was saying, "about nine Middle-Eastern types got into three cars, set the dogs loose, and left."

Chuck put the binoculars down and glowered at David. "Well, now that you've drugged a police officer, fled from protective custody, and got me all the way the hell up here, may I ask why?"

"I want to go down there," David said simply.

"Collier, you're suffering brain damage. I don't have a search warrant, which you know, legally, I would need. Even if I did, those dogs would take your face off."

"No, they won't."

"And why not?" Chuck asked.

"Because, while I was at the market, I bought three of their famous barbequed beef sandwiches—one for me and one for each dog. I laced theirs with the same sleeping powder I gave Murray. They even carried the same brand. I thought there was a certain symmetry in that. Anyway, I threw the sandwiches over the fence. The dogs were quite pleased. I figure they'll wake up sometime tomorrow."

Chuck just shook his head in amazement. "I don't believe this. I still can't let you go down there."

"Then you're going to have to arrest me. This house figures somehow in why Rebecca was killed and I am damn well going to find out what it is."

"That's my job, Dave. Just butt out and let me do it!"

"Can't do it, Chuck," David said, easily. "I even have a threat I don't want to use."

"Oh, this should be great. What?"

"How would you like the press to be turned on to this place?"

"I can't let you do that, either."

"It's already done." David spoke firmly but tried also to convey that he hated to have to do this to his friend.

"What do you mean?"

"Chuck, I know how dangerous it could be down there, so I covered myself," David explained. "I found another picture of this place in the darkroom. I packed it up in a folder along with a note pretty much explaining everything to this point, and left it at one of the real estate offices Shelly uses. Unless he receives a call from me by tonight, he messengers the packet to a reporter I know. The guy's an asshole but he knows a good story when he sees one."

"You piece of shit."

"I'm sorry, Chuck."

"No, you're not."

"It's just too important."

"You've been watching too many movies."

"And you haven't been watching enough," David said, getting animated. "C'mon, you've got to be creative! Eastwood and Harrison Ford would run circles around you."

"You'd have this place crawling with reporters before we even get a chance to investigate it."

"Then let's investigate it," David said, then whispered ". . . and be real careful."

David, with his cane, limped off determinedly. Chuck followed, wondering what hit him.

Chuck drove his police car into a majestic grove of eucalyptus trees by the fence at the rear side of the house. Since he'd had time to think ahead, David used his newly purchased wire cutters to make a passage through the fence. As they walked down the overgrown lane leading to the house, they turned to make sure the car was effectively out of sight. It was.

Getting closer to the house, they were relieved to see that the dogs were sleeping peacefully.

"I can't believe how illegal this is," Chuck said, amazed at what he'd been coerced into doing.

"Look at this place!" David was enchanted and dismayed at the same time. At one time, this house had to have been magnificent. It was white wood slate, two stories but with dormer windows testifying to at least a partial third story under the roofline. A covered porch, supported by Doric columns, stretched halfway around the house. A gazebo was placed at the corner.

Approaching the house from the back, they walked along grounds that had once been marvelous flowing gardens, now all dirt and weeds. Walking along the side of the house took them past a sunroom that must have been the focal point in days gone by and the pride and joy of the woman of the house.

Coming around to the front, David saw that the columns also flanked the front door, along with huge terracotta vases that used to hold poplars or roses or some such greenery, now empty.

The front door was painted an uncharacteristic red, which somehow looked quite grand with everything else.

David stopped in front of the house, staring. "My God, Chuck . . ."

"What?"

"This is the house that Rebecca and I used to dream of. Can you believe how we could have restored this baby to her former glory? In this condition and way out here, it probably wouldn't even have been all that expensive. We could have had a ball. I didn't know such a place really existed."

"Thank you for sharing that with me," Chuck said, dryly.

David and his new cane strode over to the house to get a closer look. Chuck reluctantly followed.

They wouldn't have been quite so casual if they had noticed the glint off a pair of binoculars watching them from the hill where they'd been moments before. An Arabic man was watching, made a cell phone call, and had a brief conversation. He then went over to his car and exchanged the cell phone for a long suitcase he kept in the trunk. He set the suitcase on the ground, opened it, and started assembling a sniper rifle from pieces in the case.

25

David and Chuck walked alongside the house, looking in the windows. On the ground floor, they were mainly seeing empty or very sparsely furnished rooms. It didn't appear as though any activity at all was going on inside. But that didn't make sense.

"Another empty one," David said, looking into another room. "We've got to get inside."

"No."

"Where do the guys go when they're here? I saw guys coming out of here myself. They sure weren't doing anything in these rooms. We've got to look upstairs."

"Dave—" Chuck started to try to talk some sense into him again, but David cut him off.

"Why have this huge place if none of it's being used? No . . . I'm going in."

"David!" Chuck called, sounding as threatening as he could.

"Maybe we'll find an unlocked door or something," David went on, his singleness of purpose driving him. "You look that way, I'll check around here."

David indicated a direction for Chuck to go and took off determinedly in the other, which led him around back. Every door he came to was locked. He tried some windows but they didn't budge either.

Frustrated, he looked around for anything that might give him an idea. He saw an old canvas tarp that seemed to be covering something. He went to it, threw it back, and discovered an old, weathered wooden cellar door that was locked with a padlock.

His attention was piqued, however, when he took another look at the padlock. It was one of the best on the market. What was an old dilapidated cellar door doing with a hundred-dollar lock on it? That made him want to get inside even more.

Okay, how? He tried to lift the door, which seemed flimsy enough but it certainly was securely locked. He thought for a minute, saw a five-foot-long two-by-four lying in a nearby pile of junk and lumber and decided to give it a try. Putting down his cane and using the piece of wood like a pile driver, he attacked the rotting wood around the padlock. A few well-aimed jabs at it broke through the door.

He then used the two-by-four to pry the doors apart until the hasp containing the padlock just fell off.

David knew what he was doing was illegal and dangerous, and he probably wouldn't have tried this if Chuck wasn't there. Even if Chuck wasn't there by his own free will, it was still comforting to David having an armed police officer with him.

"Chuck, c'mon! I found a way in."

Chuck came running around the corner just in time to see David, with his cane, disappearing down the cellar stairs.

"Jesus! . . ." was all Chuck could get out.

The basement could have been a museum. The foundation looked like it had been laid about the turn of the twentieth century and, perhaps, it had. The only room that had been built down there was a fairly good-sized pantry. The insulated coolness of the cellar made it perfect. The rest was just a large open room with some old furniture stacked in a couple of corners.

Off to one side was an immense coal-burning furnace re-sembling a huge black rusted octopus with metal tentacles that reached out to every area of the basement. Beside it was an equally large gas furnace that also looked like it had been put in many years ago. At least they didn't have to come downstairs every few hours to shovel in some coal.

David had just finished taking it all in when Chuck arrived at his side.

"Let's go up." Not waiting for Chuck's inevitable retort, David headed up the stairs.

On the main floor landing, corridors headed off in different directions. David slowed, looked, but kept on going. "We've al-ready seen this floor," he said.

The weather outside continued to be murky, casting little light inside. The effect was eerie, even inside such a lovely building. Two corridors led off from the second-floor landing. David arbi-trarily chose one and headed down it. The first door he came to opened onto a surprise.

As he stepped in, he could tell that there had probably been three bedrooms along that side of the house. The walls separat-ing them had been removed (accounting for the piles of lumber, plaster, and junk strewn around the house). The result was one huge, open long room that seemed to have been set up for some-thing specific. But what?

Chuck arrived behind David, walked in, and stopped. "Whoa. What have we here?"

"I have no idea," David said as he walked around the room. At one end were three large vats, about ten feet in diameter by four feet deep. A watering hose had been hooked up in a nearby bathroom and pulled over next to the vats. It lay on the floor, ready for use.

The middle of the room was occupied by three long tables

with folding chairs on either side. Whatever was going on, it was going to take a lot of bodies doing something at those tables. Manufacturing, maybe? An illegal sweatshop?

At the other end of the room, David made another curious discovery. He walked out on the small second-floor patio but quickly jumped back.

"Chuck, take a look."

Chuck came over to see what had gotten David's attention. The railing to this balcony had been removed. Two full steps out that door and you'd fall to the ground.

"What the hell did they do that for?" Chuck wondered.

"I have no idea," David said. Another mystery.

"And what in the world are these for?" Chuck said, walking over to the vats.

David didn't know either. "Let's check the other corridor. Maybe we could find something that will fill in the blanks," he said, already on the move back to the landing.

The two men walked down the other corridor together. The first door they came to opened into a large meeting room that could have perhaps been a ballroom in another life. Now, there were folding chairs everywhere on the parquet wooden floors. The wallpapered walls were covered with Middle-Eastern flags, banners, and slogans.

Bulletin boards had also been erected, some containing notes and notices in Arabic, others containing schematics of many types of high-caliber automatic weapons.

"Allah would be proud," David said.

"Charming," was Chuck's response, looking around.

They continued down the corridor to some large double doors that were not locked. They opened them and were amazed.

Inside, in every respect, was a *major* arsenal. Propped up and on shelves were literally hundreds of guns, from AK47s to Uzis to a variety of pistols. There were rack after rack of grenades, launchers, explosives, bazookas, and other weapons.

"I guess we found the armory," David said, looking around, somewhat awestruck, but excited.

Chuck also looked around quickly, amazed. After a moment, he headed for the door. "Let's see what else they've got here."

Chuck left. David continued to look over the vast array of weapons a moment longer, then started to go after Chuck when loud, raucous acid-rock music suddenly blared from his hearing aid. He quickly cursed and pulled it from his ear *as fast as he could, casting him into his silence.*

Frustrated, David stood still, feeling extremely defenseless. Hesitantly, he called out, "Chuck? Come back in here a minute, could you? . . . Chuck!"

Chuck didn't come back. David had no way of knowing whether he had heard him or not. He stood motionless in the middle of the room, suddenly feeling very vulnerable.

26

David shook his hearing aid and batted it a couple of times, but to no avail. It was working better as a radio than a hearing device. The sounds of life were reduced to a soft hum.

He cautiously crept to the armory door and opened it onto the hallway. The door bumped into something. Thinking it was Chuck, David came around the door to explain the situation.

It wasn't Chuck. Neither had considered that there might be a guard posted inside, but here he was, in full combat dress. Why hadn't they run into him before? He must have been asleep somewhere. Regardless, the soldier wasn't expecting anyone either, so both ended up totally surprising the other.

David's fright activated him even faster than the soldier. He dropped his cane, quickly grabbed the door, slammed it into the soldier's face as hard as he could, and took off running as fast as his leg would allow.

The corridor he was on led to two others. He made a random choice and kept running. The ear piece to his hearing aid flapped against his shirt as he ran. He felt even more frightened because he couldn't hear how close the soldier was behind him. He did know he was back there somewhere.

He came upon a door, tried it, found it to be unlocked, darted inside and quickly locked it. He stood there in silence for a moment, getting his bearings. It was an anteroom to an office. A solid-looking door dominated one wall, the only other door in the room besides the one that David just came in. He ran to it. Locked. He looked around, fighting off panic. He was trapped there.

Remembering an old trick Chuck had taught him years ago, David quickly pulled out a credit card and went to work jimmying the lock. He knew he could do it, it was just a question of whether he had the time. Fortunately, the casements were large and loose-fitting, as they were in most old houses. Each little pass with the credit card moved the bolt over practically a quarter of an inch.

He worked as fast as he could, trying not to look over his shoulder at the other door. All he could hear was the panting sound of his own breathing.

Suddenly, he got the bolt back far enough that it opened. David nearly fell into the room as it gave way. He immediately turned, closed and locked the door again. And froze.

He looked around. He was in a richly furnished, dark wood office. To David, this could have been the office of a major CEO: mahogany desk, shelves, files, computer, etc. The room was full of old-school charm; the equipment, state-of-the-art modern. He still waited, not moving.

He scanned the room in quick little spurts, always returning to the door, looking for any movement. Suddenly . . . the door knob was turning. The guard evidently had keys to these locks, probably a skeleton key. Wouldn't he then be able to open this office door, too?

David watched, still hearing only his breathing, as the knob slowly turned. He didn't know if he'd be able to hear Chuck calling to him or not. Maybe if he was on the other side of door yelling *loudly. Maybe. He couldn't take that chance. Finally, it stopped turning*

Waiting practically a full minute, it appeared that no one was going to open the door. Maybe the guard didn't have a key to the office, after all. Curious. David took the moment to look around this room in more depth. Perhaps he could find something that would make sense of the long room down the other corridor. The desk was flanked by flags that seemed to belong more to some unknown regiments than countries. Filing cabinets flanked the flags.

He quickly scanned the contents of a few drawers in the cabinets, seeing if something might catch his eye. One file did. He took a look inside and practically had the breath taken from him as fury quickly arose. He quickly closed the cabinet, tucked the file in his pants, and returned to the door.

He tried his hearing aid again, which, this time, gave him loud static. Disgusted, he stuffed it in his shirt pocket. Cautiously, he unlocked the door, slowly turned the knob, and opened the door into the anteroom.

No one was in the room. He left the office door slightly ajar as he repeated his actions with the door to the hall. Seeing no one, he quietly left the room.

He crept to a corner and carefully looked around it. He saw Chuck studying some pictures on the wall. The soldier was sneaking up behind him. He had to do something quickly. In spite of the noise it would make, David grabbed a nearby fire extinguisher, peeled it off the wall and started to run toward the soldier.

The noise made both men turn, Chuck was surprised to see the soldier behind him; the soldier was surprised to see David coming at him with a fire extinguisher. The soldier started to raise his gun but made it only halfway before David opened the spray. Actually, it turned out to be foam, which quickly encased the soldier's face.

The soldier yelled, dropped his weapon, and quickly fell to his knees, trying to clear his eyes. David deadened his pain, and relieved his personal anger somewhat, by knocking him out with the body of the fire extinguisher.

Chuck immediately started talking but David stopped him.

"My hearing aid isn't working. I can't hear you." David took the file from his pants and handed it to Chuck. "They're all here."

Chuck quickly scanned through the file. Lots of old mansions . . . including the missing one of the old house they were in. They must have been the ones drying when Rebecca was killed. David read Chuck's lips as he asked, "Rebecca's?" David nodded.

Chuck motioned for David to take a look at a picture on the wall that he had noticed. As David stepped closer to see, he also pulled out his hearing aid to give it another try. This time it worked.

As sound came back to him, he looked closely at an eight-by-ten of a group of Middle-Eastern men at a meeting in this house. Prominent in front was Shelly.

David was relieved to be able to hear again but furious about what he was seeing. "That son of a bitch! He told me he didn't recognize the place."

"I suggest we get the hell out of here and go talk to him," Chuck said, then handed David the file of pictures. "Take these back first."

"They're Rebecca's," David said strongly, then caught himself. "They're mine."

"David! I've got to come back here with a warrant or none of this will be admissible evidence. You know that. C'mon, I need you to think, here."

David wanted to argue but realized he couldn't. He led Chuck back to the office, picking up his cane on the way. David went straight to the filing case and returned the folder.

"Interesting that this room was locked," he said, "while they didn't consider it necessary to lock the armory."

They both looked around to see if they could find a reason for that. A particularly fat file got David's attention. He pulled it out, opened it and paled. "Jesus! . . ."

Chuck crossed to him, looked at the paper David was holding. It was a schematic of AT&T Park in downtown San Francisco, home to their baseball team, the Giants. The entrances were all numbered and circled. An unrecognizable word in Arabic was by each as well as a symbol that looked like an explosion.

"What the hell are they going to do?" David asked. "Blow up AT&T Park?"

"I need a warrant, quick!" Chuck said, already starting to leave. "C'mon!"

David started to follow Chuck when a smaller folder inside the fat one caught his eye. He knew he shouldn't but . . . what the hell. He stuffed it into his shirt and left.

They went back down to the cellar, peeked out and, seeing nothing, crept out. David replaced the tarp as he had found it.

"Think your dogs are still asleep?" Chuck asked.

"I guess we'll find out soon enough."

They both went to the corner of the building, looked around, and were relieved to see both dogs still out.

"Looks like we made it."

"We're not out of here yet," Chuck cautioned. "C'mon."

They started the long walk to the back fence. David thought about asking Chuck if they could check out the newly added barn while they were there, but even he knew that was pushing it. He said nothing.

"I can't believe I let you talk me into that," Chuck said, still amazed.

"I didn't. It was blackmail, but we found what we were looking for, didn't we?"

"And then some."

Suddenly, David started getting static interference from his hearing aid. He stopped and hit the unit with his hand a couple of times, hoping this wouldn't turn into another problem.

Right then, a high-caliber rifle shot rang out, missing David by millimeters. A nearby tree took the slug. Both men quickly dove for cover behind some other large trees. Chuck's gun was already drawn as he scanned the ridge the shot had come from.

"You okay?" Chuck asked.

"Much too close, but, yeah. See him?"

"No."

They watched in silence for a moment. Chuck leaned out a little more to draw a shot which followed immediately, singing past his ear. That guy was good, but Chuck now had a location for him. He quickly checked the shells in his clip, told David to stay put, and stepped out from behind the tree into the light.

With his two-handed grip he started firing at the spot where he'd seen the sniper. He waited a moment until he saw another movement and sent three slugs to that area. Chuck wasn't so bad a shot either.

"What the hell are you doing?" David couldn't believe what he was seeing. "Get back here."

"Quiet. Don't move," was all Chuck said while still intently scanning the ridge. After a full minute, which seemed like a full hour, of no shots being fired, Chuck came back to the protection of the tree.

"Seems like he's changed his mind," Chuck said casually.

"You could have gotten killed!"

"Just had to check it out. Shooting's one thing, being shot at is another. You'd be surprised how few people like that. C'mon, let's get out of here," Chuck said as he started back to where the car was parked, keeping more to the tree line this time. His eyes also never strayed from the ridge very long, but there were no more shots fired.

They were both relieved to find the car in one piece, right where they had left it. They quickly got in and sped away.

s they drove out of the hills, David turned to Chuck, still a bit in awe. "You're crazy, you know that?"

"I've known it for years," Chuck said with a laugh. "Comes with the territory."

David thought quietly. "Who knew where we were going today?" he asked after a moment.

"I checked in at the department," Chuck said. ". . . Murray . . ."

"And Shelly."

"Shelly?" Chuck was surprised. "How'd he know?"

"I told him," David admitted. "I didn't want him to keep asking around about the house for me after we'd already found it. I called him and told him about it when I let him know where I was leaving the folder with the picture."

"That was very considerate of you."

"Oh, yeah. I'm nothing, if not considerate."

"When you make your phone call to him, don't tell him anything else, please. This is another thing for us to handle, not you. Okay?"

David mumbled a kind of acceptance as Chuck pulled up at the little market and parked next to the Porsche.

"Now, drive straight home," Chuck said as David prepared

to get in Rebecca's little car. "Perhaps you've noticed, someone is still trying to kill you. I'll be right behind you."

David agreed, got in the car, and both men drove away. In a car across the street, sat two of the Middle-Eastern group calmly watching.

The trip was uneventful, which was a blessing for David. He could use a little less stimulus for a while. When they pulled up in front of the beach house, Murray was out the door, intercepting them on the front yard.

"You little shit!" he said to David.

"Murray, I'm sorry," David said. "You never would have let me go if you'd known."

"You're damn right I wouldn't have," Murray agreed, still hot.

"It's all right, Murray. He told me what he did. You couldn't have done anything," Chuck said, trying to calm Murray down a bit before turning to David. "Go make your call."

David nodded and started inside. Unfortunately, to do that, he had to pass Murray. When he reached him, Murray said, "You must have been one hell of an attorney."

David just looked over to him and smiled. Chuck and Murray followed David inside.

Ameen Basleh was twenty-five years old, the son of Iranian immigrants, and had been in the USA since he was eight. He was a naturalized citizen and had earned an AA degree in Criminal Justice. His police record was unblemished, not even a parking ticket.

As a young, bright Iranian, he was recruited quite heavily by a group of Muslim extremists who had taken it upon themselves to bring America to its knees. Plans weren't yet finalized, but they tried to get as many people in place as possible, people who would be able to use their various positions in aiding the group's cause when the time came.

Ameen wasn't easily won over. He had become quite Americanized in his last seventeen years and wasn't sure he wanted to see the demise of his newly adopted country. His parents remained devout Muslims over these years and Ameen, although not quite as devout, usually went along to services.

Somewhere along the line he found himself being shuttled off to the side into a kind of "Sunday school." He and two other young men were in this elite little group. Weekly, instead of prayers, they would be shown every atrocity ever attributed to the USA (and many that actually hadn't been). It would be hard to love the America they showed him.

He was being asked to fight for, live for, his *real* people, for his heritage, his blood. What kicked him over the top was the arrival of Bashaar. Here was a legitimate role model. Ameen had never seen an Arab like him: smart, handsome, charismatic, dedicated, and as mean as they come. He demanded respect wherever he went . . . and got it.

Bashaar became his personal mentor. He even paid for Ameen's schooling . . . as well as suggesting his choice of majors. Bashaar was not the suicide bomber type. He would rather recruit and live. Ameen made it clear from the first that he also rather enjoyed living, even in such a decadent place as the U.S., and was not interested in blowing himself up for the good of Islam.

Bashaar had no trouble with that, assuring Ameen that he, like Bashaar, would be of much greater use alive. When he got his degree, Bashaar, with a little help from some political contacts, got Ameen a rather special job.

That was a little over two years ago. Ameen enjoyed the

work, liked his coworkers and would forget for weeks at a time that he was actually a mole, part of a sleeper cell that could be called on at any time to do some heinous act. He wasn't exactly looking forward to it.

But the time did come. When Bashaar laid out the final plans for the strike now under way, Ameen laughed out loud. It was brilliant! It would embarrass America in front of the entire world as well as rob them of untold millions, which his people would be able to use to fund a full American Jihad.

Oh, and yes... they would all become rich themselves. Ameen was on board.

David came back into the living room after calling Shelly. "He wasn't home, but I left a message for him." David noticed Chuck wasn't there. "Where'd Chuck go?"

"To get a search warrant so he can do everything you just did *legally*. So, was this big adventure of yours worth me losing my badge over?"

"That's not going to happen, Murray. You know that... but if it came to it, yes. It was all there. Rebecca's pictures, the weapons from the armory heist, everything. It was pretty amazing. And Chuck, that crazy fool!..."

"What'd he do?"

"Oh, just stood out in the open, taking on a sniper with his pistol. I couldn't believe it."

"Yeah," Murray said, nodding his head. "He'll do wild things like that every once in a while. Must have worked."

"It did," David said, still amazed at it all.

"I can't believe you went in."

"Neither can Chuck. We also found a picture of Shelly out there."

"He your Arab friend?"

"Armenian. The same one who said he'd never seen that house before."

"Oh. Sounds like we may have to have a little chat with him."

"I'm sure we will when Chuck comes back," David said, drifting off toward his room. "Murray, do you mind if I leave you for a moment?"

"How far are you going this time?"

"Oh, to my desk."

"I think I can live with that. But no more funny business, all right?"

"Promise."

"Good. Now, if you'll excuse me, the Giants are playing a night game."

"Go get 'em."

"This isn't going to bother you, is it? Want me to turn the sound down?"

"No, it's fine."

David went back to his writing room. Murray immediately made the transition to game mode and was quickly very comfortable.

David walked back to his desk, pulling the blue folder from inside his shirt as he went. He waited a moment, making sure Murray was fully settled in before sitting down and opening it.

At first, what he was looking at wasn't making any sense, but after a while, it seemed to get a little less cloudy. But what he was starting to think . . . couldn't be right. He was just about to call Murray in to take a look at it, when the doorbell rang.

"I'll get it." Murray called out as he rose from the sofa and headed for the door.

Déjà vu swept over David; the doorbell was the same . . . *I'll get it* . . . Rebecca's last words to him. David got up out of his chair and tried to call out to Murray to stop but was suddenly overwhelmed by dizziness. He had to grab hold of his desk to keep from falling to the floor.

While he was getting his head back to normal, Murray came back into the room with Shelly. Murray's gun was in his back.

"I guess you found out," Shelly said.

"I guess we did," David replied, still trying to get his head clear. "Goddamn it, Shelly! What's going on?"

Shelly just nodded his head. "I came over to apologize."

"Let's sit down a minute," David said, still feeling pretty weak. He led them to the living room. David sat in the chair by the fireplace; Shelly and Murray shared the sofa. Murray kept his pistol out of sight, next to his leg, but at the ready.

David leaned forward, looking Shelly straight in the eye. "Talk to me."

"I am sorry, Dave," Shelly said. "Seeing that house just made me nervous. I don't want to have anything to do with them."

"Do you?"

"No.

David kept his gaze on Shelly. "Why don't you tell us what's going on?"

"I don't know and that's the truth," Shelly said. "I didn't know anything *was* going on."

"But, I saw you. You're a part of that group."

"Not anymore. Not for a long time." Shelly thought for a moment about how the best way to explain this would be. "Look, it would probably be best to let me start at the beginning. You know I was born in Armenia. Armenia is not basically a Muslim country but there is a contingency there. My parents were part of that small group, so I was raised as a Muslim.

"When we moved to America, we became part of our local mosque. Even back in the '80s and '90s, being an American

176

Muslim wasn't particularly easy. Many movements got started to help us out and we needed all the help we could get. The Committee for Muslim Equality used to meet in that house. I became part of that cause.

"But there was nothing hostile or militant about it. Any religion in the hands of fanatics can be dangerous, but it doesn't have to be that way. Islam, in itself, is not a hateful religion. It's really quite gentle and loving. That's the message we tried to get out. It was to help Muslim businesses and politicians and to get our needs and concerns heard. All very peaceful, political stuff."

"That seems to have changed a bit," David said. "Do you know about the arsenal?"

"I don't, but it wouldn't surprise me if they had one by now," Shelly admitted. "After a few years, it started to turn ugly. There was a faction that just wanted to hurt people. It didn't matter that they were all living better and had more opportunities here than they'd ever had before. They resented everything."

"When did you leave?" David asked.

"A few years ago. They brought a fellow named Bashaar on board, a mercenary. His job was to build an army and mastermind terrorist attacks against businesses unfriendly to our homelands. That's when I quit."

"You came here today of your own accord," Murray said. "To what do we owe this honor?"

"I was watching the coverage of the peace conference . . . today's the last day. I saw the difficulty these people have understanding each other's point of view and working with each other. You and I have no such problems, Dave, and to have this lie sit out there between us . . . I didn't like it. I had to set it straight."

David's head felt better. He went back to his desk, got the

blue folder, and handed the schematic to both of them on the sofa. "Have you ever seen this before?" he asked Shelly.

"No."

"Look at some of the stuff they're planning," David said, pointing out marked areas on a schematic. "This is the one I'm really wondering about." David pointed to another area on the schematic. "What do you think they mean by . . ."

Suddenly Murray called out, "Guys! Listen!"

Murray had just noticed a bulletin on the TV and turned up the sound.

". . . have blown up access tunnels in AT&T Park! It seems the entire stadium is under siege."

In unison, the three men stood and looked at each other, stunned.

28

A *meen, wearing his mask* and a jacket that covered everything else, got buzzed through the employees entrance leading to the San Francisco Federal Reserve Building where he worked. He reached the guard who had kidded him unmercifully since the first day.

"Well, if it isn't Jacques Cousteau," the guard said, laughing. "Working late shift on a Sunday. How'd that happen?"

"I think we've got a shipment coming in. Besides, overtime is overtime."

"I hear that." The guard registered his ID number and passed him through. Being Sunday, there were few people in their offices and just a skeleton crew of security. Ameen put his jacket in his locker, retrieved a small electronic detonator, which fit easily in his pocket, went to the employee coffee room, got himself a cup . . . and waited.

"AT&T Park and the over thirty thousand people in the stands are under siege!" the extremely excited TV announcer was saying. The picture showed smoke coming from every access tunnel to the field. "I'm now seeing people close to the tunnels falling over. Are they dead? My dear God, what's happening here?"

David and Shelly quickly sat down, eyes glued to the screen. Murray put his gun away and went to fetch his jacket.

"I think protective custody is over for the night, guys. They're going to need everyone they can get down there. I'll check back when—"

Suddenly Murray's cell rang. "Murray. . . . Yeah, Chuck. We just saw it. I'm on my way to . . . But . . . You don't really think that . . . Why is it so important that? . . . Goddamn it, Chuck! . . . All right," Murray said angrily, hung up, and threw his cell on the couch. "For some unknown, goddamned reason, Chuck wants to make sure that you don't go anywhere during this . . . whatever's going on. That I have no idea how important it is but he'll let me know later. Thanks a hell of a lot! Shit!"

Murray sat down with the others and was soon as riveted to the TV as they.

Ameen's normal job, one pretty low on the totem pole, was to sit at the guard booth by the front door of the Federal Reserve. The fact that he spoke Arabic and could converse in a couple of other languages made him a good choice. He would buzz people through the bulletproof turnstile gates as they showed their passes. He would also tell people where to stand to await tours, which happened quite frequently. There was also a bank of TV monitors there, showing key parts of the facility. Whoever sat up front had the authority to activate the entire force on duty that day, should there be any trouble up front or something that needed looking into from the monitors.

With the advent of Ameen's new headgear, it was thought that he looked too weird to be up front, so he was taken from that duty and stationed back by the loading bays . . . exactly where he wanted to be. Being Sunday, the facility was closed, but since Ameen had been assigned to the loading dock the last few days, there was nothing strange about him helping out with this shipment.

Over the years, Ameen had learned the drill that occurred whenever a large shipment came in from the Bureau of Printing and Engraving. A truck with a long, white semitrailer with no markings would show up with three or four motorcycle police in escort. Also on hand would be a contingent of the facility's own police force. The semi would back into the bay while the motorcycle police would form a semicircle barrier around the truck.

Once it was in place, they would back up to an area of the parking lot, dismount and generally, alertly, mill about until the transaction was completed.

Inside the bay, an official would open the sliding door to the truck, then open the massive state-of-the-art safe contained in the specially built truck bed. Once that was opened, workers with forklifts would hoist the pallets of bills, taking them from the truck to the elevator that took them two stories below street level, where they were counted, sorted, and safely stored.

Bashaar, with a "consultant," and sometimes even Ameen, pored over this information for months before coming up with their current plan. The impossible was being made possible thanks to their practically unlimited amount of Russian gas.

For the last couple of weeks, Ameen had been smuggling in one small gas canister at a time, which was easily hidden in a bulky jacket pocket. He stored them in his locked locker inside.

Ameen had been busy the day before this delivery. He had marked the motorcycle policemen's area with small orange rubber cones. It made it look very official and assured that no one else would park there. A small canister was attached to the inside of each cone. He also concealed one of the canisters behind the door of the parking area guardhouse while he was spelling the on-duty guard for lunch.

He had been excited and nervous arriving for work that day. Everything was in place. It was time.

Right on schedule, the semi with its motorcycle accompaniment arrived at the back gates. Sirens were off. The back of this massive building was surrounded by other office buildings. Sunday night found this area practically deserted. They wanted to keep it that way. No more attention than was necessary was called to this transaction.

The guard checked the manifest, greeted the men, all of whom he'd been dealing with for a few years, and let them in. The driver skillfully backed the semi, with its very precious cargo, into the bay, which had just been opened by one of the guards inside. There was very little room between the truck and the opening to the bay, not even enough for a man to squeeze through.

The motorcycle police formed their barrier and would hold it until the driver turned off his engine. They would then go back to their usual area and already thought it was very considerate of someone to make sure that spot was kept clear for them.

So far, everything was going just fine. Time for Ameen to go to work.

The excitement inside the baseball stadium was soon compounded by the arrival of a large, dual rotor Huey helicopter. It was painted olive green on the sides and bottom, but a steel blue on top, even the rotors. It had no ownership markings. It hovered over midfield a moment, then started to descend. Players ran for the dugouts. Even those on base realized that was suddenly of secondary importance. The people in the stands quickly became terrified when it became obvious that it was going to land on the field. Could it be a bomb?

"Please, stay calm," a man's accented voice suddenly proclaimed over loudspeakers attached to the helicopter. "We mean no harm. Stay in your seats. We will be here only a moment."

More people around the field, including many of the players, had fallen over in midstride. Immediately after the helicopter landed between the pitcher's mound and second base, fully combat-laden soldiers wearing gas masks exited the chopper and ran toward each of the smoking exits. They slid back the low wooden gates that stopped errant balls from rolling off the field and ran for the concession stands.

The loudspeaker continued in a booming, but calming voice. "Please stay in your seats. The fallen people are merely unconscious. They will awaken in about thirty minutes with no ill effects. Please remain calm."

Halfway up the bleachers, an off-duty policeman pulled the small service revolver he was never without. He took aim at the helicopter and fired. The bullets bounced off the fuselage, revealing that the copter had been armored. Machine-gun fire then erupted from its side, mowing down a line of people two rows behind the cop with the gun. Blood was everywhere. People for rows around started to panic.

"Do not fire at us!" the loudspeaker voice insisted. "As you see, it does no good and the only ones harmed are you. We wish to hurt no one."

People all around the policeman made him put down his pistol. The next strafing could kill them all. Reluctantly, he did.

All around the stadium screaming sirens grew louder as they got closer. Being broadcast live on TV, plus having half the cell phones in the place calling 911, the attack had hordes of law-men from every department on their way to AT&T Park.

Since it was late on a Sunday, very few people were in the Federal Reserve Building. Taking no chances, Ameen went into the furnace/AC room and inserted his nozzle into a hole in the sheet metal ducting that he'd cut there weeks ago. He turned on the spray and, timing it, let it spray for one full minute. He waited another full minute before taking off his jacket, which revealed his canisters as well as the uniform beneath. He then proceeded to his next target.

In a secure room, built like a bunker a floor below street level, two uniformed security police, surrounded by TVs monitoring the facility, were instead watching the TV coverage of the chaos at the stadium.

"What the hell is going on?" one wondered aloud.

"I'll bet they're hitting the box office and luxury suites," the other answered.

"Who's on site?"

"Oh . . . the world."

The banks of monitors they were paid to watch were momentarily forgotten. A few minutes ago, they were watching a mostly empty sight, except for the arrival and docking of the truck and the funny-looking little guy with the diving mask walking around. ". . . You know, the little Arab kid." They'd been seeing him the last few days and always got a chuckle when they did. They saw no one else. No big deal.

So rapt were these guards with the television, they were not aware of a small hose, the size of a soda straw, being pushed under their door. The sound of the assault on TV more than covered the almost imperceptible hissing sound that followed. The men barely had time to look at each other questioningly before they fell from where they sat.

Inside the tunnels of AT&T Park, the soldiers ran past and over bodies lying everywhere. Everyone had just finished the seventh inning stretch, so every concession stand was flush with the game's proceeds.

The soldiers cleaned them out. Three men shot the lock off the stadium office door where people had been in the process of tabulating the advance take for the game.

Everyone was gassed and nearly a quarter of a million dollars was stuffed into the soldiers' expandable backpacks.

"All right ladies and gentlemen, it's time for us to go," the voice boomed out after a few quiet minutes that seemed interminable. "Those of you who are not panicking, please calm down those who are. We wish no harm. We will be leaving soon."

Soldiers, with full packs, started appearing at all exits, running full speed toward the helicopter. In an impressive showing of coordinated timing, within a minute, all soldiers had returned and were securely in the Huey. It started to rise as the first wave of police arrived inside the stadium. They started shooting en masse at the rising craft.

"Thank you, San Francisco. Have a nice day," rang out over the stadium as the bullets bounced off the heavily armored bottom. A bazooka or some such would have been needed to pierce the armor. The minds behind this knew that policemen would be responding quickly and that shotguns and rifles would be the heaviest weapons the first arrivers would have. The armor could repel those easily. They would be gone by the time the

SWAT teams with the powerful stuff arrived. And they were. Their concern now ... how fast did the F-16s scramble from Vandenberg Air Force Base, 204 miles away?

Ameen continued to walk up and down the aisles of the Federal Reserve, looking for the few people working that weekend. Most of the ones he ran into were already unconscious. A couple were only halfway there; he helped them along with another spurt of the gas. Some realized what was happening but fell before being able to alert anyone.

Soon, the place was quiet and absolutely still. Ameen headed for the loading docks.

Once the Huey got altitude, it flew off in a southwesterly direction (witnesses in the stadium would testify to that effect). Once leaving the stadium behind, however, it started to turn, when the pilot noticed they were being followed by a small TV news chopper. It was trying to hide in any little puffball of cloud it could find, but it was still spotted.

The much larger Huey UH-1 turned and headed directly for the smaller helicopter, guns blazing. The little copter got out of there as quickly as it could.

Upset that precious minutes had to be wasted taking care of that disturbance, the Huey quickly got back into its original flight plan. Phase two of this operation was just about to begin.

David, Murray, and Shelly watched everything unfold as, by now, did most people in the country. The initial fright was over, so people in the stadium now had the freedom to panic. They didn't know if they should go near the fallen people or not. Were they contagious? Was it safe to go near the tunnels yet?

The police started arriving in large numbers just as people started running onto the field. Pandemonium would reign until someone would arrive in the announcer's booth to take over the P.A. system and try to direct some calm.

"Now's when the problems start," Murray said. "What a mess."

By the time the F-16s got into San Francisco airspace, the pilots heard from the tower at SFO that a message had been intercepted. It was in Arabic but they quickly got it translated:

> *Need help. Caught a bullet and had to put down. Am in a deserted car lot in Daly City. Come quickly.*

The directions were then given, which matched the direction the Huey was headed after leaving the stadium, and the coordinates given to the F-16 pilots who would soon be reaching their cruising speed of 900 miles per hour. The 204 miles would be covered in less than fifteen minutes. Once there, the jet's high-speed photography soon confirmed a Huey helicopter on the ground at that location. A couple of AH-64 A/D Apache attack helicopters had also been dispatched from Vandenberg but at a flying speed of 165 MPH wouldn't arrive in San Francisco for nearly another hour. Daly City law enforcement and those from surrounding areas were called in.

They arrived on scene quickly, surrounded the helicopter, whose rotors were still turning, and approached cautiously, weapons at the ready. As they prepared to storm the chopper, the lead officers suddenly threw down their weapons in disgust.

"Shit!" one of them cried out. "It's a decoy."

The others ran up to the helicopter and found, on closer observance, an old, burned-out shell of a Huey, probably bought as scrap metal and painted the same color scheme as the one at AT&T Park. Inside a small generator was running, which kept its rusted rotors turning. Next to the generator was a radio transmitter and remote control device that sent the prerecorded SOS.

The F-16s were called back and resumed their search, as did the Apaches when they arrived . . . but to no avail. There were no sightings and radar was quiet.

After watching for a while, David found that his mind went back to what he was looking at before all this erupted. He turned to Shelly, "Did you say this was 'the last day'?"

"Of the Middle-Eastern Peace Conference, yes."

"Wait a minute," David said. The blue folder was still by his chair. He pulled out some other papers he'd been looking at before Shelly arrived.

"I noticed it kept referring to 'the last day' but I didn't know what it meant. You're not going to believe this, Murray, but I think this whole thing," David said, motioning to the TV, "is a diversion. A *huge* diversion, but that's what it is."

"Are you kidding?"

"Murray, *this* is the real target." David said, handing over the papers. "Right now."

Murray looked them over with Shelly reading over his shoulder. With part of this plan evidently underway, it was easier to decipher what the schematics and maps implied.

"Holy shit," Murray said, looking at everything closer. "While most of the force is heading for the stadium . . ."

Murray quickly tried to call Chuck but got his voice mail.

That was strange. Chuck must have hit a button accidentally or something. This was not the time to be out of contact. Hopefully, he'd become aware of the situation soon. Murray hung up and called the dispatcher at the station.

He mentioned about Chuck's cell being off-line, something she already knew. She was trying to hail him on his car radio.

"Who's still around?" Murray asked.

"Right now, hardly anybody. Most of the guys are heading for the stadium, some out to Daly City, and we just had a head-on on the 280. Our other guys are working that. Are you coming in?"

"No. I need some backup."

"I've got Lieutenant Schneidmiller on the line. Would you like me to connect you?"

"Yes."

She did.

"Ray, this is Murray. Have you seen Chuck?"

"How the hell would I know?" the lieutenant said, yelling above the considerable background noise of pandemonium. "There's eight million people here, each crazier than the other. Where the hell are you?"

"Ray, listen, I know this is going to be tough, but the AT&T attack is just a diversion."

"Bullshit! A diversion? All hell is breaking loose here."

"I'm sure it is, but it's still a diversion. The real target is the Federal Reserve Bank! They're trying to knock over the Fed Reserve while every cop in town is swamped. They're probably in the middle of it right now."

"The Federal Reserve? Right. What have you been smokin', Murray? Jesus, get your ass down here! We need bodies!" The lieutenant hung up.

Murray slowly put the phone down, thinking.

"What's the word?" David asked.

"He didn't believe me. Besides, forty thousand people are going to take priority over a bunch of money."

"That's not what I heard," Shelly said.

"This is still government money," Murray clarified. "Government money doesn't vote." He walked over to the fireplace, still in thought. "Damn it, this time I'm really going to lose my badge, but I may need you guys. Come on. Let's see what we can do."

They grabbed jackets. David picked up the blue file, and they all ran to Murray's unmarked car. He hit the siren as they sped away.

As the Daly City police were scowering the helicopter shell for any evidence they could find, a group of local teenagers came running up to them, excited.

"Where are the cameras?" one wanted to know.

"Are there any movie stars here?" another asked.

"What the hell you talking about?" the sergeant in control asked.

The kids explained how they saw some guys move the helicopter shell onto the lot a few days ago. They even painted it there. When the kids asked what was going on, the men told them it was for a movie. The kids thought that was outrageously cool, that a movie would be shot in their own backyard like this and thought the police cars, officers, and guns were a part of it.

When told that, no, it was part of a police investigation and asked if they could identify the guys who built and painted the decoy chopper, they all spoke at once.

"Sure. They looked like Arabs."

he Federal Reserve Bank in San Francisco was a large, austere marble building a couple of blocks from the bay on Market Street. Other than the graceful arches that formed a colonnade along the front, the building's design was that of a great cube. It could have easily been a prison instead of the head of the Federal Reserve's twelfth district. With a little help from four other branch offices, the people working in this edifice were responsible for safeguarding and distributing all new money printed and minted for nine western states.

These states accounted for approximately 22 percent of the nation's economy. In 2005, the Federal Reserve in San Francisco had assets of 100.6 billion dollars. They processed 19.1 billion currency notes a year; about seventy-six million bills a day.

From Alaska, Hawaii, and California to Arizona and Nevada, the lion's share of all new money put in circulation passed through the immense vaults of the San Francisco Federal Reserve Bank.

In their promotional literature, they took great pride that they had never been robbed and that they never would be.

Those statements were coming under question that evening.

Ameen arrived at the loading docks in time to see that the vault in the semi bed had been opened and unloading had begun. The engine had been turned off and the police were dutifully back by the cones. Ameen casually put his hand in his pocket, flipped the switch, and everything was under way.

The cones were the most noticeable. They flew about eight feet in the air as the canister under each exploded, flooding the immediate area with gas. The explosion caused the officers to jump, but afterward they could do nothing but fall to the ground, unconscious. The canister inside the police gate shed also took care of the guard on duty, as well as anyone else who may have been in the hut.

From his other pocket, Ameen pulled a larger canister, pulled the pin on it and threw it into the middle of where everyone was working to transfer the money. Officials, guards, forklift drivers, as well as the truck driver, were quickly as out as the police officers.

Ameen pushed the buttons that opened the remaining four loading docks and ran outside to the police shed, stepped over the guard fallen in the doorway, and pushed the button opening up the vehicle gate. The millisecond it was open, four white trucks came quickly through. The trucks set about backing up to the bays.

It was quite a sight, if there'd been anyone watching. Before fully docking, the trucks unloaded their cargo of gas-masked men, all in Federal Reserve Police uniforms just like Ameen's. They first ran to the fallen policemen and carried them into the guard shed, in the unlikely case anyone should wander by. Once the area had been cleared, they went inside to man the forklifts and start the new transfer.

Ameen also turned the lights off outside, except for the dim lights that were always on. If someone were to be walking by, nothing would look suspicious.

The men started loading the four trucks with pallets of bills. This delivery was estimated to be in the neighborhood of two hundred million dollars of crisp, new hundreds and fifties. Bashaar oversaw it all and gave Ameen a fatherly hug as they stood watching it happen.

The large trucks were loaded first. They weren't nearly as large as the semi that brought the initial load. There were three twenty-four-foot-long trucks with a loading space of one thousand, three hundred and eighty cubic feet and a smaller sixteen-foot-long truck, holding eight hundred cubic feet. They were plain white and unmarked, like the other trucks that belonged to the Federal Reserve Bank. All were currently being filled.

The siren continued to blare as Murray careened around a number of corners, heading into town. Amazed by how quickly one can traverse the city streets in such a manner, David and Shelly simply hung on and tried to enjoy the ride. A short time later, Murray pulled the car into his station's parking lot. There was one other car there. Murray couldn't remember ever seeing the lot that empty.

He opened his door and jumped out. "Hang on. I'll just be a second," he said back over his shoulder as he ran inside.

David took this time to look over the rest of the contents of the folder. Shelly, in the backseat, looked over David's shoulder. Most of the papers were written in Arabic. Of primary interest to them both was a schematic map written in English, in large block letters, that included AT&T Park, but identified the Federal Reserve Bank as being the target. Elsewhere on the map was a square marked SHED. Why would that one be in English?

As they both tried to figure this out, Murray returned with a large sack that he threw in the backseat. "Open it," he said to Shelly as he climbed in, hit the siren again, and sped off.

Shelly opened the sack and pulled out three gas masks and two pistols.

"Each take a mask and a weapon and be careful, they're loaded. We may be all we've got there for a while." Murray glanced back over his shoulder to Shelly. "You know how to handle a gun?"

"Just point and pull, right?"

"Ah, the comforting joy of trained professionals."

They continued on at breakneck speed, the siren effectively clearing the way before them. They were about six blocks from the marble building of the Federal Reserve Bank when Murray cut the siren. The AT&T Park activity had even been effective at taking civilians off the street. They were probably all inside watching it unfold on television. None of the men had ever seen Sunday night traffic so light.

Heading down Market Street, a few blocks from the Federal Reserve, they saw an unmarked white truck in front of them getting ready to turn onto 2nd Street, the closest route to Interstate 80. Murray knew the government sometimes used trucks like that and would have loved to take a closer look, but time was of the essence. He handed a pad with an attached pen to David. "Get that license number."

David squinted but was just able to make it out and wrote it down seconds before the truck turned. Murray continued on, stopping when they were a block away from the Federal Reserve, parking illegally on Spear.

Market Street, usually busy, was always at its most quiet on Sunday nights, but this night was even quieter. Word had probably spread very quickly about the stadium takeover and everyone wanted to see it unfold. Soon, they'd probably be flocking to various watering holes to discuss it all and give their opinions about what happened and what should be done about it.

Murray instructed them on how to put on the gas masks but, for now, they just had them hanging, at the ready, around their necks. Seeing no activity at all, they stealthily crept up to the five-foot-tall black chain-link fence surrounding the building and its large parking and loading area. The only thing they could see that seemed out of place was four or five motorcycles unattended.

The vehicle gate was always kept closed and locked. Murray gave it a push; it swung wide open.

"They're here," Murray said. "Put your masks on. We're not going to be able to see this gas."

They did. David and Shelly followed Murray as he walked through the gate. Before them was one small white truck backed up to a loading dock. Light shown around the sides of this truck indicating some sort of activity within.

"Keep the masks on at all times," Murray said, leading them back to the pedestrian entrance. "The weapons are for emergency only. I will be going first. Please don't shoot each other . . . or me."

Murray cautiously approached the building. He found the door to the large loading area taped open. Ameen had done this so the militants could get inside after hiding the fallen policemen. Faint work lights were all that illuminated this side of the dock. Brighter lights ahead showed where the activity was.

The subdued lighting made it quite ominous when they started running into bodies lying on the floor. These were the real guards and officials that the militants had moved out of the way. David and Shelly jumped slightly whenever they ran into one.

"You're sure they're not dead?" David whispered to Murray, sounding rather hollow through the rubbery-smelling gas mask.

Murray shook his head. "Sleeping . . . hopefully. That Russian gas isn't quite as nonlethal as they like to think it is."

They continued inching along the loading area, trying to keep as covered as possible. Fortunately, there were boxes and loading crates piled around that they could hide behind. When they got close to the lighted area Murray crept ahead and took a look around the stack of boxes they were crouched behind.

What he saw was a large-scale theft of a lot of money. Six uniformed mercenaries wearing gas masks were at work. One was driving a forklift, hoisting pallets of bills into the truck. Another was assisting him in stacking. The other four were filling duffel bags with money of all sorts, old, new, whatever they could find. There was a large, armored room off to one side that was practically empty.

The men talked in Arabic and laughed easily, confident and totally unsuspecting that someone else might be near. Their weapons were leaned up against the walls, freeing their hands to loot even faster. They were having a fine time.

Murray came back around the corner to David and Shelly and told them, "I could see six of them. Their weapons are close by but they're convinced everyone around here is unconscious. They don't suspect anything, so I think we can take them by surprise. Be very quiet."

Murray then motioned for them to follow him and crept silently to the corner of the boxes. He looked back at his scared comrades and gave the thumbs-up sign. He then burst around the corner, gun drawn. David and Shelly followed.

"Freeze, all of you! Police!" Murray yelled through his gas mask. "Keep your hands very high and move away from your weapons!"

They did indeed catch them by surprise. The mercenaries were shocked, and immediately stopped what they were doing. They held their hands up but did not move.

"I said, move away from your weapons!" Murray repeated loudly.

They still didn't move. The mercenaries looked at each other questioningly, wondering what to do. They looked about ready to panic and lunge for their guns, when Shelly tried something.

"He's asking you to move away from the guns," he said in Arabic. "You'd better do it."

They moved. Murray pushed their guns even farther away from them. "Lay down, face to the floor. Spread-eagle."

Shelly also translated this and they did as ordered. Murray reached into his pocket and threw a batch of plastic Flexi Cuffs held together by a rubber band over by the mercenaries. "Cuff them," Murray said, as he used the metal handcuffs he kept on his belt on the biggest, meanest-looking one. He then started with the plastic ones himself.

David and Shelly looked at him questioningly, never having seen these except to tie off the tops of garbage bags.

"Oh, yeah," he said, realizing they wouldn't be familiar with them. "Wrap it around one wrist, then through the lock and around the other wrist, back, through the other side of the lock. Like a figure-eight."

Murray slowly applied one to a mercenary near him, showing the moves as he explained them. David and Shelly watched, saw that it was simple enough, and quickly trussed up the rest of the group, crossing their hands in back of them as Murray had done.

"Funny, how these things work," Murray explained, applying one to the last remaining mercenary. "Just that thin strip of plastic but it'll cut through your skin before it'll break. Damned effective."

They then had a chance to look around to see the enormity of the crime taking place. A few pallets of bills remained but marks on the floor showed that many more pallets had been stacked there a short time ago. They also noticed the nearly empty storage room.

"I'll bet that truck we saw was loaded," David said, looking around.

"And how many others?" Murray wondered aloud. "Shit!"

Just then, David, who had been standing off to the side of his cohorts, almost lost his gun. The hand holding it suddenly started shaking so badly that he had to hold onto the gun with both hands. Damn it. The pills evidently had to build up in his body. He'd hoped they'd start working right away.

A wave of dizziness came over him and he half-collapsed against a side wall, dropping his gun. Shelly and Murray had gone over to have a closer look at the room that had been nearly cleaned out and didn't see this. The gas masks also prohibited them from hearing the gun hit the floor.

As David tried to catch his breath and regain his equilibrium, another mercenary, also wearing a gas mask, came in through the same door they used. The new mercenary quickly sized up what was happening and drew his pistol. He approached Murray and Shelly from the rear and said in heavily accented English, "Stop, there! Drop your guns, now!"

Murray and Shelly froze, then slowly put their guns on the ground.

"Turn around."

Murray and Shelly did, hands in the air.

"Who are you?" the mercenary asked, keeping his gun trained on them both.

So far, he had not noticed David leaning against the wall behind him, trying to get his head clear. Sheer fright, David was sure, helped it become quite focused quickly. He started looking around him, having to decide what to do, fast. He was afraid he'd lose a gun-to-gun confrontation, so he let that be. Surprise may be better.

"We're the police," Murray said, forcefully. "You're surrounded and you're under arrest."

The mercenary looked shocked and confused. "Why did you come here?"

On a nearby desk, David noticed, was a large, heavy three-hole punch that seemed to be made out of iron. It took all the courage and strength he could muster just to lift it.

"Did you really think that theatrical stadium trick was going to work? Hell, half the police department is on their way here right now," Murray said, trying to keep the mercenary's attention on him so he wouldn't notice what was going on behind him. He also worked to not have his eyes look behind the mercenary and cause him to turn around to see what Murray was looking at. Murray hoped Shelly was doing the same.

"You don't think we're stupid enough to come in here by ourselves, do you?" Murray continued.

The mercenary started to shift his attention to look outside to see if there was any police activity yet. David came up behind him, precariously holding the punch over his head. The fact that this could be Rebecca's killer gave him the strength to hoist it over his head. A couple of the trussed-up troops on the ground saw David and started yelling through their gas masks at the mercenary to look behind him.

As he began to turn, David brought the chunk of iron down on the mercenary's head. As he did, both David and the mercenary fell. Murray and Shelly quickly picked up their weapons and had the remaining six, who thought they were saved a moment ago, lie back down on their stomachs. Murray separated the knocked-out mercenary from his pistol, dragged him over to the others, and attached a Flexi Cuff to his arms as well.

"Are you all right?" Shelly asked David, going over to him, helping him up.

"I just get dizzy sometimes. Did I get him?" David said.

"Are you kidding? He's not going anywhere for a while. You were great."

Murray still had his gun trained on the squirming mercenaries. "Good work, Dave."

"Thanks. Do you think we should go after that truck?"

"We have no idea where he went. He'd be on I-80 somewhere by now," Murray said. "We'd have a hell of a time trying to find them."

"Maybe not, Murray," David replied. "I've got a schematic of the whole thing, remember? There's another building marked on it that's near here, south on I-80."

"All right, that could be worth a shot, but what do we do with these guys? I'm not leaving them here with you two."

They all thought for a minute, then David got an idea. "Do you think there's still gas in here?"

"Probably," Murray said.

"Let's find out. Take off their masks."

Even through the gas mask, they could see Murray smile. "I like that," he said, and turned to Shelly. "Do it. Take them off."

Shelly put his gun away and approached the men. Since they didn't speak English, they had no idea what was coming. Once they saw, they started squirming away as much as they could until Murray came over and exaggeratingly aimed his pistol at their crotches.

"You'd better lie still," Shelly told them in Arabic. "Don't push him. He's a crazy man."

Reluctantly, they all did. They soon collapsed as the masks

were removed. Murray quickly piled all the men together. He ran to the desk where David had gotten the punch and wrote something quickly.

"All right," he said, "Let's get out of here." He put the piece of paper on one of the bodies on top as they left.

The paper read:

> *These are the bad guys. Have gone after more. Call.*
> *Sgt. Murray Townsend SFPD*

30

M urray let David and Shelly take off their gas masks as they approached the car. "But keep 'em handy. We may need them again. Where's this shed?"

"I guess it's a shed. Hopefully, we'll know it when we see it," David said as he and Shelly got in the car. "I've got a pretty good location. It seems to be about a mile south, off I-80."

"We're out of here." Murray hit the siren again and tore off for the freeway. He called in and explained the situation to the harried dispatcher. ". . . The vehicle gate is open. Repeat, use gas masks. Have HAZMAT clear it. Am pretty sure it's that same Russian gas that was used in the robberies. Am in pursuit of a light semi, white, no markings, license number 2136 PDH, south on I-80. Need backup but am proceeding. Townsend, out."

Murray replaced the radio. David was having a hard time with this. He really felt that all this would somehow end up at the grand old house, but that was *north* of town. It didn't fit that they should be going south . . . unless that truck really wasn't connected to this crime. But that didn't make sense either—there weren't regular deliveries being made from anyplace by semis on a Sunday night. No, that had to be them.

David suddenly saw the off-ramp they needed coming up and alerted Murray. Time to get off the freeway. Studying the schematic, he directed Murray to where the shed should be. They looked around at the deserted, darkened, industrial area, wondering what, in the mercenaries' minds, constituted a shed.

"It should be right up there," David said, indicating a large building ahead. Murray pulled off the road by it, turning off his lights. There was no sign of a truck.

"Doesn't look much like a shed," Shelly said.

"Let's look around back," Murray said as he drove, lights still out, and coasted the car up to the front of the building. Giving them all the "quiet" sign, they left the car, gas masks still around their necks. They left the car doors open behind them as the three walked quietly to a corner of the building where they looked around.

What they saw in back of the building, in its empty, dark parking lot, was a large truck. It was hidden quite well. The area was secluded, quiet, out of any sight lines, and no one would be around until work, sometime tomorrow.

The last bits of the truck's all-white covering was being peeled off, revealing a large, colorful MAYFLOWER MOVERS, complete with logo, painted on the side.

" 'Shed' as in 'shedding your skin,' " Murray said softly to Dave. "Good call."

The mercenaries finished peeling back the vinyl-like covering, threw it in the back of the semi, then prepared to climb up into the cab.

"We've got to act now," Murray said. "C'mon!"

Murray ran around the corner, weapon drawn, and aimed at the men. David and Shelly followed, guns also drawn.

"Freeze! Police. Don't even think about it. Climb down and keep your hands very high." When the men froze but failed to climb down, Shelly again translated. The men reluctantly climbed down and raised their hands.

Murray went up to the men, his pistol aimed at their heads. "One at a time, starting with you," he said, indicating the man closest to him. "Very gently, throw your weapon over here."

Shelly translated and the men reluctantly complied. At that moment, Bashaar and Ameen walked out of the building, laughing, unaware of what was going on. One of the mercenaries saw them and shouted out, warning them in Arabic, "Run. Police are here!"

With outrageously fast reactions, Bashaar and Ameen had their weapons out and had quickly located their enemies. They started firing as they ran for cover toward the side of the building.

Murray, David, and Shelly, who were quite exposed out in the parking lot, darted back toward the building as well. Unfortunately, all they could find there were bushes. They might have been able to hide from sight but if anyone decided to pepper the shrubs with rounds, they'd have been history.

The mercenaries had other things in mind. The ones that Murray had stopped quickly picked up their weapons and ran behind the truck. Murray and his small posse then heard a car start up on the side of the building where the two new mercenaries had disappeared. Tires squealed as they ran to that side of the building.

By the time they got there, they saw a small black car—not disappearing down the street as they'd imagined, but disappearing around the side of the building where Murray's car was. The three continued around, after it. Soon, they heard the disheartening sounds of two shotgun blasts, followed by two pistol shots . . . then more tire skids.

By the time David and the others got to Murray's car, the semi was being driven away, escorted by the small black car. They also saw the source of the noise: two shotgun blasts through the hood of the car, and just in case that hadn't thoroughly trashed the engine, two bullets had been put into his left-side tires.

Murray immediately called in to see how his backup was coming and found that there would be none for quite some time. Everyone was still dealing with the seemingly endless pandemonium at the stadium. People were starting to wake up from the gas and were feeling pretty rough. There were also the few poignant cases of people not waking up. No one with authority could be spared from that site at the moment.

Murray was furious, until he saw a taxi coming down the street. Maybe they weren't totally out of it yet. He quickly ran out in front of the cab, holding his badge high, in clear view, forcing it to stop. The driver started to tell him that he was on his way to pick up a fare. Murray told him to scoot over and to consider his cab commandeered.

David and Shelly got in the back, Murray drove as they went after the "Mayflower" truck. He let the driver call in to send another cab to the address he had been going to. Following David's hunch, he headed out north. They went many miles, but no truck. Semis couldn't go that fast. The speeding cab would have overtaken them if they were still on the freeway. Evidently they'd turned off somewhere along that stretch of freeway. Unfortunately, it could have been anywhere, and the schematic held no more clues.

Murray decided it was pointless to continue searching the freeway. They would have loved to have gone on and checked out the house, but since they hadn't been able to follow them, there was no probable cause for a search. Also they'd all seen this bunch at work, and Murray didn't want to go out there without a trained army behind him. David and Shelly had been great, but keeping them in harm's way any longer would be irresponsible.

This was definitely not the time to screw up. A warrant and plenty of backup would be assembled tomorrow, assuming the stadium mess could be cleaned up by then. For the moment, it was time to take David and Shelly out to the beach house and give the taxi driver back his cab. It was a bit of a drive, but Shelly's car was also there and Murray thought he owed them.

It seemed like a week since David had slipped Murray the sleeping powder and had had his adventure with Chuck in the old house, but it had actually just been that morning. With all that had happened that day, plus the fact that it was after two the next morning, David realized he was exhausted. Actually, it had just caught up with him. A moment ago, he felt fine; now, he didn't know if he could stay awake until he got home.

He did, barely. Murray didn't want to get out of the cab because he was afraid the driver would speed away and he'd be out of a ride again, so he leaned over the backseat before David or Shelly got out.

"You guys were terrific," Murray said. "Great backup, I appreciate it a lot."

"You weren't so bad yourself," David said as they started to get out of the car.

"Hey, you, Shelly," Murray stopped him. "I'll try not to pull a gun on you next time I see you. This wouldn't have worked without you. Seriously. You done good. Real good."

"Thanks, Murray," he replied. "And I am going to enjoy doing without that gun part."

Murray bade them a good night and promised to keep them in the loop as to what transpired from then on. Shelly was nearly as tired as David but turned down an offer to crash in the guest room. His own bed sounded like nirvana. Opting to talk the next day, instead of then, they thanked each other. Shelly drove off home and David, gratefully, went inside.

David's head had been on the pillow roughly 1/16th of a second before he was out.

31

There was one thing about Rebecca David had never been able to quite figure out. Sometimes when she had been working on something long and hard and had thoroughly exhausted herself, she was afraid she wouldn't sleep that night because she might be "too tired." This never quite computed for David. When he was tired, he went to sleep. When he was *really* tired, he slept even better and longer. The concept of being "too tired" didn't have a place in his psyche at all.

Until that night. He had never had such an action-packed, stress-filled day as the one just completed. Blissful sleep came immediately . . . for about three hours. It was five o'clock in the morning and he was still wiped out, but his mind was whirring away with way too much information to sleep.

In the short time he'd slept, he had another dream about Rebecca. Thank God this wasn't another one of her getting killed. It had actually been quite nice, he remembered. The two of them were picnicking on top of a small hill. The Navaho rug was laid out under them and covered with great food and drink. The sun was warm and clear. A grand day.

Below them, they watched a group of men playing a game. They were dressed in football uniforms but weren't playing football. They would start in a football huddle but would then run off in different directions, then run back. They seemed to be having a marvelous time, as were David and Rebecca watching them . . . until it came to him.

He felt embarrassed that he hadn't recognized immediately that the men in the field, a few days earlier, were rehearsing running from the helicopter through the stadium tunnels and back. He had gotten so caught up in the drama of the moment, he hadn't put the two together. His mind filled in the blanks for him. They were together now.

Another link with the old house. That house. He knew perfectly well that that group was there right now using those weird things David and Chuck had seen. He was also sure they had something to do with the stolen Federal Reserve money. It was frustrating that Chuck and Murray were so handcuffed that they couldn't act on something they knew was going on.

But wait! That might have been the idea that woke him up and kept him awake. *He* didn't need a warrant. And if John Q. Citizen (him) happened to see something suspicious and called it in, the police would have to come investigate, wouldn't they? . . . Especially about a crime this big? It might take a while because of all the stadium mess but . . . of course they would.

He knew Chuck would take care of it, but when? With everything that he also had to take care of, would the militants still even be at the house? David decided that Chuck and the department may need just a bit of a shove.

He turned on the light by the bed and looked at the picture of Rebecca that he kept there. (This was the smallest of the ones that kept getting replaced in the living room.) He looked to find approval in her eyes . . . and found it.

———

That was why David was out of bed at five-ten in the morning and on the road by five-thirty.

The old mansion and its grounds were in a valley with higher points all around it from which David should be able to get a good view of what was happening below. He chose not to go to the same one he and Rebecca had gone to before, the one the sniper had also used to attack him.

He drove past what he knew was the road to the house and went to the next road, hoping it wouldn't be too far away and would still provide a good view of the house.

He hunted around for a wooded place where he could hide his car. The eucalyptus and redwood groves that were so prevalent a few miles south were pretty spotty around here, but there were some. He finally found one big enough to work. It was a bit farther away than he'd hoped but through his binoculars, he still got a decent view of the house. It would have appeared deserted except for one small thing: the dogs were put away. A good sign.

The mercenaries were down there. He was sure of it. If they'd only gotten a look inside the barn . . . David was beginning to wonder if he could come around in back and take a quick look himself when he suddenly got the feeling he wasn't alone.

He turned to see two mercenaries with rifles pointed at him. His heart sank. Fear and anger suddenly attacked the pit of his stomach, making him feel nauseous.

"Stand," one of them said in accented English. David did. The other put his rifle down, pulled out a length of rope, and tied David's hands behind him. They led him to a jeep they had parked nearby.

As they got in and drove away, David realized how ineffective his hearing device was. To not be able to hear a jeep driving up behind you . . . that's pretty darn ineffective. Damn it!

It was no great shock that they took him to the house. They

parked in back of the barn where there was the tan canvas-side troop carrier truck, the small black car he'd seen the night before, and two other cars. They couldn't be seen from the front and, since there was no road behind the barn, it was a pretty safe place to keep cars out of sight.

Trussed up and at gunpoint, a disheartened and frightened David was led across the backyard to the house. A guard stationed at the back door opened it for them, closing and locking it behind them. The main floor seemed fairly empty, rather like when David and Chuck had visited the place earlier. They directed him upstairs.

Here was the difference! This was a hotbed of activity. He just got a glimpse down the hall where the large room had been made, but there seemed to be people all over. He was led down the other corridor to the office where he'd found the folder.

Sitting behind the elaborately carved desk was Bashaar, who stood and came around the desk as David was brought in. He walked directly up to David and punched him in the stomach, doubling him over.

"I have already seen you much more than I like," he said with his thick Middle-Eastern accent.

It took David a few moments to get his breath back and to stand again. They looked at each other eye to eye for a moment. It didn't catch. David didn't remember the first time he fleetingly saw Bashaar's face. His demeanor would have been considerably different if he had known he was looking Rebecca's killer in the eye right then.

Suddenly, Bashaar started yelling to someone outside the room in Arabic. Soon, someone entered. David turned. He couldn't believe what he was seeing. Before him was . . . Chuck!

32

As soon as *Chuck saw David* he gave him a powerful back-of-the-hand slap across his face, knocking him to the ground. With his hands still tied behind him and his nonworking leg, it took David a while to stagger back to his feet. David no longer felt fear, he was furious. Chuck and Bashaar watched. Neither lent a hand.

"What the hell are you doing here?" Chuck asked angrily.

"You son of a bitch!"

Chuck slapped David again, this time not quite hard enough to knock him down.

"You are a piece of work, Collier."

"You are *with* these people?"

"Yes, I am. They have a grand vision of the future and I am glad to play a small part in helping to bring that about." Chuck turned to Bashaar and had a conversation with him in Arabic. David was getting one surprise on top of another. When they finished their talk, Bashaar gave one last, hateful look at David and left the room.

When he was gone, David turned to Chuck. "You even learned their damned language? What are you, a goddamned terrorist now?" David asked angrily.

"Shut up," Chuck bellowed. He walked to the door and

looked out. "My only problem is what to do with you now," he said loudly, then closed the office door. He motioned to a chair in the corner. "Sit down," Chuck said as he pulled a chair over by David.

"I'll stand," David said defiantly. "Or are you going to knock me down again?"

"Damn it, Dave. You make life very difficult for me."

"And just imagine how bad I feel about that," David spat back. "Did you kill Rebecca?" David asked, his hands straining against the ropes that held them.

"Of course not!" Chuck said adamantly, while still trying to keep his voice low.

"You know who did."

"I think so. I'll take care of it, so just shut up a minute." Chuck looked around again to make sure no one was about, but lowered his voice anyway. "This is a setup. I've been working on this sting for a year and here you come trying to blow it for me."

"You knew all this was going to happen?" David asked.

"Hell, I helped plan half of it."

"Why the hell are you helping them plan these things if you're just going to turn around and arrest them? Couldn't you have stopped it before it happened?"

"Sure, I could have, but for what? These are worker bees, not the big guys. There's only one semi-honcho here and that's Bashaar, the guy you just met. I'll take care of him personally. The others I want are in the Middle East. They run a good part of the show over there."

"What can you do about that from here?" David wondered.

"Follow the money," Chuck said. "And there's a bunch of it to follow. Actually, there would have been a hell of a lot more if it hadn't been for you."

"And Murray. And Shelly."

"But you were the instigator, the bulldog, the one who wouldn't let it go. If Murray had only kept you home where I gave you both explicit orders to stay . . . Well, I'll deal with him later. Damn it, I wanted to tell you so many times but I couldn't. Any leak of any of this and it wouldn't have worked. Not even a whisper. I couldn't throw a year's work down the drain. I had to keep on. Still do."

"Where's this money going?"

"Basically, everywhere. They've got over a hundred million dollars here. They can buy nukes, technology, people, whatever they want. The main one I'm trying to stop is the funding of an all-out American jihad. That's their baby. That would have been financed by this money," Chuck said, then added, "and it still will if I don't handle it right."

"Why not just turn the whole operation in?"

"I told you, all we'd get are little fish. I want the ringleaders, the ones that would actually make a difference if they were gotten rid of. That's all starting to happen."

"How'd you get involved in this in the first place?"

"Because I know the Federal Reserve Bank here," Chuck explained. "Remember before college, and even after a bit, I worked security over there? I put in about two years at that place. On the chance that I might know where some weak points could be, Bashaar came to me with a big bribe; a million bucks if I gave them information that would allow them to pull this off."

"And you went for it?"

"No. I knew how much money could be at stake. I said I'd do better than that, I'd even help plan it . . . but for ten million. Once I pointed out how much money they could get, ten mil didn't seem like that big a deal."

"So what happens now?" David asked.

"As usual, you came along at the exact wrong time. Now's

when it's all paying off. Contacts are being made with the very people I got in this for. You are a distraction I don't need right now."

"You even learned Arabic," David said, still amazed about that one.

"Hey, wouldn't you learn Arabic for ten million bucks?"

"I thought you were going to turn them in?"

"From *their* point of view, Dave. Think about it . . . an American on the inside of a plot like this. They have to totally trust me, that was difficult. Learning the language went a long way."

David just looked at Chuck, not sure whether to believe him or not. "That's why you stepped out in front of that sniper, isn't it? So he would recognize you?"

"Do you think I'm really stupid enough to step out in front of a sniper's rifle? The asshole hadn't made me yet. I had to make sure he did before somebody got hurt. Nobody here is going to do anything to me. I've made myself instrumental in everything that happens from here on. They need me."

"So you actually knew what all those things were in that big room."

Chuck laughed. "Hell, I designed the whole room. These rag-heads have no idea what a dollar in circulation is supposed to look like. Listen, I've got to get back to work but let me show you what's going on here."

"Then what happens?"

"First, I'm going to try to keep you alive until this is over; it should only be a day or two. Realize that I might have to be a little rough. I am sorry, but we're back to establishing no doubt about me in their eyes. That's what's going to keep you alive and me in this game. Follow?"

"I guess."

"C'mon," Chuck said as he stood and helped David out of

the chair. "By the way, most of the people here can't speak English, but some do. Play this all the way—you never know who might be listening."

He had David walk ahead of him into the outer room, then into the hall, which was empty. They went around to the other corridor, which was a different story—people were everywhere.

Chuck gave David a rough push into a doorway. "Oh, good timing," Chuck said as he noticed something. "You wondered about why the railing was taken off the balcony. Take a look."

David saw a forklift truck lifting a pallet of new, crisp bills from the yard below up onto the patio. Workers quickly slid it inside. While it was there, the forklift was loaded again with large crates full of, presumably, bills that had reached the other end of whatever they were doing there. David could see the forklift taking the new load out to the barn, where the trucks probably were.

Money was everywhere, especially on top of the long tables. About twenty men were working there, arranging and packing loose piles of bills.

"The money from the jewelry store paid for most of this."

"You were involved in that, too?" David hadn't figured out the big picture yet.

"So, what are the main problems with freshly printed money?" Chuck went on without acknowledging David's comment. "Consecutive serial numbers and, of course, that freshly printed look. Hard to avoid. Remember the vats?"

Chuck roughly pushed David in front of him down toward the other end of the room, where the vats were, to a rather bizarre sight: the vats were full of money. David then saw a man turn on a hose and douse the money with water. He sprinkled in a small bucket of soft dirt, a little bleach, and some other chemical that did God knew what, then climbed in the vat and started kicking and walking around like he was stomping grapes.

Chuck smiled proudly. "Those are my little low tech inventions. I call them my 'Scrooge McDuck.' Remember in the comics when he was always swimming around in his money in his huge vault? Well, that's what we're doing here. We're mixing up the serial numbers and aging the bills. A little water, a little dirt, a few other magic ingredients, a little stomping, a little wrinkling . . . Voilá, you've got a used bill."

David saw that the men along the tables were working with these distressed bills. In spite of his situation, David almost laughed when he noticed two men in turbans at the far end of the table with electric hand irons. They were ironing bills that had emerged from Chuck's little aging ceremony a little too crinkled. It was a funny sight.

He didn't have long to enjoy it. As he watched, Ameen came in the room, saw David, quickly crossed over to him and gave him a backhanded slap like Chuck had, only harder. This, too, knocked David down. Again, he had to struggle to his feet on his own.

"I'm getting real tired of this," David said as he finally regained his feet.

"Why couldn't you have just butted out?" an irate Ameen said. "Nobody was getting hurt. It wasn't even your money!"

"Have you ever heard the name Rebecca Collier?" David asked tightly.

"No," Ameen said.

"You might want to look into that before bragging too much about nobody getting hurt."

"Okay, time's up," Chuck said, stepping between the two. He called, "Fadi," to one of the armed men nearby who seemed to be guarding the place. The man came over to him and talked briefly with Chuck in Arabic. Ameen angrily walked away. Chuck grabbed David by the shoulder, threw him over to the guard and walked away.

The guard roughly led David the other way, back to the stairs. He was then marched down to the basement and led over to the pantry he had noticed there before. Even though it was daylight outside, it was still fairly dark in the basement.

The guard lifted the crossbar that locked the pantry, opened the door, and fiercely shoved David inside, causing him again to fall down. David saw that the room was about fifteen feet square and seemed to contain nothing but cans of goods on shelves that ran around the room on three sides. The guard closed the door. David could hear the crossbar being lowered back into place, effectively locking him in.

David was halfway to his feet again when he heard a hissing sound. He looked in time to see a faint aerosol spray coming from under the pantry door. No! They were gassing him. Trying to stop himself from panicking, David tried to remember if gases rose in the air or fell.

He opted to go with rising, so picking a wall the farthest away from the door, he fell to the ground and put his nose as close to the junction of wall and floor as he could. He thought possibly he could stave it off until . . . but then . . . maybe not. The world suddenly turned black.

33

A few hours later, David couldn't tell if he'd opened his eyes or not. The basement was now pitch black, no light coming from anywhere. They must have given him a serious dose of that stuff. David forced himself to stand up and stretch. His hands were still tied behind him and hurt. The ropes were too tight to allow for proper circulation. He had a headache and felt like he might retch all over everything.

He leaned against a wall of the pantry for a few minutes. After a while he started feeling better. He knew that everyone hadn't survived the gas attacks. It appeared that he had, although what he'd been spared for, he still wasn't sure.

David still couldn't believe Chuck was a part of this. It was so out of character, but a sting this size would really be something. What David couldn't quite grasp was why Chuck had to help them do so much damage, if he was just going to catch them. Of course, he understood about getting the leaders, he just couldn't help thinking that so many people shouldn't have had to die in the process. Couldn't there have been a better way?

He remembered that two women had died in that jewelry store break-in and he thought a soldier had died at the armory, too. And what about the people who'd been strafed and died at the baseball stadium? Those were a lot of lives to give up for a sting.

Physically, David was starting to feel better. He could tell the gas effects were wearing off. Soon, he wanted to move, but it was so black, he knew he had to be careful. With his hands behind his back, he wouldn't be able to protect himself at all if he fell.

He carefully crept around the perimeter of the room. It had appeared rather flimsy, he thought, but kicking the walls in a few places showed him that it was solidly built. If he was going to get out, it wouldn't be through those walls.

Most of the shelves were empty but some contained cans. He'd have to wait until morning to see what kind. That reminded him that he hadn't eaten anything in at least a day. The more he thought about it, the hungrier he got. Ah well, there wasn't anything he could do about it anyway, better to think of something else.

He felt his way around until he came back to what he thought was roughly where he had begun. Not much there. All he could do for the moment, at least, was think. Had he blown it again? Caught, maybe killed this time? No, he couldn't let that happen. Tracks had not been left. They were started. They were under way but if he died in this house he knew damn well that scumbag would not publish Rebecca's book. A story or two of his might make it into print but that wasn't the point. Rebecca had to leave a trail, too.

And her killer had to be caught. There were no alternatives. Her killer . . . Rebecca. Suddenly, David felt like he'd been kicked in the stomach. Rebecca! She was killed by one of this group, he had no doubt about that. Was she another who'd been sacrificed for Chuck's sting? How much had Chuck known about it? Could he have stopped it? David knew Chuck could be unscrupulous if he felt a need for it but even he wouldn't do something as heinous as that. Would he? Could he?

David couldn't even imagine Chuck taking a turn like that, but then he was finding things out about Chuck that he never thought could happen. It was too confusing, too painful.

The thought of it made him feel sick again. Angry, pissed, furious, helpless . . . and sick again.

David suddenly was very tired. The hour or so of gas-induced pass-out didn't make up for the lack of sleep he'd endured for the last few nights. He tried to lower himself to the floor easily. He made it about halfway down, then fell the rest of the way. He felt drained. In spite of everything, he fought sleep for a minute. There was just so much to do . . . so much to figure out. But, it would have to wait until morning.

Too tired or not, David slept deeply, for a long time.

It was a beautiful day at the beach house. Rebecca was making them a picnic to take out on the beach. She had her bathing suit on with one of his white shirts, worn open, over it. David was on the patio, watching her through the open slider. He wondered how many years of marriage it would take before he got tired of looking at her.

She was opening a can of cranberry sauce, a pop-top. It opened, but not all the way. She had to pull on the lid itself to get it off. In doing so, she cut herself.

"Ouch! Damn it."

David quickly came inside. "You all right?"

"Oh, yes. I'm just being a klutz. I don't want to get blood on your white shirt. I keep forgetting how sharp these suckers are. I'll be right back."

She left to go back to the bathroom, to clean herself up and probably put a bandage on the cut. Glad that it hadn't been more serious than that, David went back to the chaise lounge on the patio.

He was awakened from the dream by a soldier who didn't speak English. It didn't matter, he brought breakfast. It was morning; sun streamed into the basement from a number of small sources. He also untied David's hands and led him over to a corner of the basement where he could relieve himself. Never had a pee felt so good. That seemed like Chuck's influence. David couldn't quite imagine his Arab hosts being considerate enough to think of little things like that.

He was able to use his hands to eat the cereal and toast and get some feeling back in his fingers. When he was through eating, the guard tied him back up again and, not having said a word, left, locking the pantry behind him.

David looked around him; it was daytime. Chuck had mentioned that it might only be a day or two. Until what? Until they killed him? He hoped Chuck was as influential with those people as he thought he was. Evidently, he was planning to double-cross the Arabs. It seemed to David that it would be much easier for them to take Chuck out of the picture when they were through with him. But Chuck was a smart man. He'd have himself protected somehow.

David tried again not to think about Chuck being involved with Rebecca's murder. He was sure Chuck never would have let that happen. At least he thought he was sure.

So, what was he to do now? Just sit around to see if they would kill him or not? If he tried to escape, would that reflect badly on Chuck again and mess up his sting?

It did make a certain sense, the way Chuck had explained it, and David could see how he had definitely gotten in the way of Chuck's plans. Maybe he should just wait it out, give Chuck a chance to get these guys without his interference. He sat down against a wall and proceeded to wait.

A few things then occurred to him that changed everything.

By all rights, David should be dead. Look how many attempts there had been on his life, attempts that had not worked strictly because of luck or timing: the hospital, the blown-up car at his old law firm. (Murray had thought someone had tapped his phone, but David remembered that Chuck had been in the room when the phone call inviting him had come in, the same call where David also got the okay to park in his old spot.)

And what about the sniper when he was with Chuck? There was no doubt who he was gunning for. But maybe the sniper really hadn't recognized Chuck. He certainly stopped soon enough after Chuck made sure he saw him.

But the others! Could Chuck have known about them? Being as involved with everything as he was, could he have *not* known?

Even after the guy killed Rebecca and took out after David, he was trying to kill him, and damn near succeeded. How important was this sting to Chuck? Or how important was the ten million dollars?

Chuck could have told him. He should have told him. He was a lawyer, for Christ's sake, he knew how to keep a secret. They were also friends. Good friends. They went back a long time, shared a lot of memories over the years.

David started getting upset again and that made him antsy. He had to move, had to do something. He struggled to get to his feet again and paced around the pantry, thinking. That was when he remembered the dream he'd had earlier, and laughed. Oh, Rebecca, she'd done it again.

Cutting herself with the can lid was a pretty good way to remind him that he was surrounded by a bunch of sharp objects. Objects that just may be able to cut his ropes. Deciding to give this a try, he walked over to the pantry shelves and selected a large pop-top can of peaches. He turned his back on it so he could pick it up, then fumbled with it to get it in a position where he could open it.

He found he wasn't quite as limber as he thought he was. With his hands tied behind him as they were, he had a very limited range of motion. He struggled to get his hands high enough to lift a can from the shelves. Then he had to maneuver it so that he could hold it with one hand and pop the top with the other.

Easier thought than done. No matter how he tried to hold it, the only finger on the other hand that he could get under the pop-top was his little finger, the one with absolutely no strength.

Perseverance won out. Bit by bit he was able to work his little finger under the pop-top until he could actually slide his finger inside the loop. Then he had the leverage to open it.

To add a further insult to everything, when he finally got the top pulled back, the liquid ran all over his pants. He could just imagine how sticky they'd be when they dried. He pulled harder and got the lid free from the can; peaches went everywhere.

David then tried to find a way to hold and maneuver the lid so he could use it to saw through the ropes. He tried a number of ways before he finally settled on one that seemed to work.

He didn't have enough strength in his fingertips to actually cut through the rope so he ended up wedging the lid between himself and a wooden shelf. Placing the lid against the ropes, he then leaned back against the lid, putting pressure on it and sliding back and forth.

The main problem was that he couldn't get more than about an inch of movement as he rocked. Ah well, that could still work, just might take a little longer.

His fingers also cramped. David had to set the lid down a couple of times and walk around some. He stretched and moved his fingers as much as possible before he went back to resume work on the rope.

It did take a while but the lid was, indeed, sharp and it did cut through the rope. It felt so good to shake the rope free and let circulation return to his hands. Thank you, Rebecca.

Now . . . for the pantry.

34

Moving and flexing his hands and wrists as much as possible, he looked around his little prison. It appeared to have just been slapped up, spaces between the boards, not a straight line in the place, but it was solid. He tried again to kick loose a board or two, but had the same results as before. None.

The door was effectively locked by a two-by-four crossbar that lay in metal holders. If he could only find something that could lift it up. There were small cracks between the boards, even on the door, but they were too small to push anything through . . . except maybe . . . the lid.

Using the good ol' trusty lid, David was able to insert it in a crack between boards on the door. He still held onto the pop-top side but was able to slide the whole lid through, which meant it stuck out the other side of the door a good three inches.

The crossbar was held about an inch out from the door itself by the hardware holding it. That left two inches of lid that could be applied to the bottom of the crossbar and, hopefully, lift it.

When he got it in place, it actually cut into the wood a little, which gave it good traction, but the crossbar was heavier than David hoped. He had to put a finger under the lid to give it enough leverage to lift the bar. It did, but cut his finger pretty good in the process.

As soon as one end of the two-by-four was lifted above its metal holder, David pushed the door open, which caused the crossbar to clatter to the floor with a racket that he hoped they wouldn't hear upstairs. He froze and listened but heard nothing. Having that empty first floor as a sound buffer may have saved him.

David now found himself trapped in the basement. He went back and opened another can of peaches and proceeded to eat them while checking out the state of the basement.

The first place he looked was at the old, rickety door that he had smashed through when he and Chuck first went out there. He noticed that the hundred-dollar lock was still there but, this time, on a brand-new, sturdy door.

The inside doors leading upstairs into the house itself were also locked, but he wasn't sure he would have gone that way even if they'd been open. What else could he find? It was a typical cement unfinished basement, David concluded as he walked around the entire place, just the one door outside and small, high windows. Perhaps he could break one, but he didn't know if he could climb up that high and squeeze through the opening. They were pretty small.

Not much else was there except piles of lumber and junk, the electric furnace, and that big old coal monster. David thought for a minute about how difficult it must have been to have kept a place as big as that heated by coal. He wondered how often someone would have had to come down and add more coal to the fire. Would there have been a servant for just that purpose, he wondered? Or, maybe, coal burned longer than he was imagining. He really didn't know.

But, an observation came to him. Regardless of how long it lasted, there had to have been a supply of coal and a way to get it easily into that furnace. David went behind the huge furnace. There, protected from view by the large metal ducts that still reached out ominously to every corner of the house, was a coal bin.

It was a windowless cement room of about fifteen square feet. Any coal that might have been there had been burned decades ago, but the room remained. As did the coal chute above.

David remembered the stories from his grandfather, how they'd get coal deliveries, have the truck back up to their coal chute (everyone had them) and shovel the coal down the chute until it reached the desired depth in the room. The coal truck would then close up the chute and move on to the neighbors.

David faced a few problems. There was indeed a coal chute but it was in the ceiling, about fifteen feet above him. The door on the chute would surely be locked—from the outside. Plus, he didn't know how much time he had. Chuck or any number of his mercenary pals could come down to look in on him any minute now.

Whatever he was to do, David knew he'd better do it quickly. He added his empty can of peaches to a rubbish pile. He then checked the other two piles down there, looking for anything he could use. They mainly consisted of lumber and lath and plaster from the walls that had been removed from upstairs, but there were also the occasional broken pieces of furniture.

David figured out how he could pile some of these on top of each other and reach the chute door. He dragged over a bookshelf, a table, and a three-legged chair and was in the process of trying the right combination of stacking when a new thought hit him.

Doors were designed to keep people out. That meant that the hinges were on the inside. If they had been on the outside, all someone needed to do to get in was to take the pins out of the hinges. Did the same apply to coal chutes? Since there were no windows in the coal room, it was hard to see clearly, but he couldn't make out any hinges.

Then it occurred to him. Of course not, the chute door had to open out, therefore the hinges would have to be on the outside. Damn. He could climb all the way up there and still not be able to open the door.

He thought about the basement doors he had broken to get in the first time. He went back to take a look and almost laughed. Somebody else was thinking as he had. The new doors had been put in with the hinges on the inside, designed to keep people out. Of the double doors, one side was nailed solidly closed, the other came up to meet it. There was probably a rope or some such on the outside to aid in pulling up the door. It still would have been a bit cumbersome for the person using the door outside, but much safer.

The pins were in too tight to remove by hand, but a rapid search turned up a threepenny nail. David took off his shoe, used the heel as a hammer and, with the nail, pounded the hinge pins until they were pushed through and the basement door fell in. He didn't wait around to see if anyone had heard that.

He put his shoe back on and ran as fast as his leg would allow to the closest tree. Then he paused a moment to see if he had alerted anyone. For the moment, the coast seemed clear. He ran from tree to tree, trying to keep himself shielded from sight of the house as much as possible. Nobody seemed to be running after him just yet.

Soon David was off the property and could openly run a bit more. He had to stop and rest many times but, eventually, he made it across the little valley where the house was, and up the small hill, behind which was his hidden car. At least, he hoped it was still there.

He found the stand of trees in question and was very pleased he had taken the time to park it out of sight. He was also quite glad that the squad hadn't seen fit to come back and find out how he had gotten out there. His little Morgan was waiting. He quickly drove away, not allowing himself to relax until he had put some road miles behind him.

As he drove, David felt himself physically sink deeper and deeper into the seat. He realized he was totally exhausted. Also, his hand was starting to shake again. Being so wiped out probably didn't help that any either. He should get his pills. The doctor seemed to intimate that the shaking could be a symptom of something else. Great, that was all he needed.

He just wanted to stay alive long enough to fulfill his promises. That's all. If the pills would help do that, so be it. He headed for his house.

As he got close, David realized that might not be the wisest of moves. Chuck, once again, and not without reason, would be furious with him. Who knew how many bad guys could be watching his house right then?

He came at his house from a direction he hardly ever used. He pulled over behind a parked car a few houses down the beach from his own and watched. Did he detect any movement? Any people sitting in cars, waiting? Anything at all out of the ordinary?

David waited a few minutes. It seemed quiet but he also knew he couldn't count on that. Those guys were good. If they didn't want David to see them, he could be pretty sure that he wouldn't see them.

"Hey, stranger."

David practically jumped through his convertible top. He turned to see Daley standing next to his car.

"Who are you trying to sneak up on?"

"I'm actually trying to see if anyone's sneaking up on me," David clarified.

Daley straightened up, looked around. "Looks all clear to me. No sneaks." She leaned back down to the Morgan's low window. "Listen, would you like to come in for a minute? Have an iced tea or something? I don't think anyone will come looking for you here."

As awkward as he felt about it, he had to admit she had a point. No one would be looking for him at her place and a glass of iced tea sounded like heaven. David just then noticed that he had parked in front of her house and that it was actually her car he was hiding behind. That meant that her garage was empty.

"At the risk of sounding too paranoid, would you mind if I put my car in your garage while I'm here?"

"Hey, just because you're paranoid doesn't mean they aren't out to get you," Daley said, walking over toward the garage. "Let me get the door for you."

David watched Daley in her white shorts, bright yellow top, and long tanned legs as she raised the garage door for him. As he drove inside, he had to admit . . . she was a piece of work.

They sat at her kitchen table, relishing the iced tea. He explained about needing his pills but also how good it felt to just relax for a moment. He stared out at the beach, surprised by how quickly he'd gotten used to it and how much he had looked forward to seeing it every day. Daley was watching him.

"You really look like hell, you know?"

"I've had kind of a tough couple of days."

"When's the last time you ate?"

David thought. "I had some peaches."

"Good," Daley said. "Peaches are good. What else?"

"Uh . . ." David actually couldn't remember the last meal he had.

"Did you eat yesterday?" she persisted.

"I'm not sure."

"Tell you what," she said, scooting back from the table and going to the refrigerator. "I made Amanda one of these this morning; still have the makings. You like ham and cheese?"

"Sure, but you don't . . ."

"Good. It'll be ready in a sec. Why don't you move to the overstuffed guy in the living room. Just relax for a bit."

David thought about arguing but was just too tired. Besides, a big soft chair sounded about as good as a sandwich . . . about as good as the iced tea.

He got himself comfortable. Daley soon arrived with the sandwich and more iced tea on a tray. "Now, give me your keys. Where are these pills?"

David fished the keys out of his pocket and told her where to find them. "But if you see anything or anyone suspicious, don't go in. Promise?"

"Sure, a little adventure is nice but I don't have a death wish." She smiled, thought for a minute. "I'd better go in by the back. It's more open and I could see better if any unruly sorts are hanging around."

"Good idea," David agreed.

Daley smiled again. "See? That's what comes from watching too much TV. See you in a bit."

She left by her back sliders, which were similar to David's. He relaxed and tore into the sandwich. Never had ham and cheese elicited such unabashed delight. Truly the best sandwich in the world . . . and the chair was so comfortable, so . . .

David was sound asleep by the time Daley returned.

35

David awoke in a strange bedroom. Once he remembered where he was, he was relieved to find he was alone. That was one complication he didn't even want to think about. He also didn't want to go into how he got there or who undressed him.

Daley had taken care of everything though—there was even a bathrobe at the foot of his bed. He put it on and walked out into the house, noticing, actually for the first time, what a charming, tidy little home she'd made for herself and her daughter. Very comfortable. It might have had something to do with a woman's touch but that was another area he didn't want to go near at the moment.

Daley was emptying the dishwasher when David walked in, somewhat surprised that it was morning. He had figured at first that it was just later in the afternoon. Guess he had been a little more tired than he thought.

The coffee she gave him tasted as good as the iced tea, as did the eggs, which soon followed. David took his pill, thanking Daley profusely for everything. He fended off her questions as best he could, promising that, one day, they'd sit down and the whole saga would be told.

He cleaned himself up, dressed, and used his cell phone to call Murray's office to make sure he was in. Stressing the importance of all they had to speak about, he made an appointment to meet him at the station in an hour.

After the call, David went to Daley and thanked her again for being so kind. He'd barely gotten the thanks out when she stepped up to him and planted another kiss on his lips. She then walked off, telling him that she was going to open the garage door for him.

He met her just outside the front door. "Look, Daley, I really do appreciate everything but I'm in no position mentally or emotionally to get involved in anything right now."

Daley looked at him like he was nuts. "I know that, silly person," she said as she kissed him again. "Don't even think about it. I'm just a friendly sort." With that she trotted off to the house, waving as she closed the front door. David just stood there for a moment, shook his head in wonderment, and headed for his car.

A half an hour later, Murray was waiting, but David didn't know if he was ready for the tale he was about to hear.

Murray wasn't. He tried to interrupt about a hundred times before David finally convinced him to listen. He could ask all the questions he wanted later. David went through the whole thing: how he'd gone back to the house again; how'd he'd gotten captured and had been taken to their boss; most importantly, what he had learned about Chuck! (Murray had a lot of trouble being quiet right around that part.)

David told of Chuck's acting tough, then explaining about the year-old sting; about Chuck even having learned how to speak Arabic; about the aging and mixing of the bills; about Chuck's ten million bucks; right up to David being gassed and locked in the pantry until he escaped.

After having such a tough time being silent during David's story, Murray sat quietly when David finished. After a moment Murray asked softly, "Do you believe him?"

"I don't know, Murray. I'm really ashamed to say that but . . . honestly, I don't know." David had been pacing the office, too riled up to sit, but he sat now. "I think I was starting to believe him until I realized that Rebecca was killed by guys that were working with him. Did Chuck know about that? Did he authorize it? These same guys came within a hair's breadth of killing me. How much was he involved in any of that?"

The two men sat quietly and thought for a while. "I don't know if I believe him," David repeated, mostly to himself. He then reiterated what he had told Murray at the beginning, that he was sworn to secrecy. If this was, in fact, a sting the size Chuck said it was, they didn't want to blow it for him. Still, everyone was going to have to keep their eyes and options open.

David asked if they'd learned anything from the mercenaries they trussed up at the Federal Reserve.

"Not a damn thing," Murray said. "They're strictly grunts. They didn't even know where the house was. Whenever they were taken out there, they were in the truck with the sides down. They didn't really know anything about the operation. They were only told about their own small piece of the pie, and all they knew was that they were going to be rich and really stick it to America. That was all they needed to know."

"It is curious, though . . ." Murray added after a moment.

"What?"

"Chuck hasn't been in touch with anyone here since all this came down, not even me. Requested an emergency leave of absence right after the stadium thing. Your story puts it all in an interesting light, doesn't it?"

"How could someone pull something like this off alone?" David wondered. "Wouldn't he have to be working with someone somewhere? Someone who knew he was inside? What if that place got raided? He'd be arrested along with everyone. He'd have to have someone else. Unless . . ." No! David shook that off.

The two men thought for another moment, until Murray was called away on an unrelated item. David used this time to check his answering machine at home. Chuck had left a message, pissed.

"David, goddamn it! What the hell are you trying to do? Are you trying to purposely blow this thing for me? Well, you're doing a damn good job of it. Jesus! Call me!"

David wasn't sure he wanted to.

Murray listened to the message when he came back. Neither knew quite what to do. Years of friendship and trust from both of them stopped them from bringing in the whole department. They were going to give Chuck a chance to make it all pay off but they also had to be prepared in case he didn't.

Murray sat David down to make a map to the old house, in case they had to bring in the SWAT team. It was frustrating knowing that the bad guys and the money were there and they couldn't do anything about it. Well, they could, but for now, they wouldn't.

"Which brings up an interesting question," Murray said, unprompted. "How the hell long are we supposed to wait? They could be futzing around out there for a month while we're here with our finger up our nose."

"I don't think so, Murray. Chuck said that it was all coming together in the next couple of days. That's actually like today or tomorrow. It shouldn't be that long."

"So, if they're going to be moving all that money," Murray said, walking over to a large wall map of San Francisco and the surrounding area, "how would they be doing it? If it's going to be that soon, everything should be in place now—trucks, boats, planes . . . And whatever happened to that helicopter—the real one?" he added as an afterthought.

"Last seen heading inland from the stadium, I think. By the time they discovered the other one was a decoy, it seems like the real one was long gone. Could be anywhere."

"Well, not exactly. It was heavily laden with men and all that armor. It couldn't have too huge a range, could it? Damn, I wish we could bring in some others on this. I've got some math geeks who would be perfect to hunt all this up. Instead, I've got to do it myself. Shit!" Frustrated, Murray started to leave his office. "I'll be back in a bit. Help yourself to whatever."

David sat quietly for a moment, wondering what he could do. He got up and also looked at Murray's wall map. A heavy helicopter could only fly at, what . . . seventy, eighty miles an hour at best. And for how long, he wondered . . . two or three hours? That right there gave them a workable parameter to investigate, but he imagined the police were already doing that. They were probably scouring those areas right then.

To the east of San Francisco were numerous little towns, little places where a large helicopter would be noticed and remembered. But where else could it have gone—out to sea? But the helicopter was last seen heading inland . . . which is exactly where any self-respecting terrorist would fly if their eventual destination was offshore, wouldn't he?

All right, David was getting excited now. Where could they have landed offshore within that flight parameter? The various small islands around didn't quite fill the bill. They were either inhabited, which would be no good for the mercenaries, or deserted, which would make them too obvious and easy to spot by search planes.

Where then? A ship? Maybe a big one, like a freighter? That might work, the shipping lanes weren't that far out to sea, but far enough to not be seen from the mainland. This was looking better all the time to David. Okay, all he needed now was to find out what ships were in the vicinity two days ago.

Actually, he realized that he needed a ship that was still in the area, unless everything had been processed and shipped out of the old mansion already. That seemed unlikely.

One of the truest observations made of attorneys, David thought, was that they didn't know everything; they didn't need to . . . what they needed was to know how to *find* anything, and that they did. David had always prided himself on being able to do just that. It was time to dust off that skill.

He had a Rolodex at the beach house that any young attorney would have killed for but he'd have to do without that for now. David found a phone book on a nearby bookshelf, looked up a number, and dialed it.

"Coast Guard," the voice on the other end of the phone answered.

"This is Sergeant Collier of the SFPD. We're still working on that AT&T Park / Federal Reserve operation and could use some information." (David also dusted off his skill at lying in the line of duty.)

"You bet. What can we do for you?"

"We need to know what ships were calling at the harbor all last week and this."

"All of them? That's thousands of ships, sir."

"Actually, just the large ones, freighters . . . like that," David said.

"Sure, I could look that up for you. Should I fax or e-mail them to you when I get them? Should just be a few minutes."

"Uh, yeah . . . but . . ." David was stuck for the moment, when Murray came in. "Murray, what's your fax number here?"

Murray told him and David repeated it. "And if you also could include who each ship is owned by and registered to, we'd appreciate that as well."

"I'll get you what we've got, sir."

David thanked him and hung up.

"You getting creative again?" Murray asked.

"Yeah, but I don't think you'll mind too much," David said as he sat Murray down and told him his reasoning. "At sea just seemed to be the best place to hide a helicopter that size full of a bunch of Arab terrorists. I requested info on all the large ships around here the last couple of weeks."

"On whose authority?" Murray wondered.

"Uh . . . Sergeant Collier?"

Murray just shook his head and sat down at his desk.

A few minutes later, the fax started printing. Murray grunted when he saw it was being sent to Sergeant Collier. "Was that a battlefield promotion you got?" Murray asked dryly.

"Something like that."

As the list came through, they were surprised that there was so much activity concerning large ships. Neither had realized San Francisco had that busy a port. They both read down the list, looking for anything that might jump out at them. Their attention was first drawn by one ship from Yemen, two from Saudi Arabia, and two more from Pakistan. Murray made a note, assuring that they would be searched first.

David read on, then started to laugh. "Don't bother, Murray. It's not any of them. This is the one we want right here." He pointed to one on the list: a freighter named the *Solana* flying the French flag.

"Look who owns it."

Murray looked closer and read, "Kingsnorth Bros., LTD. English."

"Right. A Spanish name on a French ship, registered in England, whose main offices are in Pakistan," David said, smiling.

"How do you get all that?" Murray said, looking over the printout again.

"Remember The Paramount? That dumpy hotel where the mercenary army was staying? Looking into that, we learned it had been bought not long before by the Kingsnorth Brothers . . . from Pakistan."

"It doesn't sound Pakistani."

"Exactly."

"How sure are you of this?"

"Way beyond a shadow of a doubt," David said confidently. "That's where you're going to find them . . . And probably the helicopter, too."

"All right. Let's find out where it's from, where it's going, what and who is on board." Then Murray stopped himself. "Goddamn it! How long are we going to wait on Chuck? I don't want to muck things up for him, but if you're sure about that ship, between it and the old mansion, we've got these guys!"

Suddenly, the phone rang. Murray answered it, listened for a minute, put his hand over the receiver as he looked over at David.

"It's Chuck."

36

Murray, is Dave there with you?" Chuck asked over the phone.

"Yeah."

"I thought he might be. Put this on speaker . . . you won't have to repeat everything."

Murray did. "You're broadcasting."

"Okay. You are one sneaky son of a bitch, Collier. Now I see how you were able to let all my perps go years ago . . . you're crafty."

"I don't particularly enjoy it," David said.

"Yeah, well . . . sorry about all this, I really am. Thanks for not just storming the place when you got out. I guess you must have believed me a little bit, huh?" Chuck asked.

Followed by silence.

"All right, enough small talk," Chuck said over the speaker. "If you were going to pull this shit, at least you pulled it at the right time. It goes down tonight. I'll tell you where and when you can recover the money and the troops."

"We already know about the *Solana*," Murray said. "I imagine the rest would still be at the house . . . maybe in the trucks out back?"

"Damn! You guys are good. They even painted the top of that chopper the exact color the sea would be at that time of day, weather permitting, Amazing. Actually the trucks are already on the road and you'd have a hell of a time trying to figure out which ones are ours. I can save you a lot of time."

"Why don't we just take them, Chuck? What are we waiting for?"

"Murray, think for a minute. I've been with these guys since they were garden-variety terrorists. They hadn't even stolen any money yet. What could possibly be gained by simply getting the money back?"

"You tell us," Murray said frankly.

"I told Dave about following the money. It's working out just as we planned. We've got the honchos following the money over here . . . with our blessings."

"Excuse me?"

"Listen, this is a lot of money. It took this amount to get them over here. We never would have been able to extradite them . . . and what I've gone through to set this up, Jesus! What a bunch of yo-yos. No wonder it's such a mess over there. The latest big problem I had to work out for them was how to disperse the money without them killing each other for the others' share. That was a lot of fun."

"What'd you do?" David asked.

"The UN's Middle-Eastern Peace Conference just ended. A lot of the very honchos we want, ironically enough, were here for that conference. It's no real big surprise that nothing got accomplished. Anyway, the Saudi ambassador is throwing a big 'do' for all the delegates and their families tonight at the Fairmont Hotel. Fancy dress, limos, the whole shot. Awards and honorariums will be given out. Very civilized . . . unless you knew that the main reason many of them even came to the conference was to be here to personally oversee their portions of hundreds of millions. As if they don't have enough back home. Jesus!

"Of course, because of the tension a lot of Arabs in one place causes," Chuck continued, "the ball will be protected by the SFPD and the FBI. Also, we keep these guys from killing each other so they can go home, organize their groups, and kill us. They're getting a big kick out of this."

"You got the FBI on this?" Murray asked.

"Yeah, actually I've got to get out of here. As you can imagine, I'm kinda busy right now. There's a guy named Quinn Mc-Gowans with the FBI that I've been working with for most of the year. Thank God he's going to be taking care of the money. That's one headache I don't have to deal with. He should be down at the station about now. Go meet him, he's a good guy. He's going to be going over the security plans for the gala tonight. You'll also get your personal instructions from him, Murray."

"Sorry we doubted you, Chuck," David said.

"But you didn't all the way and I appreciate that," Chuck said. "I would have had a tough time believing me, too. Wish us good luck tonight, Dave. I'll see you guys soon."

Chuck clicked off. David and Murray just stared at each other, amazed.

Special Agent Quinn McGowans of the FBI was indeed a good guy and a staunch fan of Chuck's.

"You have no idea what this guy has put up with this last year. He worked all day with you," he said, motioning toward Murray, "then spent the nights with this bunch, planning one of the largest heists ever to happen in America. Not bad."

"I can't believe I didn't know," Murray said.

"Well, it was just so big we couldn't take any chances at all. My wife just found out about it today. This is a biggie. So . . . Murray." Quinn referred to a clipboard he was carrying. "I have you driving a limo for a honcho from Iraq, via Afghanistan, via Pakistan. He'll be accompanied by a wife, girlfriend—maybe both, knowing these guys—and probably a bodyguard or two."

"What's going to happen?" Murray asked.

"We needed a way to separate the dirtbags from their entourages, and we found it. Actually, Chuck, did; this was one of his babies. This is, essentially, an awards banquet. Speeches are given, awards for various things are handed out, and on and on . . . Saudi Arabia's ambassador to the United States, who's springing for this thing, is the first speaker and he's a long-winded sucker. We know he's good for at least half an hour. That's how much time we've got. We want to be through and out of there by the time he finishes.

"You ought to see the statues, by the way," Quinn continued. "They're real cute, little golden Bedouin tents on a base. You open them up, and inside is your prize. Pretty neat. Anyway, Chuck came up with the idea of having our honchos come backstage before getting their prizes. That's when we could nab them. The only problem is that it hasn't been set up that way. The only one that really knows that, though, is the personal secretary to the ambassador who planned this whole thing. So Chuck will go to him first, claim that there is a security problem that he, the primary planner, in his infinite wisdom, is the only person capable of solving.

"He will then go backstage with Chuck, whom he knows is in charge of security for the whole thing. The secretary will instantly have duct tape over his mouth, be handcuffed, and will be shuttled out the back door into a waiting limo and taken to the station.

"After which, young polite Arab boys will go to each of the honchos and invite them, one at a time, to come backstage. They will ask, why? The boys will smile knowing smiles, and say something like . . . 'Well, if you happen to get an award, it would be good if you were already backstage to be ready to easily walk out and receive it.' The men will then smile, look knowingly at their wives or mistresses (Yes, I am a damn important person), and follow the boys. The bodyguards will want to come along but the honchos will tell them to stay put. It would be an act of cowardice to be protected inside a ballroom of one's peers. Twenty seconds later, he'll be hog-tied and sitting in the back of your car."

"My car?" Murray asked.

Quinn looked again at his clipboard. "Actually, I have you fifth in line dropping off your group. When they have gone in, follow the limo in front of you around to the side of the Fairmont and await the arrival of your new trussed-up passenger, accompanied by a special agent. You then bring them to the station."

"What do you think will happen when the rest of them find out?" David asked.

"We're anticipating pandemonium," Quinn said casually, "but by then we'll all be long gone. For the rest, if they want to get cabs and fend for themselves, fine. For those who don't, buses, food, and lodging will be provided, as well as getting them to their planes the next day.

"As soon as the men are in custody," Quinn continued, "a massive raid will be mounted against the freighter *Solana*, and teams will be dispatched to intercept four very expensive trucks—actually, thanks to you guys, I guess there's just three now—heading for Chicago, the proposed home of the American Jihad."

"What about the house?" David asked.

"Oh, yes," Quinn said with a smirk. "You spent some time in there, didn't you? God, Chuck was pissed."

"Is there anything left out there?"

"Not much. All the money's gone. We'll have follow-up crews out there, of course. It's still a crime scene and loaded with evidence. Well, listen, guys," Quinn said, standing up, "I'm about talked-out here. Chuck wanted me to bring you up to speed and I think I have. Why don't you come with me, Murray, and we'll get you coordinated with the other drivers. Dave, nice to have met you, even if you did almost screw us up."

"I'm glad I didn't. Nice meeting you, too. Good luck with it all."

"Thanks. When Chuck gets the money back and we can put this puppy to bed, maybe we can all have a drink and laugh about it."

"I'd like that."

"Good. Me, too. But right now, we got some bad guys to get. Come on, Murray. See you later."

The men shook hands. David and Murray exchanged half waves, knowing they'd talk again soon. David sat as the magnitude of it all flooded over him. Pretty amazing stuff. When he was ready, he returned to his little Morgan and drove back to the beach house. Life there suddenly seemed a lot simpler.

37

David had forgotten to check the mail, and it had built up for a few days in the box. Most of it was bills and advertisements, but there was a note from *Atlantic Monthly* that David's piece was going to be printed in the edition two months from then. Very good.

He also heard from the publisher he had blackmailed into printing Rebecca's mansion book. He was following true to his word (David *had* him) and needed a cover letter or some text to set up the photograph collection. That was progressing also. Even with all that had happened and all that was happening, David still felt good about that. Inching steadily forward.

He sat down at his desk, glad to get his mind off all this duplicity and back on Rebecca, back working for their legacy, their tracks, back to where he wanted to be, where he belonged. He was preparing to get on it right then, when something occurred to him. Isn't it strange, and sometimes maddening, he thought, that as soon as you take your mind off a subject, how many times it comes slamming back to your consciousness with an observation not picked up on before? This was one of those times.

He'd barely started on Rebecca's book when, suddenly, David remembered Chuck saying he was thankful that Quinn and the

FBI were taking care of the money. But hadn't Quinn, moments later, said something about "when Chuck gets the money back"? It seemed, as far as the FBI was concerned, Chuck was taking care of the money, in the short term at least.

But, wait, what money were they talking about? Quinn said that a raid was being called in on the *Solana* and a group was after the trucks headed for Chicago. The FBI would clearly be in control of that money. What other money was there? Somewhere in all this, Quinn felt that Chuck was responsible for a certain amount of this money. Chuck stated he was glad that he didn't have to worry about it.

So, what was it? Had these guys not communicated correctly? With possible multimillions at stake, that didn't really seem likely. Could Quinn be lying? Could Chuck? David felt terrible doubting his old friend like this, but it seemed more likely that Chuck was lying than Quinn, even though he'd just met him.

David didn't like feeling that way but couldn't deny that it was there. It was, probably, living out that charade about the house with Chuck. He'd lied so smoothly and effectively that David knew he could be doing it just as smoothly and effectively now. Damn it! So what should he do?

If the FBI was waiting for Chuck to bring them some of the money, that meant Chuck wasn't under the gun for it . . . he had some time. They knew he was currently pretty damn busy and would wait. If he chose not to turn it in . . . by the time the FBI realized that, he could be long gone.

Perhaps it would be best to get this clarified while the cast of characters could still be accounted for. Chuck would be running the security for the banquet and involved with shuttling off the honchos backstage; Quinn would be occupied in the process . . .

somewhere. But Murray would be fifth in line at the side of the Fairmont Hotel.

Hoping he was doing the right thing, David threw on a jacket and ran out to Rebecca's little Porsche. As much as he loved his Morgan, he had to admit her Porsche was faster, especially through the switchbacks. Damn! Why hadn't he thought of this in town? He was getting tired of this interminable drive.

He felt pretty certain that he'd run into very few policemen on the way. He knew where they were. He drove off as fast as he could, headed for Nob Hill.

The majestic Fairmont Hotel has reigned as a bastion of San Francisco's elite society since it was first built in 1907. Actually, it was built a few years before that but was nearly destroyed, along with everything else in San Francisco, in the earthquake and ensuing fires of 1906. It was immediately rebuilt and still stands today as one of the finest hotels in America.

It draws patrons from all over the world, and in 2006 finished an eighty-five-million-dollar face-lift. The refurbished lobby can't help but amaze with its massive multicolored marble columns holding up the gilded ceiling, three stories above.

The banquet for the Peace Conference delegates was being held in the Venetian Room, which was an upscale nightclub for over thirty years. It was currently one of the most fashionable banquet rooms in San Francisco big enough to hold a gala the size and scope of this one. The amount of gilt in the room would have made a czar proud.

The room was full of some of the richest people in the world. The gentlemen were either in floor-length flowing robes or in two-thousand-dollar suits (their robes probably cost that as well). It was a little strange seeing the women in Dior gowns with their heads covered, but they all made it work rather glamorously. Flower/candle centerpieces softly lit each table. The Saudi ambassador took his place in the center of the large stage that dominated one side of the room. He started his speech.

Shortly thereafter, Chuck, in a tuxedo, went to the ambassador's secretary's table with his situation.

As David got closer to the hotel, he began seeing intimations of what he knew was going to be happening soon. Street barricades were lying at the ready to block off streets at a moment's notice. Police cars, marked and unmarked, seemed to be everywhere. Their drivers stood around, waiting, having yet one more cup of coffee before all hell broke loose.

David managed to skirt them, though they really weren't stopping traffic just yet. He passed rows of tour buses and their police escorts, waiting to transfer the unsuspecting throng back to their hotels.

Arriving at the hotel, David found that there was no parking anywhere even close, so David parked in a yellow zone in front of a fire hydrant and prayed that this night would not culminate with a fire. He parked in back of the mammoth building; he had seen no activity to speak of when he drove by the front, so he knew everyone was inside. Everything was probably already under way. He ran directly to the side, looking for Murray's limo.

Yes, it was under way. By the time David located Murray, he was third in line and moving up. David ran to his window and started to explain about the money and the different takes on it. Had he noticed that? Should they do something while they still knew where everyone was?

While they spoke, everything inside the hotel was progressing. The Saudi ambassador droned on, as promised, punctuated only by waiters calling on and escorting certain members backstage. (Ostensibly. Actually, the door led to the kitchen and down some stairs to a side door used for deliveries. The limos were lined up outside that door.) Everyone knew the awards would start after this speech, so no one thought anything of it as the men were, quite proudly, led away.

Except Bashaar. He was actually the hero of the moment for planning and pulling this whole thing off. He would be the last to be honored, he knew, but the whole thing bothered him. The other dignitaries had just arrived from the Middle East. They suspected nothing. He, however, had helped the ambassador's secretary plan this evening, down to the seating charts. Nothing had been mentioned about taking people backstage first. There was no reason for it; the ballroom wasn't that large. Besides, all the honorees were seated close to the front.

Making it look like he had to go to the restroom before he got ready to be honored, Bashaar got up, excused himself from his table for a moment, and left, accepting congratulations from many on the way out of the room. He met eyes with Ameen, all dressed up and thrilled to be in this company. A slight motion of Bashaar's head was all that was needed for Ameen to also excuse himself from his table and quickly join Bashaar.

"Something's not right," Bashaar told Ameen when they reached the corridor. "Come."

Bashaar took off at a dead run to the front door and outside, Ameen close behind. A couple of doormen and ushers wondered what the hell they were doing.

Running out to the front steps, Bashaar looked around. At

first glance, it appeared very quiet. A closer look revealed buses parked a couple of blocks away. They hadn't been there a few minutes ago. He ran to a side of the building, nearly a block long, but saw nothing of interest. With the questioning Ameen by his side, he then ran to the other side. There seemed to be a line of limos closer to the back of the buildings.

Glad that he had stayed in as good, if not better, shape than the men he led, Bashaar ran down the side toward the back of the enormous Fairmont. Ameen was already puffing behind.

They walked along the line of limos thinking it odd that they were back there. Everyone would be leaving by the front door and the limos were usually pre-placed there to be available at a moment's notice.

What Bashaar saw next froze him in his tracks. Not far in front of him was David Collier talking to someone in a limo. What the hell was he doing here?

David, still talking with Murray, noticed a slight movement off to his side, casually looked over in midsentence, and locked eyes with Bashaar, not a car length away. Oh shit! Bashaar turned and took off running, Ameen not far behind.

"Damn it, Murray! It was Bashaar. He saw me."

Murray jumped from the car. "Which way?"

David pointed. "There." Murray could see the figures running along the building. "Drive. Take them to the station," Murray said over his shoulder as he gave chase.

The limo in front of them had just pulled up so David quickly got in the car and moved Murray's limo up behind. Soon an FBI special agent ran out escorting a very pissed off Arab dignitary/terrorist. He placed him in the backseat of the limo in front and drove off. David then pulled up to the back door and waited. He was next.

He didn't have long. Barely a minute had passed—David

was worrying about how Murray was doing—when another twosome came out the door. The back door of the limo was opened and a duct-taped, handcuffed gentleman in robes was escorted into the limo. Actually, he was fighting back quite viciously and had literally been thrown into the limo, the agent following.

David quickly drove out of there. The Arab was making as much noise as he could through the duct tape. "Can it! You'll have plenty of time to talk, believe me," the agent said, then seemed to notice David for the first time.

"Who the hell are you?" he asked, threateningly.

"I'm David Collier. I'm a friend of—"

"Where's Murray?" the agent cut in.

"A couple of the guys got loose, Bashaar and another one. Murray went after them."

The agent was still holding his irate captive down but took a second to move the gun over to David's head. "One false turn out of you and you're history. Got it?"

David managed a "Yes, sir." He tried very hard to make it to the station without screwing up.

 $\mathcal{S}$ *ince no one at the station* knew David, they had only his word for his impromptu involvement. They didn't want to put him in jail, but they did confine him to Murray's office until he showed up. That took about an hour. Murray came in tired and not pleased.

"I got the young one. He wasn't nearly in that good a' shape," Murray said, pouring himself a cup of coffee. "I cuffed him quick but couldn't catch up with Bashaar. Shit!"

"I'm afraid it's my fault again, Murray. If Bashaar hadn't seen me you probably could have gotten him."

"Don't worry about it. Bashaar had already figured something was up. If he hadn't seen you, he'd see the next person shuttled out the door wearing duct tape and handcuffs . . . about ten seconds later. That would have done it."

David was surprised to see Chuck and Quinn come in a few minutes later. They would be going back to the scene soon but wanted to make sure the other prong of their sting was working. They had every cell phone number of every person at that ball. They were all important people (especially, in their own minds), all very irate, and every one of them got on the phone to call and "have something done about this!" They were not used to such treatment . . . have never been so humiliated in their lives . . . heads were going to roll, etc.

Every call was being traced, many tapped and taped, backed up by warrants and court orders. Chuck and Quinn had done everything right and already connections were being made to people and areas not suspected before. Chuck was as happy as he was relieved. It would have been horrible if he'd gone through all that he had and then have it not work. He looked over and winked at David. Fortunately, with no thanks to Mr. Collier, that hadn't happened.

David wasn't quite as comfortable with this whole situation as Chuck seemed to be. David still wondered about the money and tried to bring it up innocently.

"Have you heard yet how the raids have worked? Did they recover all the money?" he asked.

"Everything seems to be going as planned," Quinn replied. "The *Solana* has been boarded and helicopter, money, and men apprehended behind a large firewall, without a shot being fired. Not bad. That was the stadium money, chump change."

"We didn't even care if they made it," Chuck added. "Actually, we thought the F-16s would have scrambled quicker and that chopper wouldn't have had a prayer."

"How could that not have made a difference?" Murray wanted to know.

"The whole stadium thing really was just a diversion. Either way, it served that purpose. The people involved knew only what they were doing. They weren't even fanatics, just low-grade mercenaries that would do anything for a buck. In this case, a lot of bucks, but none of them knew anything about this. The stadium money was to pay for that whole operation—the helicopter, munitions, uniforms, lodging, all of it. The rest was theirs, so if they got caught, killed, or put in jail . . . it didn't matter."

David thought about the people who died at the stadium but decided that it was not the time to bring it up.

"The mother lode is in the trucks," Quinn said. "You, of course, stopped the little one but three of the big mothers made it out. We've already gotten two and are preparing to move in on the last one."

"Is that it?" David asked, still fishing for the money connected to Chuck.

"There's still twenty or thirty million of the Federal Reserve's money down at the docks," Chuck said easily. "It was supposed to be loaded on board the *Solana* when she docked tomorrow."

"Wouldn't they have found the helicopter?" Murray asked.

"I'm sure it or the troops wouldn't have been on the ship at the time. We were sort of a surprise to them," Quinn said, smiling. "Actually, it was quite a firewall they built. If we hadn't *known* that the men were there, we probably wouldn't have found them."

"What happens to the money at the dock?" David persisted.

"Chuck and his boys bring it in tomorrow. It's currently locked up and under guard. Other than a few pissed-off Arabs, I'd say we had a pretty successful night."

Was that it, David wondered? Could everything really be explained that simply and easily? Alerts had gone off in David's mind; what caused those? Was he really that crummy a friend? It sure seemed like it.

"We still need Bashaar," Chuck said, unaware of the mental turmoil going on in David's head.

"You know him better than anyone here," Quinn said. "Do you have an idea of where he might be?"

"Well, the problem is that he's a smart little shit. He knows we're having this conversation right now. He's not going to be anywhere close to any locales that I may have for him."

"What do you suggest?" Quinn asked.

"Don't forget, Bashaar worked on this operation for a year, too," Chuck said. "He's not real happy right now, in fact, he's downright furious. His two least favorite people in the world as of now are David and me. He will not leave this area without a major effort to have his revenge on at least one of us, I can promise you that. Well, Quinn, we better head back to our mess."

"Yeah, we created it, we've got to clean it up." Quinn turned to David and Murray and explained, "It only looks like a mess. Actually, it's playing out just as we'd planned. The irate second-echelon calling for help, pulling what strings they think they have, is one of the main benefits of this whole thing."

"And, Murray, I want you on Dave detail again tonight," Chuck said.

"For Christ's sake, Chuck!"

"Don't give me a bad time. Everybody else is busy, you know that, and Dave's got to be watched, especially tonight."

"You're always welcome to the 'Murray memorial couch,'" David said, trying to lighten it up a bit.

"Not tonight," Chuck said to Murray. "I want you outside."

"Chuck!"

"Two reasons. First, Bashaar will see you. He'll know that Dave is being guarded but he won't know how many more you may have with you. It might buy us a little time with him, let us set something up where we're in control. Secondly, you'll like this one, I'll get you relieved as soon as I can start pulling guys away from the stadium. And we won't be disturbing Dave when we change over."

"Oh, that's fine," David said. "I'm too keyed up to sleep right now anyway. Got some writing to do."

"Doesn't change a thing," Chuck said, standing. "All right, you two get out of here, we'll go back to our illustrious group and we'll all be in touch later."

Chuck and Quinn left and drove off to the hotel. Murray followed them, driving David to Rebecca's Porsche, parked by the fire hydrant. David approached and let out a groan. Even with all the mayhem that was still going on around the Fairmont, someone had taken the time to write him a ticket. Murray pulled it off the windshield.

"I'll see what I can do," he said, putting it in his inside coat pocket.

"You're a good man, Murray."

"Yeah, yeah, yeah. Don't get too creative in that little toy car. I'm right behind you."

"Yes sir."

Off they drove, in the middle of the night, for the beach house.

Murray situated himself outside with a minimum of grumbling. He walked around for a while before finding the perfect spot. He needed a place where he could see most of the house, be hidden but not too hidden, but where he would also be protected. Finally finding such a spot, he sat down with a thermos of hot coffee that David had made for him. That should do until he was relieved.

Inside, David made himself a fire in the fireplace, built a drink, sat down on the couch, and looked deeply at the gorgeous picture of Rebecca. God, it seemed like weeks since he'd had the chance to just sit down and be with her like that. After reliving moments and revisiting feelings, something that always seemed to happen at times like these, David raised his glass to her.

"To you and me, kid."

As he brought his glass back down, he noticed his hand was starting to shake again. The pills had been doing such a good job, he hadn't even concerned himself with his hand or what the ramifications of all that might turn out to be.

Of course, it had been a long, nerve-wracking day since he'd taken his pill. He wondered if he should take one then but thought better of it. He'd wait till morning. So his hand shook a little. So what?

He went back to his writing area to get to work on Rebecca's text but soon had to move. As much as he normally loved it back there, somehow he felt farther away from Rebecca and he didn't want that. The little four-by-six picture didn't quite cut it. He grabbed his trusty laptop and returned to the living room, setting up shop on the couch in front of the fire . . . and with Rebecca.

After a while, David got up and went to the bar next to the fireplace. He replenished his drink while his mind continued to whir away at possibilities. The squawk from Murray's police radio outside reminded him that he was being monitored. It was rather nice to have forgotten about all that for a moment.

There was then a drone as Murray was speaking to someone about something David couldn't make out but which, he was sure, didn't have anything to do with him anyway. But it was distracting.

Well, he could certainly do something about that; he simply removed his hearing aid, *placed it on the mantel and went back to work.*

Yes, that was more like it. He was becoming more comfortable in his silence. The beach house was lit only by the fireplace and the one lamp by the sofa that he needed for writing. Those were the types of nights that he and Rebecca loved the most. The ones he missed the most. The quiet little nothing nights.

It was perhaps an hour later when David stood, took his laptop into the other room, and printed out a couple of pages. As they were printing, he stretched and realized how tired he felt. It had been one hell of a day . . . actually, a hell of a week. Ah well, hopefully all that was being wrapped up.

He took the newly printed pages, picked up his drink, and silently started to proofread his first draft while walking back into the living room.

"The time you spend with these mansions on the following pages will transport you to a time when man was striving for the best. Life was not reduced to the lowest common denominator. The technology of their time was not nearly as advanced as ours to-day, but, somehow, their goals seemed more lofty.

How many houses or units could be crammed onto a given space didn't even enter their minds, nor did how they could sub-divide the acreage, give everybody a bit less and make a lot more money."

David was so engrossed in reading and editing his words that he failed to see the shadow of a figure standing outside. He continued walking and reading in silence.

"No, at that time the goal was quality. To be spacious, lovely, and built to last. Gardens and grounds were factored in, as were views, privacy, and comfort.

These were special homes built for special people and were de-signed to make them feel even more so."

David returned to the sofa by the fireplace.

"It was a unique and special time in America. The pride in these magnificent buildings still shows today.

Please enjoy these offerings by the photographer Rebecca Collier. If you take with you even a little feeling about what life can be instead of settling for much less without a fight, Mrs. Collier will be very pleased."

David looked off into the fireplace. "And so will I," he added quietly.

He paused a moment and took what looked to be the last sip of his drink. Figuring that was enough for the night, he got up, turned the light by the sofa off, and returned the glass to the kitchen. On the way back, he noticed a flash of light outside. The figure outside had just lit a cigarette.

"Hey, how's your coffee holding up?" David called out, assuming it was another cop guarding him. "Just wave if you'd like me to brew another—"

Suddenly the glass window in front of him exploded. David was thrown violently back into the room as a slug slammed into his shoulder. He lay on the ground shaking, in silence, overcome by pain, fatigue, and confusing, confusing fear.

39

David quickly scooted back into the still-darkened kitchen. Fear, shock, and instinct took over as he tried to hide in the shadows. The pain in his shoulder made him want to cry out but he knew he couldn't. He fought clumsily to his feet and went as swiftly as he could through the kitchen to his writing area. The lamp on his desk had been left on. He quickly turned it off.

The only light in the house now came from distant streetlamps shining through the windows, the moonlight, and the dwindling fire in the fireplace, creating long, dark, flickering shadows.

The writing area was out of sight of the living room but, not being able to see or hear, David had no idea what was going on in the other rooms.

He examined his shoulder, which hurt like hell and made his left arm practically impossible to move. The slug had hit some bones for sure, he could feel them, but by the size of the hole in his back, the bullet may have passed on through. He supposed that was a good thing.

David knew he was bleeding pretty badly from where the bullet had exited, so he leaned against a wall to put some pressure on it to slow the bleeding. Tears ran down his face from the pain as he continued to fight crying out and revealing his position.

When he couldn't take it anymore, he moved slightly away from the wall, took a few deep breaths, and tried to think. He soon realized he couldn't just stay there and await being executed. He crouched his way back to the kitchen and armed himself with a carving knife. He then crept along the cabinets, keeping well into the shadows, watching windows and doors intently for any sign of movement. He crawled past his bar, inching toward the mantel and his hearing aid.

Trying to avoid the light of what was left of the fire as much as possible, David reached up to grab his hearing aid. It was gone! He felt all around. He hadn't dropped it, he was sure. It had been there! Fear shot through him. Someone was inside!

He quickly lurched to the other side of the fireplace and crouched behind a chair, feeling outrageously vulnerable. His left arm didn't work, his left leg barely worked and, oh yes, he couldn't hear. He settled in behind the chair so clumsily that he bumped a small table and toppled the vase that was on it. He saw it hit the hardwood floor and silently shatter.

Immediately after, the plaster flew from where a bullet hit the wall, inches from his head. David dived for another shadow and spun, but couldn't see where the shot had come from. The gunman must be using a silencer again. David thought he'd be able to hear a gunshot even without his hearing aid, but he heard nothing. The crippling effect of his malady became even clearer to him. He froze for a moment, fighting back pain and panic.

In the midst of it all he suddenly remembered that the human mind can only have one dominant emotion at a time; let that be anger! Don't panic, get the son of a bitch!

Get back to thinking. Think better. Be creative! He knew he couldn't wait this person out and was sure he'd be shot before he'd gotten a door halfway open to escape. The house was too small to stay hidden in for long. Through it all, an idea started to emerge. Soon, David had a plan.

He reached back to the fireplace and replaced his carving knife with a poker. The TV was nearby. He turned it on and cranked the sound to full volume. David could hear it slightly but knew it was much louder than that. The vibrations he could feel and the glowing LED lights assured him of that.

He staggered over to where the radio was and turned it on and up all the way. That sound going through his motherboard and stereo speakers would be loudest of all. Yes! Even David could hear this. It was on the same station Daley had turned on when she had come over with dinner. The cop outside would have to hear that . . . if he was still there. If he was still alive.

An image of Murray being dead flashed through his mind, but David fought quickly to let it go. No! That would not help right then. Suddenly a wave of dizziness came over him. He had to stabilize himself to stop from falling over. He froze until the wave passed. He tried to clear his head and think again . . . be smart.

He looked over at the telephone. A chill visibly went through him when he saw that the line had been cut.

Having no idea where his cell phone was at the moment, David sat and waited, petrified. His rapid breathing sounded to him like he was underwater, or when he was wearing one of the rubber gas masks.

He carefully scanned the house. He used his never-unpacked boxes as cover, comforted ever so slightly knowing that his stalker couldn't hear him. He searched for movement, any movement. There was none.

Suddenly, the music/noise David could hear stopped. What had happened? He could hear nothing; the vibrations had quit. He was so situated under the stairs that he couldn't see if the LED lights were still on or not. Maybe there was still sound that he just couldn't hear.

The last vestiges of the fire in the fireplace, the moonlight, and the distant streetlights were still the only lights. He waited in un-suspecting silence for a while but was too keyed up to just sit. He went looking. He concentrated on staying in the shadows and kept his poker high in case he ran across someone. Creeping along the wall, back by the stairs, David's fears were realized: the TV was off. He spun to check out the radio and stereo and saw that their dials were dark as well. Someone had cut power to the house. So much for his equalizer. He suddenly felt more vulnerable than before.

As this new wave of fear hit, David saw a figure of a man outside the window across from him. Before he had a chance to react, he saw the flash of a gun. The window between them silently broke. David didn't feel any new pain so he assumed the man had missed. All of a sudden, a dark-clad man jumped on him from the stairs above.

Panic again surged through David as he fought to get out from under the man. He did, and started to violently bludgeon the man with his poker as viciously as his one arm would permit. The man just lay there. David looked closer and got another chill: the man was Bashaar. Still closer scrutiny revealed that he was already dead.

David's attention flew back to the figure outside the window. He watched the figure as he walked by the windows on the way to the back door. The figure opened it and came in. With the power off, very little light, and no sound, David couldn't identify him. He still clutched his poker, ready to strike.

"Who is it?" David asked, still sounding to himself like he was at the bottom of a well.

The figure took a few steps toward David before enough light fell on him for recognition. To David's relief, it was Chuck, silently talking to him.

"Chuck, thank God," David said. "I can't hear anything. He took my hearing aid."

David leaned back against the wall, partly from relief, partly to stem the blood that he knew was still seeping from the shoulder exit

wound. The pain shooting through his body made him instantly re-
gret that choice. He dropped his poker.

Chuck searched Bashaar's body, finding his gun first and pocket-
ing it. He then found David's hearing aid and tossed it to him.
David caught it with a wince and quickly put it on, returning him
to full sound.

"Oh, Chuck. Great timing," David said, trying to get his
breath.

"Are you all right?" Chuck asked.

"Not really."

"Did you get hit again?"

"Yeah. Can you believe it?"

"I'm sorry, Dave," Chuck said, concerned.

"I should be getting used to it by now, you'd think, but I'm
not. It hurts like hell."

Both men stood in the flickering afterglow of the fire, unsure
where this was going next. David bent over, looking closer at
Bashaar. "He was the one who came here that day, wasn't he?
He was the one who killed Rebecca?"

"Yes."

"Did you know about that?" David asked when he stood up.
He waited for his answer, looking Chuck straight in the eyes.

"Only afterward. There wasn't anything I could do."

David looked down at the crumpled corpse for a moment.
Inner rage started to fill him until he couldn't hold it anymore.
With all the power he could muster, he hauled off and kicked
Bashaar as hard as he could. The body flopped over and slid a
foot or two. David glared down at it with loathing . . . when a
question occurred to him.

He slowly looked up at Chuck. "Why didn't Murray come in
when he heard the noise?"

Chuck held David's look but said nothing. A hardness had come into his eyes, a hardness David remembered when he and Chuck had been on opposing sides of a situation. Were they now? Could Chuck's frustrations of years ago still be festering inside him?

Chuck slowly took Bashaar's gun out of his pocket. For the first time, David noticed Chuck was wearing gloves.

"Where was Murray, Chuck?" David repeated, the cold feeling of dread starting to come back over him.

"I'd relieved him a few minutes before," Chuck said, casually holding the gun.

David froze. Was the gun starting to turn toward him? No, it couldn't be. David couldn't believe what he was seeing. "So, Murray wasn't here?" David said, haltingly.

They both jumped as a large black presence came barreling through the door.

"No, but he is now," Murray said, looking down at Bashaar on the ground. "Good shot," he said to Chuck, then looked around the house. "What the hell are you two doing standing here in the dark? Jesus, where's your fuse box?" he asked, not waiting for an answer as he went off to find it.

David was still staring at Chuck. Did he really see a hint of a smile as Chuck put the gun back in his pocket?

"I'd called him off knowing he was anxious to get home," Chuck said, taking off his gloves. "It took me a little longer than I thought to get here. Luckily, I got here in time."

"Yeah . . . luckily."

Suddenly hard rock music started blaring from the speakers. David immediately lunged over to the stereo/radio and turned it off. Chuck got the TV.

"God, that's obnoxious," David said, still reeling.

"We'd better get you an ambulance," Chuck said as he walked away, pulled out his cell, and put in a 911 call.

"That's what did it, right there," Murray said coming back into the room, turning on a couple of lights. "Your sexy friend Daley called my cell. She knew something was wrong. She could hear the radio blaring all the way over to her place and she knew you would never do that . . . especially not *that* music."

They both smiled for a moment, remembering the earlier confrontation about the station.

"She got me before I was too far away. Glad she kept my card," Murray said, then noticed David's bleeding. "Are you hit bad?"

"Chewed my shoulder up pretty good, I think."

"Ambulance will be here in a few minutes," Chuck said, coming back to the group. "Well, guys, by my count, this should be it."

"What do you mean?"

"I think this caper's over. This is the last of the bad guys right here," Chuck said easily, looking down at Bashaar, purposely avoiding David's questioning look. "Sorry I mistimed that switch," Chuck continued, "but we'd better call this in, Murray. The coroner's going to want to come out and we'll have to . . ."

Chuck and Murray walked off talking cop stuff as though nothing else had happened. Maybe it hadn't.

David sat on the edge of the couch cushions, not wanting to get blood all over everything. He stared into the dying embers of the fire, then up to Rebecca overseeing everything and wondered how she would have felt about all that transpired. His life had been considerably different from the one they had known. The wonderful life they had known.

David looked over at Chuck and wondered what to think. Would he really have shot him with Bashaar's gun? It would have looked like Chuck arrived a moment too late to save his friend. But, why? It sure seemed like he was considering it, or was it just David being weird again? As Chuck said, the caper was over now . . . or was it?

Sirens could be heard in the distance. David's life was just about to change drastically again. But to what end? He didn't know. There were fewer questions that remained, but the ones that lingered were pretty powerful. He still intended to get those answers but . . . probably not that night.

Pain and fatigue got to him. He settled back down onto the couch to wait. Yes, that felt much better. He'd deal with the blood later.

40

Six Months Later

It was a nice day at the beach. It was a little overcast but that was all right. It kept it from getting too hot. David was having a party and, like the moving day party, it started on the deck and spilled out onto the beach. Many of the same cast of characters were at this party with a few notable exceptions.

Chuck was not there; Murray and his wife were. Shelly, Sol, and his wife, Kay, were also there. Daley and Amanda were new invitees, as was Nurse Judy. Other past coworkers of David and Rebecca rounded out the group. Everyone seemed to be having a fine time drinking wine or beer and discussing great thoughts with one another.

Rebecca was represented by a large picture on a table. The Navajo rug was draped over the railing. David's bandages by now were minimal. The party had actually started out on a rather somber note, with everyone treating Rebecca's picture like a shrine. David wanted more of a celebration and had evidently done a good job of convincing people to lighten up.

David was in a good mood, sipping his wine, talking and enjoying everyone. Sol, Kay, and Judy were looking at a book and some magazines on a table.

As David walked up to them, Sol said, "Very impressive."

"Thank you. I think so, too."

"*California's Magnificent Mansions of the Thirties* by Rebecca Collier," Kay read. "Very nice."

"This last picture doesn't quite fit, though, does it?" Sol asked, turning to the last page of the book, the one containing the old, white mansion.

"Well, that shows what can happen to these great old places without love."

"I'm sure it was magnificent at one time," Kay said, looking at the picture.

"I'm sure it was," David agreed. "It was also Rebecca's last photograph. Seemed fitting"—then, lifting the mood somewhat— "And . . . after all the conspiring I had to go through to get this done . . . once they saw the pictures, they got very excited about it. I think they did a great job."

"What's this other one?" Judy asked, indicating the *Atlantic Monthly* magazine.

"Take a look."

She did, and read, "'You Don't Know Me, but I'm Your Father.' A short story by David Collier." Judy looked over to David. "Did this happen to you?"

"No, my folks are a whole different story; might be just as interesting actually. This is based on a friend of mine who met his father for the first time in college. It was pretty amazing."

"I'd like to read it," Judy said.

"I hope you will."

"This is a lovely testament to Rebecca, David," Kay said, still looking through the mansion book.

David just smiled. "Yeah."

"What are you going to do now?" Judy asked.

"You know, Judy, I haven't a clue. I've been so involved with fighting through a rather raucous present, to try to preserve and honor the past, I haven't even given a thought to the future. I'll let you know."

"Please do."

David saw a group off to the side that he needed to talk to. "Excuse me for a minute, please. I've got to go fuss over some people."

He walked over to where Murray and his wife were talking with Daley and Amanda.

"Look at this, a meeting of my heroes."

"It's a lovely party, David," Daley said.

"Thanks to you folks"—he winked at Amanda, who smiled— "I'm here to have it."

"Dave, I don't think you've met my wife, Cherice," Murray said. "Honey, this is David Collier."

"Needless to say, I've heard a lot about you. Nice to finally meet you, Mr. Collier."

"Nice meeting you as well, Mrs. Townsend, but it's David."

"And it's Cherice."

"Done. Now we've gotten that out of the way," David said. "I'm sorry I needed to borrow your husband for so long. Thank you."

"As long as he comes home in one piece, I can deal with it," Cherice said, looking proudly at Murray.

"Thanks to him I'm in one piece. Without Murray, God knows what would have happened. In fact, would you mind if I borrowed him again for just a minute?"

She granted permission and David and Murray walked off to a corner of the deck alone. "I mean it, Murray, you made all the difference. I really wouldn't be here if it wasn't for you."

"Well, I don't think I would have been able to do as much if it hadn't been for you and your harebrained exploits," Murray said, with a twinkle. "It actually is a wonder you're still alive."

"I know," David said, smiling. "Any news from Chuck?"

"You know he requested a prolonged leave of absence."

"Yeah, the day after all this came down."

"You heard about the money?" Murray asked.

"I heard they recovered all but ten million."

"Curious number, don't you think?"

"Curious is exactly what I thought," David said. "Do you think we'll ever see him again?"

"No. He's probably got blond hair and is living in Rio or Tuscany somewhere. Everything else connected with the sting went beautifully, by the way. We found and arrested a number of people here with some very nasty ideas and we've got inroads all over the Middle East that we didn't have before."

"That's good," David said looking out at the sea, sipping his wine. "Not much good came from Rebecca's and my major adventure at the beach but I am glad it all wasn't for nothing."

"I'm not sure it was worth the price you paid for it but, no, it wasn't for nothing."

David took a look at the time and excused himself. Laboriously, he climbed up on a bench, waved his good arm, and called for his friends.

"Hello, there. Let me have your attention, please. Could I have your attention?"

They all quieted down and looked at him.

"Thank you, I just love attention."

His friends laughed and groaned until David held up his hand again to quiet them.

"Sorry about that. It's not often that anyone gets a chance to speak to, literally, everyone who means something in their life. I have that pleasure right now. I just want to thank you all for being such good friends to Rebecca and me. I hope you will all be in my life . . . as long as there's a life to be in. You are all quite special. Thank you again for coming."

Sol helped him climb down from the bench and another round of chatting began.

A couple of hours later, nearly everyone had gone. Daley and Amanda were the last to leave. David was seeing them off down at the beach, since they had such a short walk home.

"Thanks for inviting me, too, Mr. Collier," Amanda said.

David bent over and gave her a hug. "Wouldn't have it any other way, kiddo." He stood, looked at Daley. "And thank you for it all. Really."

Daley stepped up to him and gave him another big kiss. When she finished, she stayed right there, looking at him, two inches from his face.

After a moment, David said, "I know . . . you're just a friendly sort."

She smiled and gave him a quick kiss on the nose. "You take good care of yourself. Thanks for today." David just nodded as the two ladies started the walk down to their beach house.

He limped back to the stairs and slowly climbed up to the deck. Once there he turned off the easy soft rock he'd had playing on the radio and turned on a preset stereo CD of some lovely classical strings. He walked over and lay down on the chaise lounge looking out to sea.

Rebecca's picture was on one side of his view, the Navajo blanket on the other. Before him was the table with the books, the ocean beyond. David's hand had been shaking again. He had to wait for a spasm to pass to have another drink of wine.

David was quietly staring out to sea when Shelly came back out on the deck. "Are you okay?" he asked.

David looked over to him. "Sure."

"Are you sure you're sure?" Shelly asked, coming over to him.

David didn't answer right away. "You know that big, beautiful house, Shelly?" David finally asked. "Now that your old group is out of there, it just got sold to a development company. They're going to tear it down."

"Condos?"

"Looks like. Can you believe they're going to be able to get twenty of them on that lot? Pretty amazing, huh?"

'Unfortunately, stuff like that happens every day."

"Did you know Rebecca gave me this rug?"

"I did know that. The book is really great, Dave. She'd be very pleased."

"Well, tracks have been left," David said, still staring at the ocean. "Just a footprint here and there. You might have to look for them, but that's all right. They're there."

"Dave, are you sure you're all right?" Shelly asked after another silent moment.

"You might be confusing something being wrong with something being . . . different," David said softly, then added, "Or maybe I had too much wine. Anyway, thanks for your concern, Shelly, but I'm just fine. Really."

"Sure you don't need anything?"

"Nope."

"All right," Shelly said, starting to leave. "You take care of yourself."

"Will do."

Still feeling something was amiss, Shelly hesitantly left.

After a moment, David silently toasted the sea and beyond

and finished the last of his wine. He set the glass down by Rebecca's picture. He took it, settled back again, and studied it. Then he held it to him and turned his attention back to the sea.

As he settled deeper into the lounge, David slowly turned the volume on his hearing aid up. Soon he was surrounded, inundated by the classical strings and the crashing of waves. A tear started working its way down from the corner of his eye as he smiled, overcome by joy, satisfaction, relief, and anticipation.

It was a grand picture: the ocean stretching out, blue, calm; the ocean fog coming in, just as it should. Wonderful. David saw and loved it all. The ocean sounds and music continued quite loud. After a few moments, David seemed to doze off. A few minutes later his hand stopped shaking. David looked more peaceful than he had in months.

Relative calm on a not so sunny Sunday at the edge of the world.